D0209571

STORIES *from* HOPE HAVEN

Christmas Miracles

CHARLOTTE CARTER

Guideposts
New York, New York

For my father, Edwin M. Carter,
a church elder and a good man.
Thanks, Dad, for all you did.

The Best Medicine by Anne Marie Rodgers

Chasing the Wind by Patricia H. Rushford

Hope for Tomorrow by Patti Berg

Strength in Numbers by Charlotte Carter

A Simple Act of Kindness by Pam Hanson & Barbara Andrews

The Heart of the Matter by Leslie Gould

Well Wishes by Anne Marie Rodgers

Measure of Faith by Patricia H. Rushford

Cherished Memories by Patti Berg

Christmas Miracles by Charlotte Carter

Chapter One

"WHAT ARE YOU DOING?"

Standing in the middle of the lobby of Hope Haven Hospital, Anabelle Scott stared up at the fourteen-foot Christmas tree that had been erected more than a week ago. Now, two hospital custodians appeared to be taking the tree down. Taking it down the day after Thanksgiving? Why on earth would they do that?

Eddie Blaine, a broad-shouldered handyman in his late forties, was carefully removing ornaments from the tree and placing them in a plastic storage box.

"We're doing what the CEO ordered," Eddie said from his perch near the top of a twelve-foot ladder.

"Why did Albert Varner want the tree taken down?" Her movements jerky, Anabelle yanked the hand-knitted scarf from around her neck and stuffed it in the pocket of her heavy coat. She had just arrived for her morning shift as nurse supervisor in the Cardiac Care Unit and hadn't made it upstairs yet. "It's more than a month until Christmas. Is there something wrong with the tree?"

"Not that I know about." Hap Winston, older than Eddie by a good twenty years, held the ladder steady for his co-worker. "Varner didn't say why it's coming down, and we didn't ask. We just do as we're told."

Anabelle imagined Hap Winston had been doing as he was told here at the hospital for longer than any other employee; he had been named Employee of the Month innumerable times due to his dedicated efforts.

"Are we going to get another tree?"

Hap held up one hand in surrender and shrugged. "Don't know."

His plastic storage box now full, Eddie eased down the ladder and handed the box off to Hap. Picking up a second box, he climbed back up.

Scowling, Anabelle drew her lips into a thin line and shook her head. In the more than thirty years that she'd worked at Hope Haven, there had always been a Christmas tree in the lobby during the holiday season. And during the past ten years, Hope Haven held a Christmas party for all the children who had been patients that year. The cafeteria dished out ice cream, and Santa handed out gifts donated by hospital visitors and staff. Some of those children, particularly those from families struggling with big medical bills, were unlikely to receive any other gifts for Christmas.

"What about the Christmas party for Hope Haven Kids? And their presents?" The party wouldn't be the same without a tree.

"Don't know." Eddie grunted as he extended his arm to full length in order to reach an ornament.

"Well, I'm going to find out what's going on." And the person she needed to talk to was the hospital social worker, Janice Thompson, who organized the yearly event for the children. Janice made contact with the families and created cute little Christmas tree ornaments for each child. On the back, the card noted the child's first name and initial, the child's gender and age, and the youngster's Christmas wish.

Janice shared an office in the Human Resources Department on the first floor. She was just taking off her coat as Anabelle walked in.

"Janice, I'm glad I caught you," Anabelle said. "Do you happen to know why Eddie and Hap are taking down the Christmas tree?"

Janice cocked her head, which shifted her long hair to hide part of her face. She stared at Anabelle a moment before she finished hanging up her long coat on a coat tree. "What are you talking about?"

"Apparently, Albert Varner ordered the Christmas tree in the lobby taken down."

Two spots of color appeared on Janice's cheeks. "Why on earth would he do that?"

"Precisely my question. I thought you might know."

"But the Hope Haven Kids' party—we've always had a tree for the party. And what about the tree ornaments donors select to give a child a gift?"

Anabelle just shook her head, Janice's concerns mirroring her own.

"I'm going to see what's going on." Janice strode out of the office at a fast clip, her long legs making it hard for Anabelle to keep up. When Janice reached the lobby, she came to an abrupt halt.

"Wh— You can't take down the tree!" The shock raised her usually calm voice to almost a shriek.

"We're just following orders, Ms. Thompson," Hap said.

"But . . . but what about the kids' Christmas party? And the tree ornaments? What have you done with those?"

"Saved 'em for you right over there." Hap pointed to a low table covered with magazines and the pile of green cardboard trees.

"Oh, thank goodness."

Scooping up the ornaments she'd created, Janice glanced around the lobby. Lines of concern formed on her forehead. She walked to one of the two decorated barrels used to collect the donated gifts. She peered inside the first and then hurried to the other side of the tree to the second barrel.

"What happened to the gifts that were here?"

"I don't know anything about any presents," Eddie replied, climbing down the ladder.

"Didn't see any here when we came in," Hap confirmed.

Janice covered her mouth with her hand and her face reddened. Her eyes grew wide. Her gaze darted around the lobby.

"Someone has taken the presents for the children!" Janice looked on the verge of panic.

"Oh dear . . ." Anabelle's heart sank into her stomach. "Maybe someone put them away for safekeeping."

"Without telling me? There were a dozen or more presents here when I left work Wednesday night." Her forehead pleated into a baffled frown and the muscles around her eyes tightened as though she might cry. "I'm going to report this to security. The children's gifts have been stolen."

After commiserating with Janice, Anabelle realized she had to get to work and start her shift. Ignoring the lobby elevator, she walked upstairs to the third-floor employee lounge. Built originally in 1907 and modernized several times to better serve the people of North Central Illinois, Hope Haven Hospital was founded by Winthrop Jeffries, a minister and doctor who believed patients should receive care not only for their bodies but for their spirit as well. That, in Anabelle's view, meant a Christmas tree in the lobby was an appropriate display to remind both patients and visitors of their need for spiritual good health. So was giving Christmas gifts to little children.

She squared her shoulders and pushed open the stairwell door to the third floor. She'd find out why Albert Varner had banished the tree from the lobby, figure out how to reverse that decision, and find out what had happened to the gifts that had already been donated.

She went directly to her locker in the staff lounge, hung up her winter coat, and slipped into the white lab coat she'd brought with her from home. Taking a moment, she checked her appearance in the small mirror on the back of her locker door. She sighed, noting there were almost no signs of pepper left in her salt-and-pepper hair, which she wore short with feathery bangs.

Two of her fellow nurses were getting coffee in the kitchen area, and she joined them. A plastic cornucopia with fruit spilling out of it rested on the counter. The Thanksgiving decoration would no doubt be replaced soon with red poinsettias and holiday garlands.

"Good morning, you two," she said.

"Hi, Anabelle." James Bell, a rugged-looking nurse who could pass as a lumberjack, shot her a welcoming grin. "Cold enough for you?"

"It was twenty-two degrees when I let Sarge out for his morning run around the yard. He didn't stay outside long." Her beloved one-year-old German shepherd–mixed-breed puppy was quickly growing into his overly large feet. There were times when his awkward antics were downright silly and usually endearing. Except when he decided to dig up nonexistent bones in her husband's flower beds.

Wearing yellow scrubs with a tiny teddy bear print, Candace Crenshaw lifted her Styrofoam cup of coffee in greeting. "Just as well I didn't have to get Howie out of his nice warm bed this morning to go to school. He never would've made it, he was buried so deep under the covers."

Anabelle remembered how her three children used to do the same on especially cold mornings. Widowed young four years ago, Candace had been struggling to raise her two children and adjust to being a single mom. Fortunately, she had her mother living with her to help out, not to mention the support of Heath Carlson, whom she'd started dating recently.

"Did you two see what Eddie and Hap are doing to the Christmas tree in the lobby?" Anabelle asked.

"I saw them messing with the tree when I came in," James said. "I didn't think much of it. What are they up to?"

"They're taking it down."

"Down?" Candace echoed.

James tossed his empty cup into the trash. "Why are they doing that?"

"That was precisely my question," Anabelle said. "They don't know why. Varner told them to, that's all they said. Not only that, but the gifts that had already been donated for the children's Christmas party are missing."

"Missing?" Candace's eyebrows drew together. "As in stolen?"

"Janice is checking with security now," Anabelle said. "No one had told her about the tree coming down, either."

Shaking her head, Candace said, "Maybe the tree is diseased. Or people with allergies have complained."

"Maybe. Although no one's complained before, that I know of," James said.

Anabelle was about to elaborate about why the tree was important, but the staff room door burst open, admitting Elena Rodriguez, an ICU nurse, all bundled up in a parka, snow boots, and wool cap.

"I think I got frostbite just by walking in from the parking lot," she announced. "It's cold out there." She glanced at the three of them. "What did I interrupt?"

"We were talking about the Christmas tree in the lobby and the presents for the children," Anabelle explained.

Elena looked at her blankly. "What about them?"

"Varner is having the tree taken down," James said.

"And the presents are missing," Candace added.

Elena's dark eyes widened in shock. "Why would he do that? What happened to the gifts?"

The operative questions of the day seemed to be Why? and What? "Janice Thompson is trying to track down the missing presents. As soon as I can, I'm going to ask Mr. Varner what's going on." She and Albert Varner had known each other for many years. While they weren't exactly social friends, they were close and respectful co-workers.

"I doubt Varner's going to be in today," James said.

"Probably not. Some people actually get four days off for Thanksgiving," Candace pointed out.

"Then I'll ask him when he gets back on Monday." Anabelle checked her watch. She had taken long enough getting to work. "After all these years, it's just plain foolish for the hospital not to have a Christmas tree and the party for our Hope Haven Kids."

Telling her friends she'd let them know what she found out next week, Anabelle took the stairs to the second floor. She retrieved her clipboard from her office, slipped on her reading glasses, and checked the patient census in the Cardiac Care Unit. Some years ago, the hospital had upgraded their equipment, including the installation of computers to track patients, supplies that were used, and even the dispensation of medication.

Despite having been trained on the system and being forced to use it, Anabelle still preferred her own handwritten records. Call her old-fashioned, but she trusted the way she'd always handled her nursing responsibilities.

She chewed on the end of her ballpoint pen. She was also old-fashioned about wanting a tree in the hospital lobby to celebrate Christ's birth. Some traditions shouldn't change.

That evening, Elena's husband Cesar called to say he'd be late getting home for dinner. Since he'd been promoted to detective on the Deerford police force, his hours were usually regular but sometimes a case required him to work late.

Elena had already put Isabel, their six-year-old granddaughter, to bed and was in the family room reading her Bible study book by the time Cesar walked in the door.

He shrugged out of his parka and bent over to kiss her. "Sorry I'm late."

"It's all right. I kept your dinner warm in the oven."

"Thanks. I'm late because I was watching hours of videotape at Hope Haven."

Elena closed her book and set it aside. "At the hospital?"

"Yep. We got a call about a bunch of gifts for kids that had gone missing."

"Oh, right. Everybody at the hospital was talking about that, and the fact that Albert Varner ordered our lobby Christmas tree taken down. Anabelle was really upset about the whole thing."

"So was the social worker who's in charge of the kids' Christmas party." Sitting down in his recliner, Cesar stretched out his legs. "Problem is, I've looked through hours of surveil-lance tapes and haven't spotted a soul leaving the hospital with an armload of wrapped presents."

She frowned. "Does that mean they're still in the hospital somewhere?"

"Don't know. Truth is, there aren't that many surveillance cameras around the hospital. If it's an inside job or somebody familiar with the hospital took the presents, maybe the perpetrator knew how to avoid getting caught on tape."

"It's terrible to think someone associated with the hospital would steal gifts meant for little children. What are they going to do with them?"

He rubbed his eyes with the heels of his hand and ran his fingers through his short dark hair. "Maybe sell 'em at a swap meet or out of the back of a car. Trouble is, we don't know for sure what was in the packages that were taken, so we don't know what we're looking for."

"Whoever took the presents must have been desperate. Even so, that person should be ashamed."

"You've got that right." With a weary sigh, he got up from the recliner and headed into the kitchen.

Worried about how hard Cesar worked and how discouraged he appeared, Elena followed him. Maybe dinner would lift his spirits.

Saturday morning, Anabelle sat across the kitchen table from Cameron in their home two miles from the hospital. Cam's hair and neatly trimmed mustache had long ago changed from black to gray, but his eyes were the same bright blue as they'd always been and sparked with intelligence. After more than forty years of marriage, Anabelle still thought he was the most handsome man in Deerford.

Sarge had planted himself right next to Anabelle, his tail sweeping the floor. He looked up at her with his big brown eyes, pleading for just a taste of her scrambled eggs or a bite of bacon. She was tempted. . . .

"Don't do it, lass." Cam's voice held a hint of laughter. "No table scraps, the veterinarian said. They'll make him fat."

"I know." She popped the last bite of bacon into her mouth. "Sorry, Sarge. Cameron's right."

With a melancholy whine, Sarge lay down on the floor and rested his head on his front paws. His tail beat once on the hardwood before giving up the effort.

"That dog knows just how to push a person's guilt buttons," Anabelle said, smiling. "A stranger would think we never feed the poor thing; he can put on such a convincing act."

"The amount of food he goes through in a week is enough to feed a whole pack of dogs. If he keeps that up much longer, he'll be as big as a horse."

"In which case, Lindsay Belle will be able to ride him all day long." Anabelle doted on their first grandchild, seven-month-old Lindsay. She didn't get nearly enough cuddle time or chances to babysit, having to share that honor with Lindsay's other grandmother. And, of course, Anabelle worked full-time at the hospital, cutting the number of hours she was available to help out Ainslee by babysitting.

The doorbell chimed.

"I'll get it." Cameron pushed back from the table. At the same time Sarge came to his feet. The dog trotted after Cam toward the front door, happily wagging his tail as he looked forward to a little action in his quiet household.

"I'll clean up the dishes." Picking up their plates, Anabelle carried them to the counter and rinsed them off. Through the window over the sink, she had a view of the pasture and barn, which Cam had used to store his landscaping equipment until he retired, turning the business over to their son.

"It was the mail carrier." Cameron returned to the kitchen carrying a large box, Sarge weaving around his feet in order to get a peek. "What did you buy this time? It's heavy."

"I don't know. Put it down and let me see." Excited to see what had arrived, she wiped her hands on a nearby towel. She'd been busy on the Internet lately ordering Christmas presents for family and friends.

Clearing space on the oak table, Cam set the oversized, un-wieldy box down, found a knife, and opened it.

Anabelle clapped her hands. "Look, it's a present for Lindsay Belle."

"Another one?" Cam stepped out of Anabelle's way.

She quickly removed the packing material to reveal the contents. "It's a little walk-and-ride car. Her name's stenciled right across the hood. See?" With Cam's help, she lifted the pink toddler car out of the box. "Isn't it adorable?"

"Walk-and-ride?" Cam lowered his eyebrows and flattened his lips. "Lindsay can't walk yet."

"She's already beginning to pull herself up to her feet in her playpen. She'll be walking in no time." Anabelle attached the push handle to the back of the car. "Oh, she's going to love this."

"That's what you said about the sixteen presents you've already bought for Lindsay that are stashed in my office."

She scowled at her husband. "I haven't bought her that many gifts."

"Well, let's see." He began counting them off on his fingers. "White fake-fur snow boots . . ."

"She needs to keep her feet warm. The boots are adorable."

"A storybook with her own picture and name in it."

"Babies love pictures of babies. I can read the book to her."

"The frilly dress with matching panties." He ticked off a third finger. "A ball that plays music, a snowsuit, a bouncy chair—"

"Oh, all right. I've bought a lot of presents for little Lindsay. That's what grandmothers are supposed to do. We can afford it."

"True. But are you sure Lindsay's mother will like you outdoing Santa Claus in the gift department?"

A prick of guilt niggled at Anabelle's conscience. She'd been accused more than once of trying to take over. But this was different. "Ainslee will understand. I'm sure she will."

Cam cocked his brow. "The baby's only seven months old. She'll be overwhelmed. She's too young to even understand what Christmas is all about and would be just as happy crawling around inside the cardboard box your walk-and-ride car came in."

Lifting her chin, Anabelle folded her arms across her chest. "Well, I understand what Christmas is about, and it gives me great pleasure to give gifts to my family, particularly to my only grandbaby. Besides, she'll be eight months old by Christmas."

Chapter Two

LATER ON SATURDAY AFTERNOON, ANABELLE WAS STILL fussing about the way no one seemed to appreciate the joy of Christmas and its traditions as she drove to the grocery store in town.

She'd loved Christmas morning when her three children were young. She'd been married almost twelve years and had given up on ever having children before she'd gotten pregnant with Evan at age thirty, and she'd rejoiced in her motherhood every day since. Particularly during the holidays.

Evan had always been up first to check on the presents under the tree. Then he'd raced back upstairs to wake his little sister Ainslee. And later, after Kirstie was born, he'd carry her downstairs as well. Their little faces had been alight with excitement as they opened their presents.

She could barely wait to see that glow on little Lindsay's cheeks this year.

Perhaps that was one of the reasons the banished Christmas tree at the hospital and the missing presents for Hope Haven Kids was so worrisome. She could barely wait until Monday to have a talk with Albert Varner.

Though the grocery store's parking lot was crowded, Anabelle pulled in just as a car was pulling out of a spot near the door. Her lucky day!

She angled her car into the spot before someone else could beat her to it. They'd had snow the week before Thanksgiving, but now all the mounds of dirty snow and slush had melted and dried up. She always hoped for a white Christmas, but often Mother Nature didn't cooperate.

Anabelle started her shopping in the cereal aisle and then made her way to pick up a loaf of the whole-grain bread Cam preferred, and finally reached the dairy section at the back of the store.

"Hello, Anabelle. How are you?"

With a pang of annoyance, which she chided herself for, Anabelle turned to greet Ainslee's mother-in-law, Louise Giffen. As always, Louise was well turned out, her rich burgundy sweater complementing her fair complexion. She wore her sandy-brown hair pulled up and back from her face, and simple gold hoop earrings dangled from her ears.

Anabelle tried not to envy the woman's youthful vitality. "Hi, Louise. Did you have a nice Thanksgiving?"

"Yes, indeed, and have you heard the exciting news?" Louise was practically bubbling in her eagerness to share. The pitch of her voice had risen with excitement and the words tumbled out of her mouth in a rush.

Anabelle had to stop and think for a moment. Ainslee hadn't mentioned anything special. "What news is that?"

"George and I, along with our son who lives in Baltimore and his family and Doug and Ainslee and Lindsay Belle, are all going to Disney World for Christmas. We've rented a condo."

Anabelle's jaw went slack, and her heart dropped into her stomach. "You're all going to be gone for Christmas?"

"George and I will be going down the weekend before. I don't think Doug has decided when they'll fly down yet. He gets so busy at work, you know."

Another customer wanted to get into the dairy case, so Anabelle pushed her cart aside, placing it between herself and Louise, which gave her a little time and space to gather her wits. The disappointment she felt, the shock that she wouldn't be with Lindsay for the baby's first Christmas, was a blow she hadn't expected.

"I really must finish my shopping," Louise said. "We're having some friends over for dinner tonight, and I have to pick up some last-minute things. Good to see you, Anabelle."

Anabelle forced a smile. "Nice to see you too."

She stood there in front of the dairy case, staring into space. The picture of the Christmas she'd visualized spending with Lindsay crumbled like building blocks knocked over by a tempestuous toddler.

This was *not* fair. How could Ainslee even consider taking Lindsay away from home at Christmas? Away from Nana Anabelle?

Somehow she managed to finish her shopping and get back home without totally falling apart. The letdown from her anticipation of the family holiday made her slightly sick to her stomach.

She carried the two cloth tote bags filled with groceries into the kitchen and dropped them on the tile counter.

"Cameron!" she called.

He appeared from his office. "What is it, luv?"

"Did you know Ainslee and Doug are taking Lindsay to Florida for Christmas? To Disney World?"

"No," he said cautiously. "I hadn't heard that. What makes you think so?"

"Louise Giffen told me. At the grocery store. Standing there, as excited as can be, she told me my grandbaby wouldn't be here for Christmas. Not here to see all the presents I—" She swallowed hard. "I'm so disappointed."

"Now, now, Annie." He took her in his arms and tugged her gently up against his chest. His flannel shirt felt soft against her cheek and he smelled faintly of the fabric softener she used. "If the children want to go to Florida, they have a right to do that."

"Of course they do. But this is Lindsay's first Christmas."

"Yes, I know, luv. We can celebrate Christmas with them on a different day. Little Lindsay won't care."

"But I had pictured . . ." She broke away from Cam's embrace. "I'm going to call Ainslee right now. I don't see how they can possibly—"

"Whoa there!" He snared her hand. "Please don't call Ainslee and tell her what she can or can't do."

"I'm not going to tell her anything. But I can certainly talk to her about staying home for the holidays."

"You shouldn't call her when you're so upset. Give it a few days until you calm down. Then you can have a nice chat with her without losing your temper or getting her dander up."

She clenched her jaw. Her fingers mirrored the same gesture. "I don't lose my temper with my children."

Cam's raised eyebrows suggested he disagreed, which really annoyed her.

Ainslee's birthday was coming up in a couple weeks. Maybe Anabelle could get together with her for lunch and talk about her holiday plans.

Candace Crenshaw laughed at her son's determined ice-skating efforts even as a motherly sense of pride filled her chest. He was desperately trying to catch up with Heath Carlson, a radiology technician from the hospital, who had become a welcome part of Candace's life. And her children's.

Recently, she'd made it a point to ask her supervisor for weekends off so she could spend time with her children. And Heath, who also had weekends off.

She'd known Heath for more than a year. Certainly she'd seen him around Hope Haven before that. But they'd only started actually dating a few months ago. She got a mental jolt realizing this would be their first Christmas as a couple.

She frowned, wondering how she should handle their new and still somewhat tentative relationship during the holidays. What sort of gift should she give him? Should she invite him to Christmas dinner? Or would he rather spend the day with his father and brother and his family?

Goodness, she hadn't had to deal with those questions since she married Dean. But he was gone now; and, as she watched the skaters, she realized her life was changing.

An agile athlete, Heath dodged through the crowd of skaters circling the temporary outdoor rink created by flooding the tennis courts at the Deerford Public Park. Taking care not to frustrate Howie too much, Heath would slow a little, let the boy get close and then speed off again.

"I'm gonna get you this time!" Howie shouted, his bright red jacket flashing past where Candace was standing on the sidelines.

"Not if I can help it," Heath countered.

In the background, someone's boom box blared out heavy metal tunes that sounded more like noise to Candace than music.

She lifted her camera, ready to take a shot when the pair circled back her way. She'd purchased the digital camera shortly before Dean had died four years ago. Only recently had she resumed taking photos again. Her grief counselor said that was a good sign, and Candace thought so too. Not that she would ever stop missing Dean; but she was getting her life back together, the weight of grief resting more lightly on her shoulders and in her heart.

She'd taken off her wedding ring three months ago, although she'd always treasure the love she and Dean had shared.

She tracked Heath around the far end of the rink with Howie close behind him. Trim and fit, Heath worked out several times a week and it showed. His blond hair and healthy physique made him look younger than his age, which was the same as hers, thirty-eight. His navy jacket hung open and he was hatless, not at all bothered by the below freezing temperature.

In contrast, she wore a knit cap, heavy jacket, and mittens. But then, she wasn't skating as hard as Heath was.

She lined up for the shot hoping no one would step between her and her subjects.

Just as she clicked the camera, Howie tagged Heath on the back. "You're it!" the boy shouted.

Heath spun around and lifted Howie high in the air. "No, I'm not!"

Howie screamed with delight and Candace snapped another picture.

Still carrying Howie, Heath delivered him to Candace. "This kid is too good. He's wearing me out."

"I can skate really fast, can't I, Mommy?"

"You certainly can, young man." Her almost seven-year-old was red faced from the cold and exertion and grinning happily at her. She cupped the back of his head. "You ready to take a break? I've got hot chocolate in the thermos in Heath's Jeep."

"Nuh-uh. I'm not tired yet." To prove the point, he dashed back onto the ice to weave his way past more leisurely skaters.

"Man, what are you feeding that kid?" Heath laughed a full-throated sound, his blue eyes squinted nearly closed. "Too bad we can't bottle up all that energy."

She grinned as she adjusted the camera strap around her neck. "Some days his energy is a bit too much for me." In kindergarten Howie had been diagnosed with ADD. She'd resisted putting him on meds at such a young age and found that lots of exercise and participation in activities such as karate helped him to stay focused.

"He sure has good coordination for his age. I wouldn't be surprised if he turned into a jock." He glanced around the rink. "Where's Brooke?" Heath asked.

"She's over on the far side of the rink with that clutch of giggling girls who are pretending not to notice the boys showing off for them." With only four months left until she turned thirteen, Brooke was teetering on the brink of puberty, which was enough to give any mother gray hair. That, and the fact that Brooke had been talking about boys lately. A lot.

"Then I guess you'll have to skate with me." He held out his hand.

She felt a little flip of excitement in her stomach. "I'm not very good," she warned, taking his hand and allowing him to lead her onto the ice.

"We'll take it slow and easy, chickadee. I promise." Ever since she'd gone birding with Heath, he'd assigned her the nickname of chickadee. Very sweet and oddly intimate.

Still holding his hand, she fell into a slow gliding step as he guided her around the rink. His steps were smooth, his grip on her hand firm. A comfortable man to be around.

"Where did you learn to skate?" she asked.

"In Port Townsend, Washington. We didn't get much cold weather there, mostly rainy, but there was an ice-skating rink within bicycling distance of home. A bunch of us kids used to hang out there when they had open skating."

"So what brought you to Illinois?" She realized she'd never asked him before.

He skated a few steps before responding. "My fiancée grew up in the Chicago area. She liked Washington but wanted to move back to be near her folks. Since my brother lives here, I came along."

Candace felt a pang of grief on Heath's behalf. His fiancée had been killed by a drunk driver. The tragedy must have affected him deeply since he hadn't found another woman to love.

"It didn't take me long," he continued, "to figure out Chicago winters weren't easy to like. When they get snow it turns to slush too fast to be good for sledding or skiing, much less skating like this."

"But Chicago does have the White Sox." She grinned because he was such an avid fan and wore his White Sox baseball cap when he went out bird-watching.

"True. Every town has its compensations." He switched position so they were skating more closely together, his arm around her waist. "There're lots of nice things about Deerford."

Warmth flooded Candace's cheeks, and it wasn't entirely due to exercise.

Elena held on tightly to her granddaughter's hand as they walked through the fabric store. Isabel wore the warm navy coat with lace around the collar that Elena had sewn for her at the beginning of the school year. It was already beginning to look short on the child. She'd have to lower the hem soon.

"I'm gonna be an angel, aren't I, *Buela*?" Using her Spanish nickname for her grandmother, Izzy's striking gray eyes sparkled with excitement.

"You certainly are, sweetie."

"My friend Hayley is going to be an angel too."

"Yes, she is." Hayley Boyd was the daughter of Elena's friend Belinda from Holy Trinity Church. Hayley was in Isabel's kindergarten Sunday school class, and they were good buddies.

"What does an angel look like?"

Elena showed her the simple pattern the children's chorus director had recommended for the kindergartners' performance at Holy Trinity's Christmas Eve service.

"See, you'll wear a pretty white dress with gold braid on it and gold wings on your back."

"Will I get to fly?"

"I don't think so, Izzy." Elena chuckled. "You'd probably fly off to the moon and then how would I get you back?"

"Yes, yes!" The six-year-old jumped up and down flapping her arms in the aisle, her long dark hair bouncing in rhythm. "I want to fly to the moon."

"Maybe when you're bigger." They stopped at a table filled with bolts of cotton fabric in a rainbow of colors, but none of them was white.

Fingering a bolt of baby blue cotton, noting its smooth texture, Elena glanced around the store. Wall shelves held bolts of various fabrics all the way to the ceiling, and there were dozens of tables overflowing with even more fabrics plus various displays of notions, from thread to ribbons.

She bent down to talk to Izzy. "We're going to have to ask for help. I don't know where to find what we need."

"This is pretty." She touched her little hand to a bolt of pink cotton, testing its texture much as Elena had. "I could be a pink angel."

"Mrs. Joiner at church wants all of her little angels to wear white this year."

Izzy's lower lip puffed out. "But I like pink."

"I know you do, but let's do what Mrs. Joiner says. She'll like that." Taking Isabel's hand again, Elena went in search of a clerk to help them. The store was busy with lots of customers shopping for fabric to make up as Christmas gifts and holiday decorations.

"Excuse me," she said when one of the clerks finished measuring a customer's cloth. "My granddaughter is singing in the kindergarten chorus at Holy Trinity on Christmas Eve. I'm looking for the fabric—"

"Oh yes, we have all that set aside for Mrs. Joiner's children. I'll show you." The middle-aged woman set off at a brisk pace down the aisle.

Elena and Isabel followed, Isabel hurrying to keep up.

The clerk led them into a storeroom. "Here we are." From a shelf, she pulled out a bolt of white cotton and one of gold chiffon for the wings.

"Yes, that looks perfect," Elena said.

With quick efficiency, the clerk pulled off the necessary yardage for the dress, cut it and then did the same with the chiffon. To the yardage, she added a precut length of gold braid to decorate the skirt and bell sleeves, boning to frame the wings, and wired silver tinsel for the halo. Finally, she placed a headband on the pile.

"That should do it," the clerk said. "Take that up to the cashier, and she'll ring it up for you."

"Thank you very much."

The clerk winked at Isabel. "I bet you're going to be the prettiest little angel in the chorus."

Isabel stood up very straight and smiled. "Thank you. I think so too."

Elena nearly choked on a laugh. Modesty was not one of Izzy's strongest qualities. Hopefully, in time she'd learn the merit of being a little more demure about accepting compliments.

Once back home, Elena parked in the carport beside the house. Izzy let herself out of the car and ran inside, leaving the back door open.

"Daddy! Daddy!"

Gathering up her purchases, Elena followed her granddaughter inside, carefully closing the door to keep the heat inside. She arrived in the kitchen in time to see her son Rafael scoop his daughter up into his arms. Dark haired with flashing black eyes, he was a younger version of his father.

Elena smiled, grateful that her handsome son was so good and caring with Isabel.

"What's going on, *mi bonita*?" he asked his daughter.

"I'm going to be an angel and have gold wings, Daddy. Are you going to come see me when I sing?"

"Absolutely. Wouldn't miss it for the world."

Elena put her packages down on the 1950s chrome and Formica table and set her purse aside. With the help of her husband Cesar, she'd redecorated the kitchen a few years ago and loved the retro style with turquoise appliances.

Bouncing in her father's arms, Izzy said, "Is Mommy going to come see me sing too?"

"I don't know," Rafael said, his jaw visibly tightening. "You'll have to ask her the next time you see her."

Elena drew in a deep breath. Rafael and Isabel's mother had never married, and Sarah had deserted Rafael and their baby shortly after Isabel was born. She'd eventually gotten herself into rehab, gotten clean and was now in Deerford working in Hope Haven's kitchen. Slowly, Sarah had been establishing a connection with Isabel, to very positive effect. Isabel was completely taken with her mother.

Elena was also fairly certain that Sarah hoped to reunite with Rafael, but knowing of the lingering bitterness in Rafael's heart toward Sarah, Elena wasn't sure the pair would ever overcome their rocky past. As much as she understood Rafael's hesitance to accept Sarah back into his life, she couldn't help but like the young woman. She also secretly hoped that the pair would reunite, if only so that Izzy could have a stable family.

Rafael lowered Izzy to the floor. "I won't be home for dinner, Mama. The band is getting together to work out some kinks in one of our new numbers for tonight's gig."

"You'll have to eat something," she said. Her son played bass and was backup singer in a small band with visions of making it big. A dream that hadn't yet come true, so he supplemented his limited income from his musical career by working part-time at the restaurant Elena's mother owned, Baldomero. He'd also begun taking classes at the local community college with the goal of becoming a police officer like his father. "I can make you a sandwich to take with you."

"I'm good, Mama. We'll pick up something along the way."

Sighing, Elena said, "If you're sure." Like every good mother, she worried about her child eating right—even though he was old enough to be on his own.

Rafael kissed Izzy and Elena on the cheek, said good-bye, and left to join his fellow musicians. Isabel wandered off, probably to play with her dolls and stuffed animals.

Picking up the bag from the fabric store, Elena carried it into her bedroom. The walnut four-poster queen-sized bed she shared with Cesar was neatly made with the wedding-ring quilt her aunt had made for them when they married. With the curtains pulled back, sunlight poured through the window, making a shadowed cross in the middle of the quilt.

She would tell Sarah about Izzy's Christmas Eve performance. The young woman had been attending Sunday services at Holy Trinity Church lately and had joined a new members group.

Yes, she'd try to catch Sarah after church tomorrow.

Elena suddenly realized this would be Sarah's first Christmas with Isabel. For the first five of Izzy's Christmases, Sarah had not been a part of the child's life.

Which now created a few complications for the rest of the family.

Chapter Three

*J*AMES HANDED HIS ELDEST SON THE ANGEL, THE last of the ornaments, to put on top of the Christmas tree they'd purchased earlier in the day.

"You get to do the honors, Gideon."

"Right, Dad." Dragging the step stool next to the tree, the sixteen-year-old climbed up, stretching to reach the top branch.

Looking on, his younger brother Nelson cried out, "Careful! He's gonna fall into the tree. He's gonna crash and burn. *Ack!* The poor tree. Woe are we." Clutching his throat dramatically, the boy staggered backward.

"Knock it off, dweeb." Dismissing his brother without a glance, Gideon slid the angel firmly into place.

With an effort, James suppressed a smile. He had to agree with Anabelle, a Christmas tree was one of the great traditions they all could enjoy. The fact that the tree had been removed from Hope Haven's lobby was more than troubling, as were the missing presents.

"Be nice, boys," Fern admonished her sons from the couch where she and their cat, Sapphire, had been supervising the decorating activities. The silver Maine coon had thus far taken little interest in the project, preferring to remain curled up in Fern's lap for her afternoon nap.

Stepping down, Gideon dragged the stool out of the way.

"Turn the lights on, Nelson," James said. "Let's see how it looks lit up." Although it wasn't late in the day, the winter sun was weak and low in the sky, casting the living room in shadow.

Nelson flipped on the lights.

"Oh, doesn't that look nice!" Fern clapped her hands. "I've always loved bay windows and now we have one. You've done a beautiful job, boys. All three of you."

She smiled at James, and he joined his wife on the couch, taking her hand in his. "Our first Christmas in our new house."

They'd finally resolved the mold problem in their former home. They'd been fortunate to rent this new house until they could sell the old one. The stairs to the bedrooms in the old house had become too difficult for Fern to manage, her multiple sclerosis causing her problems with her legs, among other symptoms such as blurred vision and slurred speech. Fatigue seemed to come much more often these days.

This new house, built by a contractor friend of James's, had been a blessing for both Fern and James. A one-story ranch, all the living area was on the main floor, plus there was a basement. The kitchen was big and well designed with an adjoining family room. The comfortable living room had a natural rock fireplace that made the room feel cozy.

After the first of the year, they'd be able to list their former house with a Realtor and hopefully get it sold quickly.

"How are you feeling?" he asked Fern.

"Pretty good, all things considered." She squeezed his hand.

"I was afraid shopping for the tree would wear you out." She'd used her walker to get around the tree lot and as a place to sit when she tired. He and the boys had brought the best trees to Fern to make the final decision.

"No, I'm fine. And you boys did all the decorating, so I'm all rested now."

Some of the tension he always felt in his neck and shoulders when worried about Fern's health eased, and his shoulders relaxed. He leaned his head back on the couch.

Her MS symptoms had been relatively mild lately, her meds doing a good job of keeping things under control. The cyclical nature of the disease drove James crazy, never knowing how she'd feel one day to the next. It didn't make Fern too happy either. Particularly the downswings.

James had never known anyone as brave and courageous as his wife when faced with difficult challenges. Not even the guys and gals he had served with in the military in the first Gulf War. An amazing woman.

"Hey, Dad." Gideon plopped down in a chair and stretched out his long legs. Based on his size 13 shoes, the high school sophomore wasn't finished growing yet.

"Hey, Gideon," James mimicked in the same adolescent style.

The corners of Gideon's mouth turned up, and he speared his fingers through his rumpled hair. Although he was already taller than James, the teenager had the same wavy brown hair and blue eyes as his father.

"So anyway, Dad, I was playing this awesome video game over at Scotty Duran's house. I was thinking maybe you and Mom could get it for me for Christmas."

Nelson tossed some wood on the fire. "Why don't you sit on Santa's lap at the mall and ask him?"

Pulling his legs up and placing his feet flat on the floor, Gideon narrowed his eyes at his brother before continuing. "The game's called Chicago Underground, and it's got all these neat tunnels and labyrinths you gotta crawl through, even some stinky sewers that bubble with green goo."

"Oh, that sounds lovely," Fern teased. "Just where I've always wanted to play, in the sewers of Chicago. Maybe your father can get the game for me too."

"I don't think you'd really like it, Mom. There's shooting and explosions and killin' and stuff."

James didn't like the sound of that. "How violent is the game?"

Gideon pulled a face and lifted his shoulders in a teenage I-don't-know shrug. "It's not bad. A lot of guys at school are playing it."

Simply because other boys at school were playing the game didn't mean James wanted his son to have his own copy.

"What's the game's rating?" he asked.

"I dunno. I didn't look."

"Then I guess we'd better find out, huh?"

"Aw, Dad." He unfolded himself from the chair and stood, shoving his hands in his pockets. "It's just a game. It's make-believe—all the characters are avatars, you know? I'm not going to go out and kill somebody just 'cause I've played some stupid video game."

"I know, son." If the game was so stupid, why would he want to play it? James wondered, though he kept the thought to himself.

"Can I go down to Scotty's house now?" Gideon asked.

James checked his watch. "Be home by six. Dinner will be ready."

"Remember to wear your jacket," Fern added. "It's cold outside."

"Yeah, sure." The boy trudged to the front hall closet, dragged out his jacket and went out the door without putting it on.

Fern exhaled an isn't-that-just-like-a-teenager sigh.

His brother's departure seemed to animate Nelson. "If you're thinking about presents for me, I could use a new scientific calculator—you know, the kind with a bunch of functions—for my Algebra II class."

James cut his son a surprised look. "What's wrong with the one you've got?"

"We're getting into some heavy calculus now. Teacher says we're going to need a fancier one."

"You'd better write down exactly what you need," Fern commented. "Your parents don't know much about calculators."

"Or what it's going to cost," James added.

"A good one costs maybe a couple of hundred."

James swallowed hard enough to down a gigantic sulfur pill. "Dollars?"

"I guess. I'll write out what the teacher said we should get." Nelson stood. "I'm gonna go read in my room. It's a book about how they invented the atomic bomb in World War II. Kind of ancient history stuff."

Fern sputtered a laugh as Nelson left the room. "Are we raising a couple of maniacs? Shooting people in sewers? Building atomic bombs? What's next?"

"I'm afraid to find out." Leaning back, James closed his eyes and rubbed them. "At least a calculator sounds nonviolent."

"I'll check online for the calculator Nelson tells us he wants," Fern said quietly. "I assume you're going to check the rating on that video game, aren't you?"

"Oh yes, and I'd venture it's not rated E for Everyone."

Raising the boys, they'd tried hard to keep them away from violent games of any sort. When they were young, they even avoided having toy guns in the house as long as they could.

But there was violence on the television even when the boys weren't allowed to watch violent programs. Every night there was violence on the news. Shootings and stabbings and war. And when Gideon had entered high school, he'd joined the Junior ROTC and thought he might like a military career.

In the current society, it was impossible to keep the boys ignorant of the violence around them. Maybe it wasn't even a good idea. But James and Fern continued their struggle to protect them from the worst of it.

Until now, Gideon had been content with nonviolent video games. James was afraid his son's preferences might have changed and wondered why.

With a groan, James stood and stretched. He'd check the rating of Chicago Underground before he started dinner.

When Cesar returned home from his own shopping expedition, Elena had the kitchen table covered with fabric, the pattern pieces for Izzy's angel costume arranged on the cloth.

"Looks like we'll be eating at the counter tonight," he commented before giving her a kiss. He was wearing jeans and his favorite wool shirt and smelled of the cold winter air.

"Don't worry. I'll have this cleaned up by dinnertime."

"Is Izzy around?" he asked.

"She's playing in her room. She was way too helpful trying to pin the pattern in place. I was afraid she'd stick herself or swallow a pin."

"I guess Rafael is out somewhere again tonight."

"The band has another gig. He left early to rehearse some new songs."

"At least he's no longer thinking of music as his one and only career goal, and he's decided being a cop is a good idea. He can always play music as a hobby."

Until recently, Rafael's career goal, or lack thereof, had caused a lot of friction between father and son. "He's finding his way, Cesar. He seems to like the criminal justice class he's taking."

He went to the refrigerator and got out a carton of milk. "About time. By his age, I was already on the force and supporting my family. He's got Izzy to think about and his own future."

"Be patient, honey. He'll do fine."

"Yeah, I know." He retrieved a glass and poured the milk. "So what are you working on now?"

"Izzy's angel costume for the Christmas Eve program at church. She'd love to have you come see her perform."

When he didn't respond, Elena's heart sank. The stubborn man seldom gave God or the church a chance since the death of his mother. He believed the Lord hadn't heard his prayers when he was a little boy, so Cesar had stopped believing in God.

Elena prayed every day that her husband would find his way back to the Lord. So far those prayers hadn't been answered but she wasn't about to give up on the Lord like Cesar had.

She'd keep her faith strong.

At church on Sunday, Anabelle was on her best behavior when she greeted Ainslee after the service.

"Hello, dear. How are you?" Tilting her head, Anabelle tried to get a peek at Lindsay, who was in her mother's arms. The baby was all bundled up in a fuzzy turquoise snowsuit.

"We're all fine." Ainslee brushed a kiss to her mother's cheek.

Cam, who was standing beside Anabelle, shook hands with Doug. A tall, slender man, his easygoing personality was a nice foil for Ainslee's often over-the-top perfectionism, especially when it came to the baby.

"Doug's going to Washington, DC, for a conference this coming week," Ainslee said. "It's a meeting of the national architect association's board of directors. He's helping to develop some national guidelines for safe construction."

"Really?" Anabelle tickled Lindsay's foot. The baby stared back at her with her big brown eyes and then blew a bubble that popped. Lindsay grinned as though she'd accomplished something miraculous and drooled onto her snowsuit. Love for the baby filled Anabelle's heart like a rising tide until it was so full her heart nearly burst.

"I'll only be gone one night and plan to be home late the next evening," Doug said.

The news of Doug's trip finally registered with Anabelle. "Ainslee, why don't you come to our house for dinner the night Doug's out of town? I was going to invite you out for lunch—to celebrate your birthday. Having dinner together with you and the baby would be even better. I'll make you your favorite German chocolate cake," she promised.

Another family wanted to get past them, so Anabelle and the others stepped off to the side of the walkway.

"Oh, I don't know, Mother. Lindsay doesn't sleep that well in a strange place."

Anabelle's shoulders tensed and she gritted her teeth. Her house wouldn't be strange to Lindsay if Ainslee would bring her over more often.

"We'll do an early dinner," she said instead.

"You go ahead, honey," Doug said. "At least you'd get a night off from cooking. And your mother is a great cook."

Anabelle beamed at her son-in-law. "Then it's all set. You can come by whenever you're ready. I'll put something in the slow cooker that will be ready to eat whenever you show up."

"Come to think of it," Doug said, an amused expression in his dark eyes. "Maybe I can get the board to delay their meeting a day or two. I'd like to come to dinner too."

Laughing, Anabelle said, "We'd love to have you, Doug. Anytime at all." Although this time, she really hoped to talk with Ainslee about their trip to Florida, and how disappointed she would be not to share in Lindsay's first Christmas.

Granted, wanting Lindsay home for Christmas might be selfish of Anabelle. But when it came to her first grandchild, generosity of spirit was a virtue she appeared to lack.

After the church service, Elena picked up Isabel from the Sunday school classroom. As they headed toward the parking lot, Sarah stood on the walkway waiting for them.

"There's Mommy!" Izzy dashed off to greet her mother.

With a delighted smile, Sarah crouched down to catch her daughter in a warm embrace. "Hi, there, my beautiful little girl."

"You're beautiful too," Izzy responded, looping her arms around her mother's neck. In her hand she held the wrinkled picture she'd colored in her class.

Elena had to admit, Sarah was an attractive young woman. Blonde and petite, she'd put on a little weight since she'd shown up in Deerford and looked less gaunt than when she had arrived. Mother and daughter were a picture in contrasts, one with a fair complexion and light hair, the other with more caramel-toned skin and naturally curly black hair. Still, Izzy's facial features and smile were all Sarah. So were her striking gray eyes.

Izzy broke the embrace. "We colored pictures of the three shepherds in Sunday school." She showed Sarah her artistic efforts. "The shepherds didn't have any sheep so I drew one for them."

"Well, yes you did." Speaking in a soft voice, Sarah confirmed the presence of a sheep with a smile. "You're a good little artist."

"Do you want to keep my picture? You can put it up on your refrigerator like Buela does at my house."

Taking the picture, Sarah studied it for a moment. "Thank you, Izzy. That's very sweet of you. It's a very nice picture."

Elena felt an unexpected stab of jealousy that she tried valiantly to tamp down. After all, she'd had literally dozens of pieces of Izzy's artwork on her refrigerator over the years and had saved them all in a folder she kept in her bedroom. She shouldn't deny Sarah the same joy and pride in the efforts of a child who had come from her own womb, however much she had failed that child initially. It was obvious now that Sarah intended to be the best mother she could be for Isabel.

"Sarah, I'm glad I caught you this morning. I hope you're planning to come to the Christmas Eve service," Elena said. "Isabel is going to sing with the kindergarten chorus."

"I'm going to be an angel!" Izzy blurted out.

"How exciting. I'll certainly come to see you."

"My daddy's coming too."

Sarah glanced toward Elena as though questioning Rafael's attendance at church.

"He usually comes to church when Isabel is in a program." Elena regretted her son didn't attend church more often, but there was little she could do about it other than pray that in time he'd change.

"I'm glad he comes for Isabel's sake." Sarah's voice held a note of sincerity.

Isabel took Sarah's hand. "Can Mommy come home with us? I could show her what we bought for my angel costume."

"Uh, not today." Reluctant to surprise Rafael by having his former girlfriend appear without warning, Elena tried to find an alternative. "If you'd like, Sarah, you could come to dinner tomorrow night. Rafael will be rehearsing with his band at a friend's house."

Disappointment momentarily erased Sarah's smile but she quickly recovered. "I'd love to come to dinner and see Isabel's angel costume. Thank you for inviting me."

"We'll look forward to seeing you." Elena said good-bye and walked Isabel to her small SUV. Each time their paths crossed, the more Elena found to like about Sarah. If things had been different, if Sarah hadn't been addicted to drugs, she would have been a good mother from the beginning. And perhaps the kind of wife Rafael needed.

Even so, the emotionally laden situation seemed fraught with potential disaster from any number of directions. Particularly since Rafael wanted little to do with his daughter's mother.

Chapter Four

ONDAY, ANABELLE USED HER MORNING BREAK to go downstairs to the administrative offices in search of Albert Varner. She'd been just as annoyed this morning to find the Christmas tree absent from the lobby as she had been Friday when Hap and Eddie had taken it down. And the thought of the missing gifts made her sick to her stomach.

The office of Penny Risser, Varner's executive assistant, resembled an overgrown jungle. Potted plants and hanging baskets were everywhere. While Anabelle admired Penny's green thumb, she thought the woman was overdoing it a bit.

"Is Mr. Varner in this morning?" Anabelle asked.

Penny didn't look away from her computer screen. "He is, but he's busy." A tiny bonsai Christmas tree decorated with miniature ornaments sat on one corner of her desk.

"I'd really like to talk with him."

"You'll have to come back later."

"Penny, please. I'm on my break. This should only take a minute of his time."

Swiveling her chair, Penny eyed Anabelle with a fair amount of suspicion. Despite having just celebrated her fortieth birthday this year, her hair was entirely gray. Somehow that added to her take-no-prisoners demeanor.

"What did you want to talk to him about?" she asked.

Anabelle had no intention of being intimidated by the woman. "Our missing Christmas tree in the lobby."

Her brows arched in disapproval. "The tree is not missing. It has been taken down."

"I'm aware of that, Penny. I want to know why it was taken down and how we can get that decision reversed."

The executive assistant's tightly curled hair seemed to quiver. "I have already broached the subject with Mr. Varner. He has not revealed his reasons to me."

That came as a surprise since Varner relied on his assistant so heavily, but it also meant Penny could be an ally in getting the tree back where it belonged.

"What about the Christmas party for Hope Haven Kids? Is that still on?"

"He's made no comment on that as yet. We have, however, asked the police to investigate the missing presents."

At least that was something. "Let me have a shot at him, Penny. He and I go back a long way."

"Yes, I know. But I don't think you'll get any further than I did." She glanced at the phone and then punched the intercom button. "Mr. Varner, Anabelle Scott is here to see you."

"What does she want?" he responded in a muffled voice.

"She says she won't take long."

"Very well."

Penny gestured toward Varner's door. "Good luck."

Nodding her thanks, Anabelle rapped on the door once and then stepped into Varner's office.

Penny's green thumb had done its work in Varner's office as well, filling the room with any number of plants that she tended.

"Good morning, Mr. Varner."

"Good morning to you, Anabelle." Standing, he extended his hand. Though not a tall man, Albert Varner was the epitome of an executive, dressed as he was in a dark suit and somber tie. Photos on the wall of his office depicted him with virtually every influential person in the county plus the governor.

Anabelle shook Varner's hand and seated herself in one of the two leather chairs that faced his desk, which was covered with several stacks of papers and reports.

Sitting down, Varner leaned forward, his clasped hands resting on his walnut desk. "What can I do for you?"

"I'm very disappointed that the Christmas tree in the lobby was removed. I can only imagine how much that must have troubled you as well." She tried to stroke his ego while still prepared to challenge him. "To remove the symbol of our Christ's birth, you must have had a compelling reason."

Color flooded Varner's face, and he picked up a pencil from his desk, rolling it between his fingers. "You're quite right. I do have a good reason to have the tree removed."

"Would you mind telling me what that reason is?"

Leaning back, he continued to toy with his pencil and avoid making eye contact. "You do realize that an executive sometimes has to make difficult decisions. The impetus for those decisions must sometimes remain confidential."

A muscle in Anabelle's jaw flexed. *Confidential, my foot! He's keeping the reason a secret because he can't justify his decision.*

"That's a shame." She tilted her head in sympathy and gave him a reassuring smile that was so tight her cheeks ached. "I know I would understand, and so would other employees, if the reason we don't have a tree in the lobby this year—the first time in thirty years, that I know about—if the reason were a substantial one."

"Yes, well . . . I'm afraid I can't reveal the specifics, but I can assure you that the action was necessary for the well-being of the hospital."

"Well-being?" *What on earth could he mean by that?*

"Yes, exactly. Which is why I made the decision I did. Now if you will excuse me." Standing, he swept his hand above his paper-covered desk. "I do have a great deal of work to do."

"What about the party for the children?"

"We can discuss that later." Sitting down again, Varner pulled a yellow pad in front of him and began writing some notes, determined to ignore Anabelle's presence.

Anabelle was not pleased to be dismissed without having obtained the information she wanted. She had little choice but to leave, which didn't mean she was going to give up trying to determine his reason for taking down the tree—then get him to reverse that decision.

She marched out of the office, gave Penny a negative shake of her head, and walked directly to Janice Thompson's office.

She found the social worker at her desk, which was covered with cardboard Christmas tree cutouts.

"Any updates on the missing gifts for the children?" Anabelle asked.

Janice started, dropping her pencil and bent down to pick it up, her hair falling to both sides of her face. "Oh, Anabelle, this is terrible. The police couldn't find a clue where the gifts have gone and I'm trying to figure out which presents were taken so we can replace them. Then I have to find a way to display the remaining gift cards so visitors, or whoever can, will buy presents for the rest."

"So the party's still on?"

Janice blinked rapidly and tugged on her right ear. "As far as I know the party is on. Have you heard something different?"

"No, but Varner isn't talking. He won't say why the tree came down and claimed he was too busy to talk about the party."

"Until I hear otherwise from Mr. Varner, I'll keep planning the party. The children so look forward to the ice cream and presents. Which means I need some way to display these." She held up a handful of little Christmas trees.

Frowning, Anabelle considered the problem. Without a Christmas tree, where could Janice hang the ornaments where the public could see them?

"Maybe I could ask my husband to make a tree out of plywood and you could hang the ornaments on little hooks."

"That would be wonderful, Anabelle. Do you think your husband would be willing?"

Oh yes, Anabelle was quite confident of that. "I'm sure he'll be happy to help out."

Anabelle left Janice and climbed the stairs to the second floor. There was more than one way to peel an orange, or in this case, ferret out Varner's secret. With the help of her friends, she intended to do just that—discover why the CEO had ordered the tree removed.

She stopped at the Intensive Care Unit and found Elena at her nurses' station watching the monitors of the patients she was overseeing.

"Think you can make it to the Corner for lunch today?" Anabelle asked, thinking she and her friends could talk more freely at the nearby Diner on the Corner than in the hospital cafeteria.

Elena glanced up. "Sure, if I can get someone to monitor my patients for me. What's up?"

"We have to figure out why Varner had the tree taken down. He's not talking."

Elena frowned. "That's odd. Why's he being so secretive?"

"Maybe when we figure out the reason, we'll know why. See you at noon."

Back at the central nurses' station, Anabelle checked with the Cardiac Care nurse on duty and found there'd been no new admissions to the unit while she was downstairs. Saying she'd be right back, she went in search of James.

She found him standing in the hallway talking with Diana Zimmer, the founder of Hope Haven Hounds, a therapy dog program intended to help hospital patients. Her dog Ace, a beautiful golden retriever, sat calmly beside her. He wore a kelly-green scarf around his neck, which identified him as a therapy dog.

"Hi, Diana." Anabelle petted Ace and scratched him behind his ears. He wagged his tail in response. "You're such a good boy," she crooned.

"Hey, Anabelle. How's your dog these days?" Diana asked.

"Sarge eats like an adolescent and is still growing. Cam's threatening to go back to work to pay for all the dog food we have to buy."

Diana laughed and so did James.

"Any behavior problems?" A professional dog trainer, Diana had been a lifesaver when Anabelle had brought Sarge home from the county shelter, teaching them how to get the puppy to respond to basic commands.

Anabelle glanced at her watch. "I think it's been at least twenty-four hours since Sarge swiped something from the house and buried it in the backyard."

"Oh dear . . ."

"I'm kidding," Anabelle admitted with a laugh. "He's still pretty energetic, but Cam seems to be able to get him to obey the basic commands, and he's teaching him a few tricks. So that's good."

James interrupted. "I've got to check on—"

Anabelle held up her hand to stop him from leaving. "Actually, I came looking for you, James. Can you do lunch at the Corner about noon?"

"I guess. Something going on?"

"We have to figure out why we don't have a Christmas tree in the lobby this year."

"I noticed that when I came in," Diana said. "There's always been one there in previous years."

"Don't I know it. And there will be one there again if we have our way."

Saying she'd see them both later, Anabelle headed for the Birthing Unit to invite Candace to lunch. Among them, they would come up with a plan to get the answers they needed.

Anabelle left the hospital a little before noon, hoping to get a booth at the diner before the big lunch crowd arrived. She bundled up in her winter coat for the short walk to the Diner on the Corner, a place often frequented by hospital employees when they tired of the in-house cafeteria food. The overcast sky hinted at the promise of snow.

As she pushed open the glass door of the diner, the scent of hamburgers on the grill greeted her along with the warm interior air.

She hung her coat on a coatrack near the door and chose a booth by the long window at the front of the diner.

Lindy Yao, a young Asian woman, appeared with menus. "Are your friends going to join you?"

"Yes, there'll be four of us." Assuming the others could get away from their patients. Elena, in particular, often had days when she didn't have time for lunch at all. Intensive Care nursing could be exceedingly demanding work.

A few minutes later, James and Candace arrived together. Candace took the seat next to Anabelle; James slid across the opposite green vinyl seat to the window.

"Have you ordered yet?" he asked.

"Not yet. I haven't been here long."

James opened his menu, although Anabelle imagined he'd long ago memorized the choices. She certainly had. Over the years, only the daily specials had changed—and those hadn't changed much.

A moment later, Lindy appeared with water and mugs of coffee for Anabelle and James, and a pot of hot water and teabags for Candace.

"You folks want to order now or wait for your friend?" she asked.

Anabelle lifted the bottom of the cheerful café curtains on the window to see if she could spot Elena. For the holiday season, the window had been painted with a nativity scene including shepherds and wise men. "I guess we should go ahead and order. Elena may have gotten hung up in ICU."

Anabelle and Candace ordered Cobb salads; James, a turkey sub with fruit on the side.

After Lindy left, James said, "If Varner wouldn't tell you why he had the tree removed, what can we do? Hanging him by his thumbs 'til he talks probably isn't a good idea." He twisted his mouth into an expression of mock agony and held up his thumbs to demonstrate.

Trying not to laugh, Anabelle hid her smile behind her hand. "No, probably not. I thought we could start by brainstorming all the possible reasons he could have for his decision, and then we pursue those until we come up with an answer."

Sipping her tea, Candace cocked her head at a thoughtful angle. "Well, we discussed earlier the possibility of someone being allergic to the tree. Maybe someone had a reaction and is planning to sue?"

"Good question." Anabelle found a small notebook in her purse and jotted down Candace's idea.

"It couldn't have been a very bad reaction," James commented. "At least I haven't had any patients admitted to my unit lately with anaphylactic shock."

"Maybe they were treated in the ER and released," Candace countered.

"I'll check the ER's records to see if anything turns up." Anabelle wrote herself a note. "What else?"

"Well," James said, "my first thought last week was that Varner or someone decided Christmas displays weren't politically correct."

Irritated by that possibility, Anabelle said, "It's hard to believe after all these years, suddenly it's wrong to have a Christmas tree in the lobby."

The diner's front door blew open and in rushed Elena, squeezing by a couple who were waiting to be seated. She slid in next to James.

"Sorry I'm late, gang. An accident victim's blood pressure tanked. The surgeon had nicked his spleen, and they had to take him back to the OR."

"That doesn't sound good," Anabelle commented.

"It wasn't. So what have I missed?" Elena asked.

Anabelle summarized what they'd discussed so far.

Lindy stopped by the table to take Elena's order of the daily special—quiche with a green salad on the side and coffee.

"Could there be a financial reason for taking down the tree?" Elena asked.

"Anything is possible," Anabelle said.

"I guess I could ask Quintessa," Elena volunteered, willing to speak to the chief financial officer's executive assistant.

"Maybe an environmental group complained," Candace suggested.

James frowned as though he was skeptical. "Like a Save the Trees organization?"

"I suppose. I'm just throwing out ideas," Candace admitted.

Jotting down Candace's thought, Anabelle said, "That's what we need to do. Think of every possibility we can come up with and see if it leads us anywhere."

"But wouldn't environmentalists be picketing Christmas tree lots instead of pressuring Varner to remove one already dead tree?" James persisted.

Anabelle shrugged. "Who knows? But let's not eliminate any possibility yet."

"Isabel has been reading *How the Grinch Stole Christmas!* It's her favorite book this time of year," Elena said. "So she'd probably point the finger at him."

Laughing, they all agreed there was indeed a Grinch in Deerford, and they were determined to ferret out his identity.

"I don't mean to pry," Candace said in a soft voice. "All of us would like to see the decorated tree back in the lobby, but you seem particularly determined to make it happen, Anabelle. Is there a reason you feel so strongly?"

"Well, it's tradition, of course. You can't just throw away—" She stopped herself as suddenly painful memories assailed her and an unexpected band of anguish tightened her chest. "I suppose I do have a special reason for feeling as I do."

Her mouth went dry. She hadn't realized that something specific had been driving her quest to restore the tree to the lobby. She had to take a sip of water before she could continue. "The year I was eight, my mother became very ill shortly before Christmas. Woman's problems, they told me. I still believed in Santa Claus, and I was upset that we hadn't put up our Christmas tree yet. Where would Santa put our presents?"

The others had stopped eating and listened attentively. Their sympathetic expressions nearly brought Anabelle to tears.

"My mother became so sick, they took her to the hospital the day before Christmas. I realized later that she'd had a hysterectomy but no one said that at the time. Not that I would've known what it was anyway.

"My father was so upset, he spent all of his time with Mother. I couldn't visit her, not even on Christmas Day. I had to stay at a neighbor's house."

She wiped her cheek with the back of her hand, surprised to find it damp with tears.

"Mother came home after spending ten days in the hospital. Christmas was long past. It was as if everyone had forgotten there was such a thing as Christmas."

Candace took Anabelle's hand and squeezed it. "No wonder you think Christmas and Christmas trees are so important."

With an effort, Anabelle pulled herself together and sat up straighter. "A Christmas tree in Hope Haven's lobby is a tradition for everyone in this town. Even more important, some of the children who attend the Hope Haven Kids' party don't receive any other presents for Christmas. Their families simply don't have the money for gifts when they're paying off huge medical bills. I'm going to see to it we don't lose our tradition."

After everyone expressed their support for Anabelle's cause, they finished their lunches and then headed back to the hospital.

Rather than return directly to ICU, Elena made a detour to the office of the chief financial officer, where she was told Quintessa was having a late lunch in the hospital cafeteria. Reversing her direction, she headed there.

The lunch crush had eased, and there were several open tables. A few employees, or maybe hospital visitors, hadn't bused their own dirty dishes, and a cafeteria worker was cleaning up the tables.

For holiday decoration, someone had draped silver garlands around the room, and there were paper cutouts of Christmas trees and gingerbread cookies pasted on the display cases. So whatever reason Varner had for removing the tree from the lobby, it hadn't affected the holiday spirit in the cafeteria. Odd.

Elena spotted Quintessa and her brother Dillan sitting together at a table in the far corner. The twins both had black hair, large expressive brown eyes, and skin the color of warm cocoa.

"Hi, you two," Elena said. "May I join you for a minute?"

"Hey, Anabelle. Sure you can." Smiling, Dillan stood. "Pull up a chair."

She sat down, and Quintessa said, "Aren't you eating lunch?"

"I already did at the Corner."

"Oh, did you need something from us?" Quintessa asked.

"In a manner of speaking. A few of us have been trying to figure out why Mr. Varner took down the Christmas tree."

"Yeah, I noticed that," Dillan said.

Quintessa plucked a pickle out of her sandwich and set it aside on her plate. "Mr. McGarry has been having a fit lately trying to balance the budget for next year. But taking down the tree wouldn't help. It's already been paid for."

Between Albert Varner and Zane McGarry, the CFO, they always had trouble balancing the hospital's annual budget.

"Could he be planning to cancel the party for Hope Haven Kids?" Elena asked.

Quintessa looked surprised by the question. "I haven't heard anything like that. He does get a little grumpy about the cost of the ice cream we serve, though. Of course, on a bad day he can get grumpy about anything."

Elena wondered if the CFO was the Grinch they were trying to identify.

"But it wasn't for financial reasons," Quintessa added. "At least Mr. McGarry didn't say anything about it to me."

Elena leaned back in her chair. It appeared there was only a small chance Zane McGarry was Deerford's resident Grinch.

But she'd have to worry about that later. Right now, she had to report her lack of success to Anabelle. Then she had to get through the rest of the day and plan what to have for dinner when Sarah came over this evening.

As she hurried through the lobby, she spotted the husband of a former ICU patient. A man in his sixties, he'd lost his wife to cancer only a few weeks ago.

"Mr. Fontaine?"

He turned slowly and stared at her with a blank look. His complexion looked drawn and pasty, and he had a day's worth of stubble on his face.

"I'm Elena Rodriguez. I was your wife's ICU nurse."

"Oh yeah." Her words seemed to take a moment to register. "Sorry, I didn't recognize you, Ms. Rodriguez."

"No need to apologize." Elena remembered how hard he'd taken the death of his wife. He still appeared to be grieving. "What brings you to the hospital today?"

"I, ah . . ." He glanced around the lobby as though he wasn't sure where he was. He shook his head as though he'd forgotten his purpose for being there. A sure sign of someone whose mind was elsewhere. "I'm picking up some paperwork. I have the maintenance contract for the hospital vehicles. The vans and service trucks."

"I see. Well, it's nice to see you. I hope you're getting along all right."

He looked at her blankly, his eyes watery and red rimmed.

"Have a good day," she told him, suspecting he hadn't had many of those days since his wife passed away. Grief could be such a debilitating experience.

Chapter Five

WHEN ANABELLE GOT HOME THAT AFTERNOON, SHE changed clothes and decided to take Sarge for a walk to clear her head. The mystery of the absent tree in the hospital lobby and the whereabouts of the missing presents continued to trouble her. With Elena's report that Zane McGarry was an unlikely candidate for Grinch, she was stuck for the moment.

She found Sarge and her husband in his office, the dog laying at his feet.

"I'm going to take Sarge for a w-a-l-k," she said.

Cam glanced up from the landscaping magazine he was reading. "It's almost dark outside."

"I know. I won't be long. I just need a little fresh air."

"Hang on." He set the magazine aside. "I'll come with you."

Despite Anabelle having spelled the word *walk*, Sarge caught on to what was happening as soon as Cam stood up. His tail wagging like a metronome for a polka, he danced around Cam's feet.

"Easy, boy," Cam said. "We've got to get our jackets."

Bouncing around like he was on a trampoline, the dog raced them to the mudroom and started to scratch at the back door.

"Sit," Cam ordered. Sarge did, and Cam hooked on the leash. "Stay."

Anabelle pulled on her jacket and looped an old knit scarf over her head. One of the reasons she'd wanted a dog was her hope that she and Cam could take walks together. Not only did the walks provide the exercise she needed, particularly at the end of the day, they also provided an opportunity for her and Cam simply to be together.

Cam let Sarge run out ahead of them, giving him a long length of leash so he could investigate any new scents since his walk earlier in the day. The dog dashed back and forth from one side of the street to the other, stopping only briefly before darting in the opposite direction.

Setting a comfortable pace, Cam strode beside Anabelle, their gloved hands clasped together. Breath fogged in front of her face, and the cold air pinched her cheeks.

In their semirural neighborhood, houses were set well back from the street and most were surrounded by a few acres of land. A few families owned horses and most had an outbuilding of some sort. She and Cam had raised their family on this street and still knew most of the neighbors, though many of the children had now moved away.

"How was your day?" she asked Cam. He'd put on a heavy peacoat and wore a baseball cap to keep his head warm.

"The usual. I went to my Rotary club meeting. Mark Cunningham's wife passed away. The funeral will probably be next weekend."

"I'm sorry to hear that." Anabelle had met Tina Cunningham, a woman in her eighties, a time or two but didn't know her well.

"How about you? Anything new at the hospital?"

"We're still trying to figure out why Albert Varner removed the Christmas tree from the lobby. So far we haven't had any luck, and he wouldn't tell me."

Sarge halted at the home of a golden retriever, who greeted him from the other side of the fence. They did what looked like a choreographed dance of recognition and then Sarge bounded on.

"Come to think of it," Anabelle said, "have you heard anything about an environmental group protesting people cutting down trees for Christmas?"

His brows inched up his forehead. "Around here, you mean?"

"Here or anywhere else. Has there been anything in the paper or on television about protests?" Anabelle didn't always have a chance to read the paper or watch the news on television.

"I can't remember hearing anything about a protest. Is that what you think happened to the tree? Varner took it down because a bunch of tree huggers got to him?"

"It was just a thought. We were brainstorming ideas."

If only Varner had told her why he'd had the tree removed, finding ways to get him to reverse that decision would be so much easier.

"There is something you can help us with," Anabelle said.

"Uh-oh. Are you finding work for idle hands?"

She laughed and told him about Janice's need to display the gift tags for the children since there was no longer a tree in the lobby.

"Sure, I can whip out a plywood tree for you and make some sort of a stand for it. I may even have some green paint around."

"It doesn't have to be real tall. Just large enough so Janice can display the gift tags." Surely Varner wouldn't object to continuing the spirit of giving during the holiday season with mere plywood.

"How does six feet sound? I can use the rest of the sheet of plywood to make the stand."

"Perfect." She stretched up and gave him a peck on the cheek. "Thank you, dear. I knew you'd want to help."

Elena was putting together chicken quesadillas for dinner when the doorbell chimed. Quickly wiping her hands on a dishtowel, she hurried to the front door to welcome Sarah.

"I hope I'm not too early." Dressed casually in slacks and a pale blue, cable-knit sweater that enhanced her gray eyes, Sarah gave her a tentative smile.

"No, you're fine. Come in. Please." Elena opened the door wider.

"Mommy's here!" Izzy screamed. She thundered down the hallway to the front door.

"Hey, little angel." Sarah picked up the child to give her a hug. "Did you have a good day at school?"

"Billy Robertson wrote purple stars in crayon all over my desk and got in trouble with my teacher."

Elena choked on a laugh as she closed the door to keep out the cold, late-autumn air. She'd heard a lot about Billy since school started. Apparently he was a real cutup. The purple stars were an addition to his usual high-energy antics.

"Oh my . . ." Smothering her own laugh, Sarah lowered Isabel to the floor. "Why did he do that?"

"He said he loves me and wants to marry me, but I told him I don't love him back." She wrinkled her little button nose. "He's too silly."

"Maybe he won't be so silly when he grows up," Sarah suggested.

"It doesn't matter. After recess, he told me he loves Louanne." Unconcerned with Billy's fickle heart, Izzy took Sarah's hand and led her into the living room. "Come see our Christmas tree."

Sarah stepped into the living room and gasped. "What a beautiful tree. And look at those glass ornaments. They're charming."

"They're all vintage ornaments. Some of them my mother had saved from my childhood," Elena said. "Others I've picked up at the Once Upon a Time store in town." Like her decorative style throughout most of the house, all the ornaments were retro, from colorful glass balls to birds inside clear ornaments. An old-fashioned gilded spire topped the tree. She'd even found a string of bubble lights and some tiny electric candles that she'd arranged around the middle of the tree.

She had put the tree up this past weekend, and it was fresh enough that the evergreen scent still perfumed the air.

For a moment, a frown tugged at her forehead. She loved the scent and sight of a Christmas tree and the nostalgia that went with it. Why in the world would Mr. Varner have the hospital tree removed from the lobby where the visitors could enjoy it?

"I have to be very careful with the ornaments," Izzy announced with exaggerated solemnity. "Buela would be very sad if I broke any of them."

"I would indeed," Elena agreed. "And you've been very good not to touch them."

Her collection of tiny period houses displayed on the fireplace mantel caught Sarah's eye. She went closer to study them. "The detail is amazing. Did you always have these too?"

"I've collected them over the years and friends have given them to me as gifts. Cesar thinks I've gotten a bit carried away, but I love them."

"I can see why."

Izzy tugged on her mother's hand. "Do you have a Christmas tree where you live?"

"My roommates and I thought we'd get one next weekend, but not one as big as yours." Shortly after Sarah had arrived in Deerford and landed a job in the hospital kitchen, she'd found an apartment nearby and a couple of roommates.

Cesar appeared from the hallway that led to the bedrooms. He'd freshened up after he got home from work, and his dark hair still looked damp. "I thought I heard voices out here. Hello, Sarah."

"Good evening. I was just admiring all your lovely Christmas decorations."

"That's all Elena's doing. My job is to get the tree set up, and she pretty much does the rest on her own."

"You help some," Elena reminded him. "Why don't you all visit a bit, and I'll finish up with our quesadillas."

"Yummy, yummy in my tummy." Izzy rubbed her hand over her stomach to emphasize her point. "I love quesadillas."

"So do I," Sarah said. "I'd like to help, if I may."

"Of course, if you'd like to."

Sarah was always so extraordinarily polite, the effort the young woman made to be accepted by the family was palpable. A pang of sympathy pricked Elena's heart. Having to tiptoe on eggshells whenever she visited the house had to be a terrible strain.

After they'd eaten dinner and cleaned up the kitchen, Elena brought out the fabric for Isabel's angel costume. She needed plenty of space to cut the material, so she spread everything out on the kitchen table.

"Here's what the costume will look like." She handed the pattern to Sarah.

"Oh, adorable." Sarah showed Izzy. "You're going to be so cute."

"I get to wear a halo like a real angel, and so does my friend Hayley."

"How exciting." Sarah sat down at the table to watch, and Izzy climbed up in her lap. Sarah laid her cheek against her daughter's dark hair.

Touched by Sarah's instinctive gesture of motherly love, Elena spread out the fabric and smoothed out the pattern pieces she'd already pinned in place. Carefully, she began cutting the fabric.

"How did you learn to sew?" Unconsciously, Sarah continued to stroke and smooth Isabel's hair.

"My mother taught me. When I was about ten, I wanted to make clothes for my dolls. So she got me started."

"When I get to be ten, I can make clothes for Dorie and her friends," Izzy said.

"You certainly may," Elena said.

Sarah raised her brows, questioning Elena.

"Why don't you go get Dorie and show her to Sarah?"

"Okay." Isabel hopped down from Sarah's lap and ran out of the room.

"She loves her stuffed animals," Elena explained. "Almost more than her dolls. Sometimes she surrounds herself with her stuffed animals and reads to them. Or at least pretends to."

"How cute. I remember seeing them piled on her bed. She has quite a collection, but I didn't know she'd named them."

Izzy came running back into the kitchen, her arms full of stuffed animals. "This is Quacker," she announced, handing Sarah a stuffed duck. "This one's Bearbear and Snuggles and Wally and Oinky and Dorie!" The final animal was an elephant with a long trunk and a straw hat perched between her big, floppy ears.

"How do you know what their names are?" Sarah asked her daughter.

"They tell me when they come to my house. Just like you told me your name."

"Of course." Looking amused, Sarah tried to repeat the names of the stuffed animals she'd just met, teasing Isabel by intentionally forgetting or confusing some of the names. That led to intense giggling on Izzy's part.

When Elena had cut out the skirt pieces, she called Isabel over. "Come see if this is going to fit you."

Isabel stood in front of Elena while she held up the skirt pieces in front of the child.

"It's too long, Buela."

"Oh, I'll hem it, honey. It'll be fine."

Elena went back to work cutting out the wide bell sleeves. Meanwhile, Izzy found a book to read to her stuffed animals and plopped herself down on the kitchen floor where she gathered her little stuffed friends around her.

"I've always wanted to learn how to sew," Sarah commented as she watched Elena at work.

"Your mother didn't teach you?"

"We never had a sewing machine. In fact, she didn't sew at all. I had to teach myself to sew buttons on if they popped off." She shrugged as if it didn't matter. "I'm not sure my mother even knew how to use a needle and thread. She wasn't very domestic."

That was a sad commentary on Sarah's mother, although Elena had known that the young woman had had a difficult childhood. Which was probably a factor in her turning to drugs. Thank the good Lord she'd finally found her way to sobriety and turned her life around.

"Maybe someday I'll have the time to take an adult education class in sewing," Sarah added. "Those classes don't cost much."

"I could teach you a few basics." The impulsive offer was out of Elena's mouth before she could stop it.

"Would you?" Her light gray eyes widened in the same way Isabel's eyes did when she was excited about something.

A spark of excitement shot through Elena. With only one son to raise and no daughters, she'd had no one she could pass on her joy of sewing to. It would be several years before Isabel was ready for serious sewing lessons. Right now, her tiny hands and childish coordination could only handle sewing kits that used yarn.

"Why don't you come here after church next Sunday?" Although she often worked on sewing projects in the evening, she could delay the angel costume until the weekend. "We can work on the costume together. It's a very simple pattern, mostly straight seams. It'll be a good project for you to start on."

"Oh, thank you," Sarah gushed, her eyes bright with enthusiasm. "I've always wanted to, you know. But I've never had a chance."

"You'll have a chance on Sunday."

Chapter Six

URING HER LUNCHTIME ON TUESDAY, ANABELLE slipped out to shop for a birthday present for Ainslee. It had to be something special. Something that would put her daughter in good spirits before their talk about the holidays.

For several years, Ainslee had been working part-time at Once Upon a Time, a vintage clothing and collectibles store. Anabelle loved to drop by. Strolling through the little shop was like a journey down memory lane, from hippie garb and wedding dresses to accessories and decorative pieces.

Anabelle counted on Ainslee's not working today and hoped the owner would give her a gift idea.

Musical crystal chimes sounded as she opened the door and stepped inside. Holiday shoppers crowded the aisles admiring the merchandise. Their chatter almost drowned out the sound of Frank Sinatra crooning over the sound system. Although

Anabelle would have loved to browse awhile, she couldn't be gone long from the hospital.

Edging past a display of belts and purses popular in the 1920s and '30s, she made her way to Dee Hardy, a co-owner of the store. A petite woman in her forties, she wore her blonde hair in a Doris Day pageboy style.

"Hello, Dee, have you got a minute?"

Dee looked up from marking the price on a perky black hat. "Hello, Anabelle. I'm afraid Ainslee isn't here today."

"I know. That's why I came in on my lunch hour. I want to buy her a birthday present and thought she might have admired something in the store."

"What a lovely idea. Let me think." Pressing her finger to the tip of her rather pointed chin, Dee scanned her shop as though mentally sorting through her inventory.

Ainslee preferred decorating her home in what she called an urban-chic style rather than the more traditional styles Anabelle liked. But Ainslee had also integrated bits and pieces of vintage accents that seemed to blend in well.

"I know!" Dee announced. "Come with me. I'll show you."

Quick and agile on her feet, Dee zipped through the store, avoiding crowded aisles and making her way around display cases so fast Anabelle had trouble keeping up.

"There!" Dee pointed to a top shelf along the wall.

"Which one?" A dozen different objects lined the shelf, any-one of which might be something Ainslee would like.

"The acrylic canister. Ainslee thought it would look smashing on her black granite kitchen counter. She could use it as a cookie jar or keep dry cereal in it. That sort of thing."

Squinting, Anabelle studied the shiny black container embellished with equally bright red spots. Nothing she'd ever want in her own kitchen, but it did match Ainslee's color scheme that included red accents.

"You're right. I think Ainslee will love it."

"Let me get a ladder, and I'll ring it up for you."

Within minutes, Anabelle was out of the shop, the perfect birthday present for Ainslee in a shopping bag, and on her way back to the hospital. The canister was sure to make a hit with her daughter. She'd wrap it as soon as she got home from work.

More than a year ago, James had become the leader of Nelson's Boy Scout troop, at Fern's insistence. To give him a night out, she'd told him, and to do something special with Nelson. It turned out James really enjoyed Scouting. The kids were great and he liked the discipline the boys learned as well as the respect the Boy Scouts taught them to have for their country.

Typically, the troop met on Monday night at Church of the Good Shepherd. The oldest church in town, the extensive church property included a large open space with a softball field, plus volleyball and basketball courts. The social hall, where potlucks and wedding receptions were often held, was a perfect facility for troop meetings, which had recently been changed to Tuesday night.

As a patrol leader, it was Nelson's turn to organize his patrol to present the colors and lead the pledge of allegiance.

James checked his watch. "Okay, Nelson, let's get started."

Nelson scrambled to gather his patrol together and retrieve the flags from the storage closet.

The twenty members of the troop, most of them in eighth and ninth grades, were doing their usual wisecracking and rowdy play. They all wore their Scout shirts for meetings, usually with jeans. As soon as they realized the flags were coming out, they quieted and formed a half circle in the center of the room.

Pride swelled in James's chest as Nelson marched his patrol from the far corner of the room to the center. He turned them to face the troop, and the boy carrying the state flag lowered it out of respect for the national flag.

Nelson stood at attention. "Ready, begin. I pledge allegiance to the flag of the United States . . ."

Every Scout joined in the pledge, his hand over his heart. And when the pledge was finished, they all remained at attention until the flags were placed in their holders and saluted by the patrol members.

If James taught them nothing else, showing respect for the national flag was worth every minute of his time.

"Okay, guys, find yourselves a seat," James ordered. "We've got a guest tonight, and he's going to talk to us about emergency preparedness." Most of the boys already had their First Aid merit badge. To achieve the rank of Eagle Scout, which took years and twenty-one merit badges to earn, they also needed an Emergency Preparedness or Lifesaving merit badge. Since James wasn't the greatest swimmer in the world, and he did know something about emergency preparedness, he'd encouraged the troop to go in that direction.

With a bit of jostling for a place to sit, the boys settled down again.

After a few preliminary announcements about upcoming events, James introduced their guest. "We're fortunate to have Regis Tanner, the fire marshal from the Deerford Fire Department with us tonight. He's going to talk to us about emergency preparedness, so pay attention."

"Evening, guys." Fairly new to Deerford, Regis's southern drawl was still apparent. "Thanks for having me here."

Dressed in dark slacks and a white shirt with the fire department patch on the pocket, he strolled to the table where he'd laid out an array of fire extinguishers, smoke detectors, and some handouts. Well over six feet tall, he looked to be in great shape.

"I'm going to talk tonight about how to prepare your own house for a disaster. Or, rather, how you can prepare to avoid a disaster." He glanced around the room and then picked up a smoke detector. "Who knows what this is?"

Involving the boys in the discussion, he talked about different types of smoke and carbon monoxide detectors, where they should be placed in the house, and why. He passed the sample detectors around and then moved on to the types of fire extinguishers that were needed in both houses and cars.

James sat back enjoying Regis's presentation. The boys seemed to be eating it up too.

"Okay, guys," Regis said, winding up his talk after about forty minutes. "I'm going to give you all a safety checklist. I want you to walk through your house and see if your family is prepared. In two weeks," he glanced toward James, "we'll set a few fires and try to put them out."

The boys cheered at that, and James figured that was par for the course with teenagers. They loved the hands-on stuff.

James closed the meeting and dismissed the boys. Max Witkowski, the son of Rabbi Witkowski, was helping Nelson stack the tables and put them away when his father walked into the meeting room. A man in his late forties, he wore a yarmulke that revealed a fringe of dark hair sprinkled with gray.

"Hello, James, how did the meeting go this evening?" Saul Witkowski asked.

"Good, I think. Expect Max to be checking your house for safety problems. We talked about disaster preparedness tonight."

"Excellent idea." He glanced toward his son, who was carrying folding chairs toward the storage area. "Anything new at the hospital?"

James was about to say, "Oh, just the usual," when he remembered the tree debacle. "As a matter of fact," he said, "our CEO ordered the maintenance people to take down the Christmas tree in the lobby. He hasn't told anyone why he decided to do that, so we're all in the dark."

The rabbi's forehead furrowed. "You don't suppose someone from my congregation—" He shook his head. "No, none of my people would complain about Christmas decorations. Why would they? Our faith promotes tradition as much as anyone's. Plus, if they did complain, they'd have to take on the whole town of Deerford."

Chuckling, James agreed. "Well, in the unlikely event that you hear any rumors about somebody upset with the hospital's tree, let me know."

"Will do."

Max and the other boys in Nelson's patrol had finished putting away the tables and chairs. Saul hooked his arm around his son's shoulders. "Let's get on home, son. Your mother's waiting for you."

James turned to Nelson. "Your patrol did well, son. Very sharp."

The teen shot him a grin of pleasure. Nelson seemed to strive for perfection in everything he did, whether it was writing a paper for English or presenting the colors. James couldn't be more proud of his younger son. Not because what the boy achieved was often perfect, but because he always tried.

At Cavendish House, an 1850s Greek Revival mansion owned by the Deerford Historical Society, the Deerford Quilting Guild committee members had just finished making plans for the group's participation in a citywide spring craft show.

As the group started to disperse, Anabelle picked up her empty teacup to carry it to the kitchen where two of the committee members were washing the dishes they'd used for tea and snacks.

"I think we'll have a very nice showing for the spring show," Genna Hamilton commented, carrying two empty cups and saucers. Married to Dr. Hamilton, a staff doctor at Hope Haven, Genna always looked elegant, her long silver hair worn in a sleek french twist.

"I'm sure we will. Everyone enjoys showing off their quilts. And the event often brings us new members."

"We must remember to make up some flyers about the guild and where people can take beginning lessons in quilting." Genna set her cups on the pass-through counter to the kitchen. "I saw Bill Fontaine at the drugstore this morning. He looked so sad.

Looks like he's lost several pounds since Barbara died. He must miss her terribly."

"Oh, that's a shame."

Barbara had been a member of the guild for many years. A month ago she'd died at Hope Haven of complications due to a recurring cancer.

"I noticed his car dealership has been closed recently too. All he has left of the business is the service department for repairs." So many people in the community had been affected by the recent recession, Anabelle counted her blessings that Cam had provided a good retirement for himself and that she was gainfully employed in a job she loved.

"You know what worries me," Genna said. "Barbara was helping that widow who lost her husband in Afghanistan when an IED blew up his tank. The poor dear was trying to raise two children on her own and was struggling financially. I suspect Barbara was a godsend both financially and in terms of moral support."

"Sometimes we don't take very good care of those who have sacrificed so much for our country."

"We certainly don't," Genna agreed. "To make matters worse, I heard her teenage son is on the brink of getting expelled from school. Evidently he's been in trouble ever since his father went to Afghanistan, and it's gotten worse since his dad was killed."

Turning together, they walked down the stairs from the third-floor meeting room, their shoes quiet on the carpeted steps. Oil portraits of the original Cavendish family members who'd settled in Deerford lined the stairway wall.

"Maybe the guild should try to help out the family," Anabelle suggested.

Genna stopped at the front door and frowned. "That sounds like a good idea. But you know, I can't remember the woman's name. Barbara mentioned her several times." She shook her head and then smiled sheepishly. "Another senior moment, I fear. I'll ask around. Someone will know. Or her name may pop into my head at some odd moment. I'll let you know."

"Please do. Then we can talk about the best way to help her." Anabelle pulled on her gloves and wrapped her scarf around her neck. "In the meantime, I'll put the widow and her family on my prayer list. Even if I don't know her name, God will know who I'm praying for."

Genna pushed open the door. They stepped out into the cold night air and went their separate ways to their respective cars.

Despite the middle-class nature of Deerford, there were many people like the widow who were struggling financially. Often they went unseen and unnoticed until some crisis occurred. Sometimes that was too late.

That was also why Christmas for Hope Haven Kids was such an important event. Janice always made sure the neediest children received something special for the holidays.

When Anabelle arrived home, she found Cam sound asleep in his recliner, Sarge on the floor beside him, the television tuned to the news. Cam still held the remote control in his hand.

Poor Bill Fontaine. Losing a loved one was often harder on men than on women. She wondered if she could do something to help Bill, perhaps find him a grief-counseling program. Being with others who had suffered a loss might help him get past the anguish and disorientation he must be feeling. She knew that his children didn't live close, somewhere in Florida she recalled, where they were raising their own children. So they probably weren't much help.

With his mouth open, Cam snored softly, and she smiled. At least when she or Cam passed away the survivor would have their children—and grandchild—nearby. They would provide some solace in the face of such a terrible loss.

Bending, she brushed a kiss on Cam's forehead. "Come on, sleepyhead. Time for bed."

He started, waking with a jolt. Sarge popped to his feet too.

Cam yawned. "Home already? You have a good meeting?"

"Good enough, I guess. Everyone is excited about the craft fair."

He clicked off the TV and stood. "I'll let Sarge out and be up in a minute."

Anabelle reached up to kiss him on the lips.

When she stepped back, he smiled. "Hey, that's nice. What did I do to earn a kiss?"

"I just wanted you to know I love you." Anabelle knew she was a strong woman, but even the thought of losing Cam and becoming a widow tightened a band around her chest and clogged her throat with the threat of tears.

Please, God, let us have many more years together.

Chapter Seven

WEDNESDAY, ANABELLE ARRIVED AT THE HOSPITAL AT her usual early hour. She walked up the stairs, hung up her coat in her locker, and plucked the hospital newsletter from her mailbox in the employee lounge. Putting on her glasses, she glanced over the lead article about the hospital purchasing a robotic patient to train inexperienced nurses.

"Guess that's better than letting them practice on live patients," she mumbled to herself, removing her glasses and sliding them into the breast pocket of her lab coat.

Still annoyed that she hadn't discovered Albert Varner's reason for removing the tree from the lobby, she folded the newsletter and creased it closed with a firm hand.

"So who's influential enough in Deerford to carry that kind of weight with Varner?" she asked herself aloud.

"How 'bout the mayor?" James plucked the newsletter from his mailbox.

Startled that James had sneaked up on her, Anabelle questioned his comment. "Mayor Armstrong? Doesn't he belong to Holy Trinity Church? Why would he want the tree taken down?"

"I have no idea. It wouldn't make any sense, but taking the tree down doesn't make a whole lot of sense either."

"To have influence you have to have power or money."

"That leaves me out," James said. "I'm just a cog in the big wheel that goes round and round."

Sometimes Anabelle felt like a cog as well, but someone had convinced Varner to remove the tree, which might put the kids' party at risk. It didn't seem like someone in politics would make that sort of a demand on a hospital CEO. Could someone have promised a big chunk of money to the hospital in return for taking down the tree? Varner was always looking for new sources of revenue to support Hope Haven.

Until Candace had asked her why she felt so strongly about the tree, Anabelle hadn't realized how deeply that one Christmas without her mother had affected her. More than fifty years later, the memory still had the power to bring her to tears.

"Can we find out who visited Varner in the day or two before Thanksgiving?" James asked. "That might give us a clue who influenced him about the tree."

Drawn back from her mental meanderings, Anabelle tilted her head. "What a good idea, James. I'm sure Penny keeps a log of all of Varner's visitors. I'll see if I can get a look at that."

James's blue eyes twinkled and he raised an eyebrow as if to say, "What did you expect? I'm full of good ideas." Anabelle almost laughed out loud.

In no rush to get to work, Anabelle and James slowly descended the stairs to the second floor. At this early hour, the patients were waking up, the nurses on duty making their last rounds to check their patients' status. The buzz of activity would increase throughout the day and then settle, she hoped overnight again.

The cycles that played out in a hospital were like a symphony, each person doing his or her part, sometimes as a solo, other times as part of a ensemble. Together they worked in harmony to serve the needs of the patients.

Yet the removal of the Christmas tree had created a discordant note. Several employees had commented on the absence of the tree and mentioned their surprise and concern to Anabelle.

She stopped abruptly at the nurses' station. A bright red poinsettia sat on the counter, a gift to the nurses from the family of a patient who had been discharged yesterday.

She turned to James. "Who has the most influence at this hospital?"

He frowned and rubbed the side of his finger over his chin. "Varner, I suppose. Doctors on the medical side of things."

"But Albert Varner reports to the board of directors. When they speak, he jumps. Right?"

Taking his stethoscope out of the pocket of his scrubs, he looped it around his neck and nodded thoughtfully. "I wonder if any board member visited Varner privately last week."

Candace arrived, her step light and her smile broad. "Good morning, you two. Why the serious expressions?"

"We're wondering if someone on the board of directors ordered Varner to take down the Christmas tree," Anabelle announced.

Candace's hazel eyes widened. "You're kidding. One of the board members?"

"But why?" James asked.

"That I don't know. Yet." Anabelle opened the newsletter she'd been carrying and flattened it on the counter, turning to the page that listed all seven members of the board. She tapped the list with the tip of her finger. "I'm guessing one of these people is either anti-Christmas for some reason, determined to be politically correct at the cost of tradition, or is trying to save money for the hospital by penny-pinching on the electric bill."

"But didn't Quintessa tell Elena that her boss hadn't objected to having the tree?" Candace asked.

"True," Anabelle said. "That doesn't necessarily mean all the board members were in agreement."

James looked over her shoulder at the list. "But which one?"

"That's what I'm trying to figure out." She'd have to give that some thought, but right now she needed to get to work.

Stepping behind the counter, she sat down at the computer terminal. Slipping her glasses on, she brought up the day's patient census for the CCU.

Nobody had a right to steal the Christmas spirit from the hospital or presents for little children, assuming the two acts were somehow connected. It simply shouldn't happen, and she was going to set things to right.

As she updated the computer records, she mentally eliminated Bernard Telford. The president of the board, he typically acted in a restrained way, smoothing over disagreements the board members had and finding a compromise position that kept things on an even keel.

No, Bernard Telford wasn't the culprit.

Becky Tyler, the day-shift nurse in Cardiac Care, interrupted Anabelle's thought process.

"The quadruple bypass in 201 is acting lethargic this morning." A petite woman, her green hospital scrubs made Becky look like an elf, but she knew nursing and her patients.

"How are his vitals?"

"Normal but low. I think the medications are depressing his blood pressure and respiration. He's due for another dose of meds within the hour."

Nurses weren't allowed to make changes in medication without a doctor's approval. But they were trained observers and often spotted problems before a doctor caught them.

"Has Dr. Hamilton made his rounds yet?" Anabelle asked.

"Not yet."

"I'll page him."

Drew Hamilton, a general surgeon, had been with Hope Haven for close to forty years. He believed in the team concept of medicine and valued a nurse's input.

Anabelle picked up the phone and asked the operator to page him. A moment later, she heard the page over the loudspeaker. Within minutes, the doctor called. She explained the situation, and he said he'd be right there.

Picking up her clipboard, Anabelle decided this would be a good time for her to check all of the patients in her unit.

As she walked from room to room, greeting the patients, she mentally eliminated Will West and Caroline White as board members who would complain about the Christmas tree. While they were both influential in the community, they were easygoing and not likely to raise a fuss over a long-held hospital tradition.

By the time she returned to the nurses' station, Dr. Hamilton was there writing new orders for the patient in 201.

"Good call on Becky's part," he said. "Older patients can't always process medication the way younger people do."

"She's a good nurse."

He nodded as he finished writing the order. "Genna said you had a good meeting last night."

"I think so. We got the ball rolling, at any rate. The craft fair will be fun."

He handed her the new order and left to complete his rounds.

As Anabelle continued to work, she managed to mentally eliminate all of the board members as possible suspects in the great tree caper except Emmaline Palmer and Frederick Innisk.

At lunchtime, she went downstairs to the hospital cafeteria. Hope Haven prided itself on excellent food service for both its patients and for the staff and visitors who patronized the cafeteria. Although cold sandwiches and hot entrees were available, the expansive salad bar was Anabelle's meal of choice.

As she carried her tray into the dining area, she spotted Candace and Elena seated at a table in the corner. Perfect!

"May I join you two?" Assuming she'd be welcome, Anabelle slid her tray onto the table.

"Of course," Candace said. "Although I'm almost finished with my lunch." Her soup bowl was empty, and she was working on the last of her small salad and hot tea.

"I'm glad I caught you both," Anabelle said, sitting down and arranging the dishes on her tray. "I think I've narrowed down our possible Christmas tree culprit to two board members."

Elena cocked her head and leaned toward Anabelle, lowering her voice. "You think one of the board members made Varner remove the tree?"

"I think it's possible. At least they'd have that kind of influence over him." She drizzled a little dressing on her salad and took a bite. "My first possibility is Frederick Innisk." A wealthy financial consultant, he could be a real bully. There had even been times in the past when his ethics had been questioned.

Elena snorted. "I know I used to think of Mr. Innisk as a total Scrooge, but I changed my mind. He really is more bluster than bite."

"Really?" Candace asked.

"I agree with Elena," Anabelle said. "He was instrumental in Deerford's win in the Get Fit Illinois contest. But he's still a grumpy guy, and I never know which mood he'll be in about hospital relations."

"Very true," Elena said. "Who's the other possibility?"

"Emmaline Palmer."

Both Candace and Elena remained silent and thoughtful.

"I've only met Emmaline a few times. Her husband Roger is in Rotary with Cam, so our paths have crossed there," Anabelle admitted. "Without being judgmental, I'd say she's an unhappy person. I have no idea why, but she strikes me as the sort who'd get her mind made up about something and insist whatever change she wanted had to be made."

"So how do we find out if it was her idea to remove the tree?" Elena asked.

"I'll talk to Cam. Maybe he can feel out Roger, see if he or his wife have a problem with Christmas trees. I'll also try to find out if Emmaline had any private meetings lately with Varner."

Candace stacked her dishes and stood. "Maybe Mrs. Palmer is the one with an allergy."

More likely allergic to anyone enjoying Christmas, Anabelle thought before she could halt the unkind speculation.

After lunch and her conversation with Elena and Anabelle, Candace walked back upstairs and stopped at the nurses' station. She'd been giving a lot of thought to Christmas the past few days, and not exclusively thinking about the missing tree downstairs.

"Hey, James. I need a man's opinion about something."

He glanced around as though looking for another man in the area and then grinned. "I guess that means I'm supposed to represent the view of all of manhood. Tough job, I'd say."

Chuckling, she said, "I'm sure you can handle it."

"Okay, shoot. What do you need?"

Heat rose to her cheeks and she shifted her feet self-consciously. "It's about Heath. This is our first Christmas as a couple."

"Very nice. He's a good guy."

Candace couldn't help but smile. "Yes, he is. I want to get him a Christmas present. I've been vacillating back and forth about what to get him, but everything I think of is either too personal." Warmth shot up her neck to her cheeks again as she fussed with a chipped fingernail. "Or too impersonal. It's been so long since I've been in this position, I don't know what to do."

James hooked his hip over the end of the nurse's desk and folded his arms. "You want me to come up with a gift idea for Heath?"

She laughed. "Well . . . I suppose so. I mean, I could give him a nice warm sweater, but that isn't very personal. And I've always hated giving something like aftershave that he might never use."

"I haven't been a part of the dating scene for twenty years. Fern gave me a velour robe last Christmas, but that probably would be too personal a gift for you to give Heath."

"Way too personal," she agreed.

"Does he have any hobbies?"

"He's a member of the Audubon Society and does a lot of bird-watching. He already has a very expensive scope though, and I wouldn't know what kind to get him if he didn't."

Rubbing the back of his neck, James looked thoughtful for a moment. "I remember Fern gave me a picture of herself when we were dating. I really liked that. I still carry her picture in my wallet."

"Goodness, you sound like a true romantic. But I'm afraid Heath might think that was a little presumptuous of me, giving him a picture of myself." Although not too long ago he had given Candace a locket necklace with pictures of Brooke and Howie inside.

"I don't know." He shrugged. "That's the best I can come up with at the moment. If I get any other bright ideas, I'll let you know."

"Thanks. At my age, this dating business feels really strange." She'd put off dating Heath for some time because even the thought made her feel unfaithful to Dean. That wasn't quite the problem now, but she did feel awkward about their relationship—yet more than a little pleased. She so enjoyed his company, as did her children, which was even more important to her. They needed a good man in their lives.

"You'll get used to dating. I hope something good works out for you and Heath."

"Thanks. I'll see you later." With a shy smile, she hurried toward the Birthing Unit. She couldn't remember having a problem choosing a present for Dean.

Why was it such a complicated decision when it came to Heath?

Maybe because there was more at stake now than when she'd been a college girl naively believing her happily-ever-after would come true.

When Anabelle left the cafeteria, she went directly to Penny's office.

"I have a question for you," Anabelle said.

Penny looked up from her desk. "If it's about the tree, I don't have the answer."

"No, no," she fibbed. "It's about something else. I happened to see someone with Varner a day or two before Thanksgiving. I recognized the man, but for the life of me, I can't remember his name. You keep a log of Varner's visitors, don't you?"

"Yes." Penny's voice hesitated.

"If I could just take a peek at the log. I'm sure I'll recognize the name. You know how it is when you can't remember something like that. It's been driving me crazy for days."

"Well . . . " She pulled her logbook out of her top drawer and flipped back a few pages. "Some of this may be confidential."

"Don't worry. Sometimes I just need to jog my aging memory." Anabelle smiled sweetly as she took the book from Penny.

Quickly skimming the entries, she spotted Zane McGarry's name twice. Emmaline visited Varner on that Wednesday, which meant she could be the person who had influenced the CEO. Bill Fontaine, Barbara's husband, appeared on the list once, but Anabelle already knew he had business with the hospital, so his presence made sense. There was one name she didn't recognize, however, which piqued her curiosity.

"Who's this Regis Tanner?" she asked.

"He's the new Deerford fire marshal."

"Fire marshal? Why would he be visiting Varner?"

"I'm sure it was just a courtesy call. Why? Is that the man you recognized?"

"I'm not sure." But a fire marshal could decide a tall Christmas tree with hundreds of lights on it was a fire hazard, which would mean it had to be removed. But if he'd be ordered to remove the tree due to a fire hazard, why wouldn't Varner just admit that?

Anabelle handed the log back to Penny. "Maybe whoever I saw just resembled someone I used to know. Thanks anyway."

Escaping Penny's office, she hurried upstairs. The fire marshal seemed like a potential source for the change, and she certainly couldn't remove Emmaline from the suspect list.

But suspecting someone was the Grinch and proving it were two different matters altogether.

James prepared a fresh IV bag of antibiotics for his ulcer patient. Not only did Dwaine Perry have a bleeding ulcer, he'd developed an infection as well.

Earlier, James had heard a burst of masculine laughter coming from Perry's room. His two teenage sons had been visiting him, and it sounded like they'd been having a good time.

He found his patient alone now watching television. Overweight by forty pounds, Perry was balding and gray chest hair showed around the neck of his hospital gown.

"How're you doing, Mr. Perry?"

"Fine. Getting bored."

Removing the old IV bag, James hooked up the new one. "Sounded like you and your boys were having a good time earlier."

"Yeah. I think they ditched a period or two to come see me. Their mother won't like that."

James wouldn't either if his boys cut classes for anything less than an emergency. "Say, are your boys into video games?" he asked.

Dwaine muted the TV. "Sure. Sometimes I can't get 'em to stop playing long enough to eat dinner."

"What do you do about violent games? Do you check the ratings before you let them buy a new game?"

"Naw. You can't keep those things away from kids. If you say no to something, it just makes them want it all the more. You know, boys will be boys. Mine are good kids."

So were James's boys. But that didn't mean he couldn't exercise his parental rights about what kind of video games they played or how they acted in public.

"Have you heard of a game called Chicago Underground?"

"Oh boy, have I." Dwaine swiped his hand over his face. "When the boys have some friends over and they play that game, it's like they turn their bedroom into a war zone. Bombs exploding. Machine guns or death rays, whatever they call them these days, and the boys shouting 'I blew him away!' so loudly, I expect the neighbors to call the cops."

"Ouch. That would be embarrassing."

Dwaine shrugged. "With my boys, the neighbors are used to them being on the wild side." He said it as though he was proud that his sons were out of control.

Chicago Underground wasn't the kind of game James wanted Gideon to own, even if he did play it at his friend's house.

He could only hope to come up with an alternative game for Christmas that would satisfy Gideon.

As James and the boys were cleaning up after dinner that evening, Nelson said, "I finished doing the home safety checklist the firefighter gave us."

"Good." James rinsed out the sink and dried his hands on a dishtowel. "How'd we do?"

"Pretty good, I guess. A lot of this stuff we don't have to worry about because we don't have little kids in the house."

"We still have to keep matches and knives away from you, little brother," Gideon teased.

Nelson shot him a hard look before continuing. "Since our house is newly remodeled, our stairs to the basement are solid with good handrails. And no rugs to trip us because we've got all wood and tile floors for Mom."

Gideon sauntered over to where Fern was sitting and sat down next to her. He petted Sapphire, who had curled up in Fern's lap.

"So we're good on all the safety items?" James asked.

"Well, not quite. There wasn't a wrench for the gas shutoff valve outside where it should be. I found one in the garage and taped it right next to the shutoff."

"Good for you."

"But the thing is, I was looking for the wrench, and everything in the garage—all your workbench and tools and stuff—is a mess. I could barely walk through the garage. It isn't safe, Dad. You really need to get that cleaned up."

James grimaced. "Yeah, I know. I just haven't had the time since we moved in here." Most of the time he wished he had twenty-eight hours in the day in order to get everything accomplished. Unfortunately, Earth spun on its axis much faster than that.

"Maybe you boys could find the time to help your father out," Fern suggested. "Maybe over Christmas break."

"*Mo-om!*" Gideon sat up straight. "Scotty's mom invited a bunch of us guys to go to their cabin the week after Christmas."

"That would be fine," Fern said. "You'd have plenty of time the week before Christmas to help get the garage straightened out."

With a groan, Gideon slid down as far as he could on the couch to make himself inconspicuous and pulled a pillow over his head. It didn't work.

James grinned. His wife was a genius at knowing how to handle their boys. He thanked the good Lord every day for bringing such a wonderful woman into his life.

Chapter Eight

EDNESDAY EVENING, ANABELLE BROACHED THE subject of Emmaline Palmer and the Christmas tree with Cameron at dinner.

His frown shifted his salt-and-pepper eyebrows lower. "You think she's the one who nixed the tree?"

"Well, I don't know for sure." She forked a bite of sole almondine into her mouth. "She isn't the friendliest person in the world, and she can certainly get her back up over a hospital issue if she disagrees. She was very reluctant about setting up the Wall of Hope."

"Roger Palmer is extra friendly, which figures since he's in the real estate business. He threw a lot of landscaping business my way."

"I know. That's why I thought you could talk to Roger at your Rotary club meeting. Maybe Emmaline is allergic to fir trees or something." Anabelle wasn't sure Candace's allergy theory would hold water, but it wouldn't hurt to have Cam open a conversation with that.

"I guess some people are," he conceded, scooping up the last of his brown rice with his fork.

"Then you'll talk to Roger?"

"If I get the chance. He doesn't make it to every meeting."

Anabelle would have to be satisfied with that, at least for now.

She'd arranged for her cleaning lady to come by tomorrow to have the house in good order when Ainslee and Lindsay came for dinner. Ainslee liked a germ- and dirt-free environment for her baby, a near impossible goal to achieve. Although, Anabelle had to admit, Ainslee was getting better about it.

Still, Anabelle didn't want to press the issue. She'd make sure her house was as clean as possible.

Early the next morning, Anabelle put a rump roast in her slow cooker along with vegetables and turned it on low. The hearty meal that Cam particularly enjoyed during the winter months would be ready to eat whenever Ainslee arrived for dinner.

She'd bake the special German chocolate cake with the pecan topping as soon as she got home from work.

About an hour after Anabelle got to Hope Haven, Elena came hurrying up to the nurses' station.

"While it's quiet in ICU, I thought I'd better let you know about the fingerprints," Elena said. "Cesar left me a message a few minutes ago."

Anabelle removed her glasses. "What fingerprints?"

"The fingerprints the crime scene technician took off the barrels the gifts were in."

Her heart rate accelerating, Anabelle leaned toward Elena. "Did they find something?"

"They found a lot of fingerprints. Too many, in fact. It looks like every visitor who has been in the hospital for the past two weeks peered into one or the other of those barrels."

Anabelle puffed out a discouraged sigh. "So there's no way to tell who might have stolen the presents."

"If we had an actual suspect, the police might be able to confirm he'd touched the barrel. But that still wouldn't prove much, since the lobby is open to the public."

"Looks like the police aren't going to be much help."

"Sorry." With a quick wave of her hand, Elena scooted back to ICU.

Making it a point to leave work on time, Anabelle went directly home. She changed into comfortable clothes and pulled on a rose-colored cardigan she'd knitted for herself several years ago. She liked the way the rose went with her complexion.

Quickly, she mixed up the cake batter, poured it into a pan, and put it in the oven to bake.

While the cake was baking, she brought the high chair up to the kitchen table and set three places for dinner. She found the silver baby spoon she'd used with each of her three children and looked forward to a chance to feed Lindsay. She was sure Ainslee would bring a jar or two of baby food with her.

When she thought about having Christmas without Lindsay, her chest ached. A part of her knew she was being selfish. But was it so wrong to want to share the holiday experience with her first grandchild?

Cam's truck pulled into the garage. A moment later he and Sarge entered the kitchen.

"Hi, luv. Did you have a good day?"

"Fine." She grabbed Sarge by his collar. "Sorry, boy. Ainslee doesn't like having you around the baby. You'll have to stay in the mudroom while they're here." A foolish demand on Ainslee's part. It wasn't as if Sarge would hurt the baby.

"He'll start whining if we leave him in there too long." Cam, wearing a pullover sweater and slacks, filled a glass of water from the tap and drank it down.

"It will only be a few hours. He'll be fine, won't you, Sarge?"

His tail whipped through the air as Anabelle herded Sarge back into the mudroom. She really did hate to lock him away when she knew he wouldn't cause any harm. He'd even been good about not knocking off ornaments or yanking down the tinsel on the Christmas tree in the living room. Of course, such good behavior took several commands of "Leave" until he got the idea.

"I saw Roger Palmer in town today," Cam said. "I asked him about the Christmas tree at the hospital."

Anabelle's head snapped up. "What did he say?"

"He didn't know a thing about it. He did say Emmaline has been feeling down about Christmas because none of their children or grandchildren will be around this holiday. She decided not to bother with decorations."

"I can understand the temptation," Anabelle admitted, still holding Sarge by the collar. "You don't suppose she's so depressed about the holidays that she'd demand Varner take down the hospital tree?"

Cam set his water glass on the counter. "Roger said he'd feel Emmaline out about the tree. If he finds out anything, I'll let you know."

For the moment, Anabelle would keep Emmaline on her suspect short list.

After putting Sarge away, she made a quick check of the living room to make sure her cleaning lady had dusted and vacuumed well enough to meet Ainslee's standards.

The oven timer went off. She pulled the cake out and set it aside to cool. She'd have to put the topping on later.

Popping into the living room, she saw Ainslee's car pull into the driveway out front and hurried outside to greet her.

"Hello, honey. I'm so glad you've come for dinner."

Anabelle was about to get Lindsay out of her car seat, when Ainslee said, "Mother, if you can get the diaper bag in the back and Lindsay's playpen, that'd be great. I'll get Lindsay."

Anabelle obediently walked around to the back of the Honda. She couldn't wait to get her hands on that cuddly little bundle of baby Lindsay.

Cam met her halfway up the front walk and took the playpen from her.

"How's my baby girl?" He gave Ainslee a one-arm hug that encompassed Lindsay as well.

"We're good, Pop. Thanks for having us over."

"No problem. Your mother loves having you both here. I understand we're celebrating your birthday a little early this year."

"I've heard that rumor too. These days, thirty-one is feeling pretty old."

He laughed. "You're still a spry young chicken, honey."

Inside, Anabelle switched the Christmas lights on the tree and placed the diaper bag beside the couch.

"The tree looks great, Mother," Ainslee said.

"Thank you. Your father and I put it up together. I think we both missed having you children here to help."

The tree told the history of their family's life. Every Christmas, Anabelle had purchased specific ornaments commemorating some special moment in each of her children's lives that year. She had a shiny silver trumpet to mark the year Evan started taking music lessons and baseball hero ornaments for his years in Little League. Barbie holiday ornaments represented Kirstie's love of dolls; a stone church that resembled Good Shepherd hung in memory of the year Kirstie made her confession of faith. The collection for Ainslee included a Cinderella coach and a Santa rocking horse very much like the one she'd received under the tree from Santa the year she was two.

All of her children had contributed handmade ornaments, which Anabelle had lovingly kept over the years. There were even some ornaments that Anabelle's mother had passed down to her. Those she treasured in a special way.

This year, she had hung a Baby's First Christmas ornament to celebrate Lindsay's first year of life.

Excited by the twinkling lights on the tree, Lindsay babbled her nonsense syllables and waved her little arms while her mother held her.

Anabelle reached for the baby. "Here, let me have Lindsay and you can open up the playpen."

With only a brief hesitation, Ainslee passed Lindsay to Anabelle.

"Oh, my sweet little girl," she cooed, kissing the crown of her head. In the right light, her baby-fine hair revealed a hint of red among the darker brown strands. "You're getting so big." Jiggling Lindsay in her arms, Anabelle walked her closer to the tree. "Do you see the pretty lights?"

Lindsay gurgled a response and smiled a toothless—

"She's getting a tooth!" Anabelle exclaimed, trying to get a better look at Lindsay's bottom gum and the tiny white mound there.

"I'm afraid so, and I've had some sleepless nights to go with it," Ainslee said, snapping the portable playpen open with Cam's help. "I was so glad when it finally broke through. She was so fussy there for a while."

"*Aww*, did it hurt you, baby girl?" Anabelle stuck her fingertip in the baby's mouth to rub her gums.

"Mother! What are you doing? Don't put your finger in Lindsay's mouth."

Anabelle shot her daughter a disbelieving look. She couldn't possibly count the number of times she'd put her finger in Ainslee's mouth when she was a baby. Or Evan's. Or Kirstie's. Ainslee appeared to have survived with no ill effects as had her other children. Surely Lindsay would as well.

"Let me have her back. I'll put her in her playpen now."

Ainslee lifted the baby from Anabelle's arms before Anabelle could even protest, leaving her feeling bereft and more than a little annoyed. She chose to keep her objection to herself, though, knowing she already had one sensitive subject to attend to this evening.

Once in the playpen, Lindsay did a quick walk-crawl toward the lure of the Christmas tree. One knee scooted along, the other leg bent with her foot helping to push forward. *Certainly a nontraditional mode of transportation,* Anabelle thought with a grin.

"Where'd she learn to crawl like that?" Cam asked.

"I have no idea. I asked the doctor about it. He didn't seem to think it was a problem."

"Of course not," Anabelle said. "It's her own little way of getting around. She's fine." Perfect, in fact. A marvelous gift from God.

Having reached the limit of her playpen, Lindsay plopped down on her bottom, pointed at the tree and babbled in an insistent voice.

"I think she wants out to get to the tree," Cam said.

"She's much safer in the playpen, Pop. When Louise babysits, she keeps Lindsay in her playpen or the crib. Unless she's feeding her, of course."

A knot tightened in Anabelle's stomach. "How often does Louise babysit for you?"

Ainslee looked at her blankly for a moment. "I'm working part-time at Once Upon A Time for the Christmas season. I told you that, didn't I?"

"I thought you were taking the baby to the store with you." Anabelle certainly hadn't been told that Louise Giffen was babysitting Lindsay.

"She's too old for that now. She doesn't sleep as much as she used to and gets fussy. Besides, Louise only babysits a couple of mornings a week," Ainslee said.

That mollified Anabelle only a little. "When would you like to eat dinner?"

"Oh, no rush. I fed Lindsay at home."

"Oh. Well, then," Anabelle said, picking up the wrapped gift from the coffee table. "Why don't you open your birthday present?"

Eyeing the gift with curiosity, Ainslee took it from her mother. "I feel like I'm too old for presents these days."

"Nonsense. A person is never too old or too young for special gifts," Anabelle said.

Ainslee sat down and started to unwrap the gift. Over the years it had been Anabelle's joy to watch her children's eyes light up on birthdays and Christmas mornings.

"Mother!" Ainslee cried in excitement. "How did you know I wanted this?"

"Oh, a little birdie told me."

"I'll bet the little birdie's name is Dee Hardy." Grinning, Ainslee held up the canister for her father to admire. "This will look just perfect on my kitchen counter. Thank you so much."

"You're welcome, dear." Anabelle exhaled a sigh of relief. "The shop looked busy when I was there."

"Despite the economy, it seems to be a good season for antiques and collectibles," Ainslee reported.

"And Doug. Has he called you yet?"

Ainslee's smile brought a twinkle to her eyes. "He called before he boarded the plane this morning and then again when he arrived in Washington. He said he already missed us."

Pleased her daughter still had the look of a new bride, Anabelle said, "I imagine he'll call you later tonight too."

"And in the morning." She glanced fondly at Lindsay, who was chewing on a teething ring in the playpen. "I do love that man."

"As you should. You're both lucky to have found each other."

Lindsay banged her spoon on the oak tabletop while sitting in Nana Anabelle's lap. *A few dents are a small price to pay for holding my grandbaby in my arms*, she thought.

In the middle of dinner, their conversation turned to a proposed school district tax increase. Ainslee hadn't heard about the tax, so Cam went to retrieve the newspaper that he'd put in the mudroom to recycle.

The moment the mudroom door opened, Sarge dashed into the kitchen right past Cam.

Wildly happy to join the party, Sarge danced around, his tail wagging furiously until he spotted Lindsay in Anabelle's lap. For a moment, he stood stark still then approached cautiously.

"Mother, shouldn't Sarge stay in the mudroom?"

"Let's just see what happens," Anabelle urged.

Lindsay leaned over, her little hands reaching out for Sarge. She gurgled and drooled, apparently fascinated by the creature who had appeared so unexpectedly.

"That's Sarge, honeybun," Anabelle said by way of introduction. "He's a nice doggie."

Without the need of a command, Sarge sat. His nose twitched, picking up the baby's scent. He seemed to know not to approach too closely.

"Looks like Lindsay wants to pet Sarge," Cam said.

"Touch is how babies learn." Anabelle checked with her daughter waiting for her to give the word.

"Oh, all right," she said in an exasperated tone.

"Come, Sarge." She patted her knee. "Sit. That's a good boy." She guided Lindsay's hand to the top of Sarge's head.

Lindsay grabbed a handful of Sarge's fur and giggled.

"No no." Although Sarge hadn't reacted at all, sitting patiently, Anabelle loosened the baby's grip. "We have to be very gentle with the doggie."

"He's being very patient with her," Ainslee said with a look of surprise.

Cam took the dog by the collar. "Sarge is always good with the children we meet on our walks. Aren't you, boy? He'll learn to protect Lindsay from danger. Probably herd her safely away from danger if she's about to get into trouble. I remember ol' Skipper doing that with you kids when you were little."

After giving Sarge a treat, Cam put him back in the mudroom.

Mentally, Anabelle wiped the nervous sweat from her brow. Her dream of Lindsay playing with Sarge had come one step closer to reality.

With regret, she handed Lindsay back to Ainslee in order to put the topping on the cake.

Her daughter's exquisite sigh of delight at the first bite made the effort worth the work.

When dinner was over, Cam helped clear the table while Ainslee put the baby down to sleep in the playpen.

Wiping his hands on a tea towel, Cam said, "If you ladies will excuse me, I'm going to check the evening news."

"That will be fine, dear." Anabelle was happy to have her conversation alone with her daughter.

She and Ainslee adjourned to the living room where they could watch Lindsay sleeping. A light blanket covered her as she lay on her back with her arms and legs splayed out wide, a pacifier in her mouth. Anabelle remembered the joy of simply watching Evan sleep during the early months of his life. That was true for both Ainslee and Kirstie as well, although with each baby she'd had less time to indulge in those sweet moments. Even so, every minute with them had been a blessing and a miracle.

Anabelle sat in her favorite chair, her basket of knitting on the floor next to her.

"I understand you and Doug and Lindsay are going to Disney World for Christmas," she began, her tone casual as if she were reporting the weather.

Ainslee looked up. "Where did you hear that?"

"I saw Louise at the store last weekend. She's very excited about you all being together for the holiday."

"Yes, Doug's excited about the trip too. He doesn't get a chance to see Robb and his family very often. And, of course, Doug adores Disney World."

Anabelle recalled meeting Doug's younger brother at the wedding. A fine young man with a delightful family.

"Who doesn't?" she said with a smile. "But I must admit we'll be sad not having Lindsay here with us for her first Christmas."

"I know, I'll be a little sad too," Ainslee said. "I think it should be fun. Although I have to admit I'm a little worried about all the arrangements required for traveling with a baby."

"I can see that," Anabelle said, trying to restrain the shred of hope she felt over Ainslee's hesitation. "I think I'd be questioning the wisdom of the decision too." Okay, wisdom probably wasn't the most diplomatic word, but out it had come before Anabelle could stop it.

"Wisdom? I don't know about that. I mean, it's a great chance for Doug to be with his brother's family. They haven't even seen Lindsay yet."

"Very true. I just mean that it's so difficult to travel with a young baby." Using her most nonconfrontational voice, Anabelle began ticking off the reasons Ainslee shouldn't travel so far with a baby. Aside from the fact that she didn't want to miss Lindsay Belle's first Christmas, she also agreed with Ainslee that the travel element itself was enough to overwhelm even the most prepared of mothers. "I remember traveling with Evan when he was Lindsay's age, once. It was quite . . . involved. I had to carry a car seat, plus all the things I needed just to visit a neighbor's house: a port-a-crib, a diaper bag, a stroller . . . not to mention our own luggage. I remember thinking: not again until this child can walk on his own!" Anabelle knew she was carrying on a little too long, and even she could see through her own diversion strategy, but she couldn't help herself. "It's just not easy. These days, who knows how much they'll charge you extra for your bags. And you know what a pain it is going through security."

"Oh, Mother. Why must you be so discouraging? I mean, people travel with babies all the time. I understand that it's an inconvenience, but Doug and I can manage."

"Of course you can, honey. But Christmas season is such a hectic time for travel. The planes are often overbooked and there can be weather delays. It's flu season too." Even though Anabelle felt bad for belaboring the point, she could tell by her daughter's furrowed brow that she was making some headway. Still, she kept on track. "And, come to think of it, Lindsay's too young for flu shots. It'd be terrible if she—"

"Mother, what are you trying to do?" Ainslee's lips formed a straight line and she sat very still.

"Just pointing out a few things you might want to consider." From her knitting basket, she picked up a scarf she'd been working on and slipped on her glasses. But she avoided eye contact with her daughter.

Standing, Ainslee started to gather up the baby's things and her birthday present. "Mother, thank you for the gift, and for having us over. But I think it's time to go home. Doug will be calling soon."

Anabelle knew she had gone too far.

Anabelle put her knitting aside, feeling remorseful. The last thing she needed was more strain in her relationship with Ainslee. "I'm sorry, honey. I didn't mean to make you worry. I just—"

"I know, you just want me to be prepared. I get it." She stuffed Lindsay's bib and teething ring in the diaper bag. "But the decision is ours, Mother. Doug's and mine. There's no need for you to worry. We take excellent care of Lindsay."

"I know you do, dear. You're a wonderful mother."

Ainslee picked up Lindsay and zipped the baby into a warm, snugly outfit without waking her.

Anabelle folded up the playpen and carried it out to the car and waited while Ainslee put the baby in her car seat.

"Tell Pop good-bye for me."

Standing by the driveway, Anabelle watched her daughter drive off and hugged herself against the cold. Despite Ainslee's pique, Anabelle knew she'd planted the seeds that would make her daughter think carefully about taking the trip to Florida.

And keep her close to home for Christmas instead.

At least the concerns she'd raised about infant travel were legitimate.

Rubbing her arms, she went back inside, sat down in her chair, and picked up her knitting again. The lights on the tree twinkled like the stars in the heavens. A few years ago, Cam had gotten rid of the old-fashioned lights that consumed so much electricity, replacing them with the smaller bulbs. She'd resisted at first, but now she liked these smaller lights even better.

The tree represented so many changes in her life with Cam. Milestones that had come and gone yet would always be remembered in her heart. Traditions she had passed on to their children and now, she prayed, she'd share with Lindsay.

Cam appeared from the back of the house. "Where's Ainslee? Are she and the baby gone already?"

"She went home early to wait for Doug's phone call. She said to tell you good-bye."

He slipped his hand into his trouser pocket. "Did you and Ainslee have an argument?"

"Of course not." Her knitting needles clicked together at a faster pace.

"Annie, luv, did you try to talk her out of going to Florida with the Giffens?"

"Not exactly. I mentioned how difficult it is to travel with a young baby and that I was sad Lindsay wouldn't be here for her first Christmas. That's all."

"You interfered."

The accusation stung. "I'm sure she and Doug will do the right thing."

"And we should give them the space to do just that," Cam admonished.

Anabelle knew he was right. She would simply have to live with their decision whatever it was.

With a puzzled frown, Cameron tilted his head, studying Anabelle with care. "Tell me, luv, why is it that this Christmas is so important to you, beyond its being Lindsay's first one? You're so upset, there has to be more to it than wanting our grandchild here."

She folded her arms across her chest and glanced away. "You'll think I'm just being silly."

"I never have before."

True enough, or at least rarely, but when she examined her motives closely, Anabelle was embarrassed. "It's because of my mother." She briefly reminded him of the Christmas her mother had been so ill. "Ever since then, I've cherished Christmas memories. I even wrote them down in my diary when I was a teenager. The first Christmas Mother gave me some makeup and let me wear it to church. The time my father was carving the ham for dinner and it slid off the plate onto the floor."

Cameron smiled at that shared memory.

She returned the smile. "The first Christmas you came to dinner at our house. You were so nervous."

"Yeah, I was. I remember that too." Stepping closer, he put his arms around her. "Okay, I get it. Christmas is really important to you."

"Yes, it is."

"But we still can't interfere in the lives of our grown children."

Her shoulders slumped and she rested her head on his chest. Her throat tight with emotion, she whispered, "I know."

Friday morning, James was at the nurses' station ordering an IV for one of his patients when Dr. Hamilton came by.

"How's your work schedule this month?" the doctor asked. "Taking any vacation time?"

"I'm scheduled to have Christmas Day off. The patient load is usually low, and we run a skeleton staff."

Dr. Hamilton slipped his stethoscope into the pocket of his white lab coat. "Good. I've got some surgeries scheduled for a week from Monday. I'd like you to assist."

"That would be great." James loved the variety of stepping into the OR from time to time. "I'll check with my supervising nurse."

The doctor nodded his approval, started to leave and then turned back. "The first gallbladder case, a young woman with three young children, is troubling. Jackie Yankura's her name."

He paused for a moment, frowning thoughtfully. "I wanted her in for surgery sooner, but she's worried about how her husband will handle the kids. They moved to Deerford only recently."

"You want me to ask the staff to keep an eye on him in the surgical waiting room?"

"Might be a good idea. Something about the patient—" He shook his head. "Well, I still have rounds to do and no doubt a mob waiting in my office."

With that, Dr. Hamilton hurried down the hall, turning into room 219.

James finished preparing the IV and then made a note to let the supervising nurse know about Dr. Hamilton's request that he be assigned to the operating room for the upcoming surgeries.

Chapter Nine

"EATH ALREADY MADE A BIRDHOUSE FOR US," Howie said from the backseat of Candace's small SUV. Always in motion, he kicked his legs back and forth against his seat. "How come he's gonna do it again?"

Candace and her two children were en route to a Saturday afternoon Audubon Society meeting at the library. Heath was doing a show-and-tell on how to build bird feeders. The children had recently become interested in birds, particularly Brooke, and Candace wanted to be supportive of Heath and his hobby.

"This is different." Sitting in the front seat, Brooke turned halfway around to explain. "If we want to attract all kinds of birds to our backyard we have to put up a feeder."

"I don't care if birds come or not."

Candace glanced in the rearview mirror to catch a glimpse of her son. "You like it when those pretty green hummingbirds flit by our window or when cardinals come back in the spring and perch in our tree."

"Nathan Storm says he's gonna get a BB gun for Christmas. He could shoot the birds."

Wincing, Candace shook her head. Why would a parent give a first-grader a BB gun? "He's not allowed to come around our house with a BB gun. And there'll be no shooting birds either, do you understand? They're God's creatures just like we are."

"We're bigger," Howie countered.

"But that doesn't mean we should hurt them. Just like big people shouldn't pick on or bully little people."

A shrug was Howie's only answer to that.

Located near the city park, the Deerford Public Library was built in the 1930s as part of a WPA project and was best known for the pair of beautifully sculptured lions that sat on pillars on either side of the entrance. In the 1960s, the library was expanded; and over the years it had been upgraded to include a fine collection of books and up-to-date computers for public use. During the week, a good many schoolchildren hung out at the library after school, doing their homework and waiting for their working parents to pick them up when they got off work.

Candace parked in the lot beside the library. Snow was predicted for later in the day; and the heavily overcast sky blocked out the sun, shrouding the town.

Inside, they walked past the checkout counter to the meeting room. Folding chairs sat in rows facing the front where Heath was arranging his sample bird feeders on a long table. Only a handful of people had arrived so far.

Howie went running up to the front. "Hi, Heath. We came to hear about bird feeders."

"Hey, good to see you, buddy." Heath gave the boy a smile and ruffled his hair. "You going to help me make one?"

"I dunno. Maybe I'm too little."

"We'll see." He looked up and greeted Brooke and Candace, who approached at a more sedate pace than Howie. "Hi, you two. Glad you came."

"I hope you get a good turnout," Candace said. Recently, whenever she saw Heath, she felt a renewed sense of amazement that they were a couple now, as well as good friends.

"As long as you and the kids are here, that's good enough for me." Deep creases appeared in his cheeks when he smiled, and his blue eyes sparked with warmth.

The heat of a blush crept up Candace's neck. "Anything we can do to help you set up?"

"No, I've got it covered. Thanks."

She picked out seats for them in the front row and sat down, Brooke beside her. Howie still hung around Heath to see what he was doing.

A screen had been pulled down on the wall behind the table. It looked like Heath had set up his laptop for a PowerPoint presentation to go along with his hands-on show-and-tell examples.

Slowly the room began to fill, mostly with parents and children Brooke's age and younger. Some of the adults knew Heath and came up front to greet him before taking their seats.

Glancing at his watch, Heath stepped up to the podium. "Good afternoon, folks. Thanks for coming today. The Audubon

Society is dedicated to conserving and restoring natural ecosystems for birds and other animals that benefit all of us. I'm particularly pleased to see so many children here today. If we can spark their interest in birds and the environment when they're young, they'll be hooked for a lifetime."

Reminding the audience that spring would be here sooner than they realized, he began his presentation by speaking in general terms about what they'd need to encourage birds to return to their yards and feeders every season. Then he showed slides of the various types of feeders, often with birds in the frame.

The pictures were quite good, Candace thought. She wondered if he had taken them or if they came from an Audubon Society source. She'd have to ask him later.

About the time Howie was growing restless, Heath got to the hands-on part of the program.

"I need some volunteers to help me out," he said. "How about some kids?"

Brooke's hand shot up and so did Howie's as well as those of several other youngsters in the audience.

Heath picked two kids in the back. He winked at Candace and then picked both Brooke and Howie, showing a bit of favoritism, but she didn't object. Her children seemed to really like Heath, which was important to Candace for any man she dated—not that she could imagine dating anyone else.

Heath divided the four youngsters into pairs working on two different types of feeders. The pieces of wood had been precut. He showed them how to assemble the projects.

Howie got to apply glue to the edges of the wood; Brooke nailed the pieces into place. No hammered thumbnails. Not too much glue dripped onto the newspaper protecting the library's table.

Her children seemed to be enjoying the project, so Candace pulled out her camera to take a few shots of them and Heath. One with Heath's face close to Brooke's as he instructed her almost brought tears to Candace's eyes. Both blond, they looked so much like father and daughter, she could have wept—whether out of joy or fear, she couldn't quite decide.

When the projects were completed, Heath passed out instructions to build various feeders and a list of sources for ready-to-make kits. He thanked everyone for coming, and the crowd dispersed.

Candace joined her children at the worktable. "Nicely done, Mr. Carlson. The bird feeders look perfect."

"I had some good helpers." He grinned at her.

"Heath said we can take this one home," Brooke announced.

"He says we gotta paint it before we put it outside," Howie added.

"And get birdseed at the pet store," Brooke continued. "If we get the right kind, Mom, we'll attract cardinals and finches and red-winged blackbirds."

"That would be lovely in the spring," Candace said. "Our yard would be a very busy place."

"I'll get you a pole to mount the feeder on," Heath promised. "Remember cardinals and finches like to feed at about this height." He held his hand at shoulder height. "They don't like to feed on the ground where predators can get them."

"Like cats!" Howie announced loudly. Obviously, he'd been listening to Heath's lecture about keeping cats indoors in order to protect bird populations.

"That's right, buddy. Like cats."

They helped Heath gather up his materials and carry them out to his Jeep. The snow had started to fall—big flakes floating gently down to land on the cars still in the parking lot. In a burst of pent-up energy, Howie ran around trying to catch the flakes on his tongue, his warm jacket flying open.

Brooke strolled toward their Honda carefully carrying the bird feeder.

"How's your father these days?" Candace asked Heath.

"I'd hoped he'd come today, but he's having a rough time during the holidays. They're an especially hard time to deal with loss."

Candace knew exactly what Heath meant. The first Christmas after Dean died had been especially hard for her. And she knew that Heath had also experienced the sting of grief after his fiancée had died several years ago.

"Otherwise, Dad's doing well," Heath continued. "He just likes his quiet time." He brushed a snowflake from Candace's hair and lowered his voice just slightly. "Do you have plans tonight? Can I take you out to dinner?"

His softly spoken invitation made her heart hit an extra beat. "I'd love to. I'll just have to make sure Mother plans to be home."

"Sure. I understand. Give me a call?"

"I will." Her spirits rode high on a wave of anticipation, and her footsteps were light all the way to the car.

It was almost dark when she arrived home and pulled into the garage.

As soon as they were all inside, both Howie and Brooke vied to tell their Grammy all about Heath and the bird feeder.

"Can we paint it now, Mom?" Brooke pleaded.

"Let's wait until tomorrow after church. I'll have to find you a can of outdoor paint in the garage. There should be something left from the projects we did last summer." She could only hope the paint hadn't turned to stone in the can or she'd have to make a quick trip to the hardware store.

Apparently satisfied with her decision, Brooke and Howie went their separate ways, leaving Candace with her mother in the kitchen. Dressed in her favorite sweatshirt with a picture of a spring bouquet on the front, Janet Fuller had been putting a chicken potpie together and had a streak of flour on her cheek.

Candace shrugged out of her coat. "Do you have any plans for tonight, Mom?"

"Only if you count watching a Christmas special on TV a plan. Why do you ask?"

"Heath invited me out to dinner."

"How nice, dear. You go ahead. We'll be fine on our own."

"You're sure?"

"Absolutely." She squeezed Candace's hand. "Heath's a very nice young man. I'm glad you're seeing him regularly."

"Thanks, Mom. I think he's pretty special too." She turned to leave then had second thoughts. "You know, this is our first Christmas being together. I've been scratching my head trying to figure out what to give him for a present."

"Oh, that's a hard one." Janet rinsed her hands under the faucet. "There are always ties and sweaters or a good book he might like."

"A book might work, but it would have to be something special."

"Maybe something about birds?" Janet suggested.

Candace perked up at that idea. "That would be a possibility."

"Are you going to invite him to Christmas dinner? It's our year to cook for Susan and her family."

Candace's mental gears slammed to a stop. Her older sister hadn't met Heath yet. No one in the family had except her mother. Was it too soon to be introducing him to everyone? Was she ready for that? If Heath came to a family dinner, what would that mean to her children? Candace's brain tangled on a million questions born of her own insecurities.

"I don't know, Mom. I hadn't thought about it."

"I think you should, dear. You've been seeing him a while now."

"He does have family nearby. His brother. And his father is temporarily living with him."

"Yes, I know that. But just think about it. There's always room for more at our table. Both Heath and his father would be more than welcome. Dan Carlson seemed like a very nice gentleman when I met him."

As Candace went upstairs to call Heath and change into something for the evening, she realized what a giant step it would be to invite Heath to a family gathering. The thought sent a zing of anxiety right to the middle of her chest.

Was she ready for that?

Sitting down on the side of the bed, she gazed at the photograph of her late husband on the bedside table.

"What should I do, Dean? Am I trying to move too fast?" She still missed Dean in every way possible. But the darkness of her grief had eased. Heath, she knew, had a part in lifting that shadow from her life.

With a sigh, she realized she didn't have to decide right this minute what to do about inviting Heath to Christmas dinner.

For now, all she had to do was call him about their date tonight.

Concerned about the weather report and forecast for more snow, she and Heath decided to stay in town and have a simple dinner nearby.

For once, Ripley's Diner wasn't crowded. Apparently the usual clientele had been frightened off by the weather forecast and had stayed at home. Only a few tables were filled.

A two-foot Christmas tree decorated with miniature candy canes sat on the counter near the cash register. Swags of silver garland were draped on the glass display cases featuring homemade pies and cakes.

The hostess seated them at a booth along the far wall where original paintings by local artists were on display. A watercolor of a hay field with a familiar abandoned farmhouse north of town hung next to their booth. The artist had captured the forlorn house in full surrender to time and the elements. A sad commentary on the struggles some farmers faced in the twenty-first century.

Placing menus in front of them, the hostess said, "Your server will be right with you."

For their evening out, Heath had changed into a sapphire-blue, long-sleeved, brushed-silk shirt and a nice leather jacket. She'd changed into slacks and a warm but flattering sweater.

Candace glanced at the menu, but she already knew what she wanted.

"I meant to ask you earlier. Did you take those photos of bird feeders or were they from the Audubon Society?" she asked.

"They came from the society. I'm not that good with a camera."

"Oh? I thought you were good at everything," she teased.

He grinned and dimples appeared in his cheeks. "Guess I've got you buffaloed then, but feel free to keep on thinking that. Just don't tell my brother. He'll laugh you out of the house."

"I doubt that." She'd met his brother Shaun and his wife when Chrissy was giving birth to their first child. Candace had seen the brothers interact. There couldn't have been more love and concern between them.

Heath lifted his shoulders in an easy shrug. "A little sibling rivalry is good for a family."

"I certainly get plenty of that with Brooke and Howie."

"They're good kids, Candace. You're doing a great job raising them."

A frisson of joy gladdened her heart. So often it was hard to tell if she was doing the right thing with her children. To have Heath validate her efforts gave her an unexpected lift and she tucked the feeling away to pull out again when she needed reassurance.

When the waitress appeared, Heath ordered a steak and baked potato. Candace selected chicken breast in puff pastry with an orange sauce, a real treat since she rarely prepared anything quite so fancy. The children's taste ran to the far more basic meals like meatloaf and chicken potpie.

Throughout dinner, they talked of ordinary things: the latest movies, most of which neither of them had seen, a new business center proposed on the north side of town, how they'd both like more time to travel. And they laughed, sometimes for no reason at all.

Candace was struck by how easily they conversed, no awkward silences or opposing views. Not that she felt a couple should agree on every issue. But being with Heath was simply and amazingly comfortable.

He had an uncanny way of looking at her while they chatted, his focus entirely on her as though the next words out of her mouth would be the most important words in the universe. He didn't glance away. He didn't fidget with his silverware. He didn't interrupt.

And as she thought about their relationship, she realized she was equally engaged with every word he spoke.

By the time Heath drove her home, there were four inches of snow on the ground and more coming down by the minute. The flakes flew at the windshield in big clumps, making the wipers work hard to keep up.

He pulled his Jeep into the driveway.

"It was a lovely dinner," she said, starting to get out.

"I'm going to walk you to the door, Mrs. Crenshaw. After all my effort to impress you tonight, I don't want you thinking I'm not a gentleman."

He quickly got out and came around to open her door. Her mother had left the front porch light on. As a teenager, Candace had desperately tried to convince her mother to turn the light off when she was out on a date. Janet never had. Old habits died hard.

Which Candace was sure would please Mrs. Kowalski, their loving but unabashedly nosey neighbor.

On the porch, Heath took her hand. "Thanks for going to dinner with me."

"Thank you. I don't get many nights out."

"We'll have to fix that." With his free hand, he cupped the side of her face, warming her cheek.

Slowly, he lowered his head toward hers.

When their lips met, it felt as though they were a matching pair, his and hers meant to be together. He shifted his position to wrap his arms around her and pull her closer. She leaned into him willingly.

As they kissed, the silently falling snow cocooned them in a secret world of their own.

When they broke the kiss, a sense of loss shimmered through Candace and she sighed. Heath's gaze held hers.

"In case you haven't figured it out yet, Candace . . . I love you." His voice low and tender, it rumbled through his chest, sending a wave of gladness to her heart.

Tears of joy burned at the back of her eyes when she finally allowed herself to say the words that had gone unspoken for too long. "I love you too, Heath."

He ran the back of his fingers down her cheek and he smiled. "I was hoping you did." His eyes glittered in the glow of the porch light. He took a step back. "Good night, Candace."

"Good night, Heath. I'll see you at church tomorrow." Her voice sounded husky even to her own ear.

"You can count on it."

Just before she stepped inside the house, Candace noticed the curtains on Mrs. Kowalski's window move. As she had feared, the secret world she'd briefly shared with Heath had been breached.

Chapter Ten

"COME ON IN." ELENA HELD OPEN THE DOOR FOR Sarah, who had followed her home after church. Isabel had already shot past them both to find her daddy. "I'll have our lunch ready in a few minutes."

"I'd be happy to help."

"There's not much left to do. The chicken has been in the slow cooker. I just have to heat up the rice and beans." Elena slipped off her coat and hung it on a hook in the laundry room off the kitchen. "You're welcome to come sit with me though."

After removing her jacket, Sarah followed her into the kitchen. She looked particularly nice today in a navy tunic top over a wool skirt. She wore a simple bead necklace and had twisted her blonde hair, which she'd let grow recently, into a knot at her nape. Elena couldn't help but wonder if the young woman had dressed to impress Rafael.

In the other room, Elena heard Izzy giving Rafael a blow-by-blow description of her morning at Sunday school.

Retrieving two pots from a cupboard, Elena began putting on the rice and beans to heat.

Isabel dragged her father into the kitchen. "Buela's going to teach Mommy how to sew today. Then Mommy can teach me when I get bigger 'cause I'm her little girl."

"You're my little angel," Sarah said with a smile.

"Hi, Sarah." Rafael acknowledged the mother of his child with a brief nod. He hadn't shaved yet, and he was wearing old jeans and a knit shirt that had seen better days.

"Hello, Rafael. Good to see you."

"Yeah." Moving to the stove, he checked to see what Elena was cooking. "We going to eat soon?"

He started to stick a finger in the beans to sneak a taste, but Elena whacked his hand away. "Soon enough. I won't let you starve, I promise."

"But your cooking's so good, I can't wait. Besides, I'm hungry."

"Me too," Isabel piped up.

"If you're so hungry, Rafael, then you can set the table for me. Your father's helping a friend from work fix his brakes, so we can eat here in the kitchen."

"I can set the table." Sarah jumped to her feet and went to the drawer where Elena kept her place mats.

Rafael stepped back out of the way, a curious look on his face.

"I can help you, Mommy. Buela lets me sometimes."

"Of course you can help, angel. You're a big girl now. What color place mats should we use today?"

"The red ones for Christmas!"

"All right. You put these on the table for me, and I'll get the silverware."

"I can count them too." Carefully doing her task, Izzy counted each place mat as she arranged them on the Formica table.

Stirring the beans, Elena wondered how much of Sarah's enthusiasm to set the table was because she wanted to be a good mother and how much was again due to a desire to impress Rafael. Elena feared Sarah would be disappointed if her motivation was the latter. Rafael had shown little or no interest in resuming his relationship with his daughter's mother.

When everything was ready, Elena served up the meal and carried the plates to the table. Rafael sat at his usual place with Isabel next to him. Sarah sat across from their child.

"We'll say grace," Elena announced, bowing her head. "Dear Lord, thank You for bringing us together to enjoy the meal that You have provided. We thank You for the fellowship of the Lord's house this morning and pray that You will continue to bless our family. Amen."

"Amen! Amen! Amen!" Isabel chirped. "Now we can eat."

Elena smothered a smile and suspected the others did as well. Not 100 percent angel, Izzy could be a little rascal when she wanted to.

They ate in silence for a while and then Sarah asked, "How's your band doing?"

Rafael looked up briefly. "Okay, I guess. We're booked most weekends for one or two nights."

"That's good," Sarah said.

He shrugged. "Not great though. We're trying to get some more steady gigs but it's tough."

Sarah tried to appear interested and sympathetic, but Rafael didn't keep up his end of the conversation.

Feeling sorry for Sarah, Elena changed the topic to sewing and what she and Sarah would work on that afternoon.

Rafael finished his lunch first. "Hey, mi bonita," he said to Isabel, "if you eat all your lunch, I'll take you down to Baldomero for dessert."

Beside her, Elena sensed Sarah shrink.

Izzy cheered. "I get flan for dessert, Buela. Do you want to come too?"

"I can't, little one. Remember? I'm going to give Sarah a sewing lesson." She glanced at Rafael. He looked innocent enough—no malicious intent in his eyes or cynical smile on his lips—but she suspected he had an ulterior motive to escape the house as fast as he could with Sarah here.

As if he sensed her skepticism, he said, "I promised Grandma Baldomero I'd do some computer work for her. If I go now, I'll get Izzy out of your hair for a while so you can sew in peace."

"I'm not in Buela's hair," Izzy objected.

"How 'bout I get in your hair?" He plunged his fingers into his daughter's dark hair, mussing it and making her shriek with laughter.

In the midst of Isabel's giggles, Elena noticed a look pass between Rafael and Sarah, an instant of shared delight in the child they had created together. Elena's breath caught. Perhaps there was yet a way that the Lord would bring these three people together to form a family of their own.

"All right, you two." Elena waved Rafael and Izzy away from the table. "Go, go. We'll clean up, won't we, Sarah?"

Still smiling at Rafael, Sarah said, "Of course."

After Elena started the dishwasher and Sarah finished wiping off the table, Elena sat her down at the sewing machine—which Elena had moved from her bedroom to the living room for today.

"So you can get a feel for the machine and how fast it goes," Elena said, "we'll start with a couple of leftover swatches of material and stitch those together. Then we'll start work on Izzy's costume."

Elena showed her how to thread the machine and how the needle could be adjusted and how to set the length of the stitch she wanted. She demonstrated the stop, start, and reverse button and how to adjust the speed from slow to fast.

Shaking her head, Sarah asked, "How do you remember all of this stuff?"

"I've been at it a long time. My grandmother has an old treadle machine she still uses and thinks my computerized machine is too complicated for her."

"Either way seems a little daunting," Sarah admitted.

"Don't you worry about a thing. You'll catch on in no time." As Elena had gotten to know Sarah better, she'd come to realize the young woman had a good head on her shoulders. If she'd gotten a better start in life, a more involved mother who had pushed her to achieve, she would have gone far. She still could.

Matching the edge of the two scraps of fabric, Sarah lowered the foot, set the sewing speed to slow, and guided the cotton cloth beneath the needle. The material started to bunch.

"No need to push the fabric under the needle," Elena said. "The machine will pull it through at whatever speed you've set."

"My hands are sweating."

"You're doing fine. Stop sewing just before you get to the end, and we'll turn the fabric."

"Oh boy . . . how do I stop it?"

"Same way you started the machine."

Her forehead furrowed, the tip of her tongue peeking out of the corner of her mouth, Sarah managed to bring the machine to a halt. She leaned back in her chair exhausted and looked up at Elena. "I'll never get the knack of this."

"You will if you keep trying." Elena sensed encouragement and praise would be the best teachers for Sarah, two essential elements that had been missing from her earlier life.

After a little more practice on the swatches, Elena set her to work to sew the first seam putting the angel skirt pieces together.

When Sarah finished the seam, she held up the skirt, a huge smile crinkling the corners of her eyes. "I did it!" She examined her work more closely. Her smile devolved, shifting her features into a frown. "It's a little crooked right here."

"It's fine. The costume doesn't need much tailoring."

Still studying her shortcomings as a seamstress, Sarah said, "I don't suppose Rafael would be all that impressed with my sewing." She raised her head, her eyes glistening with both hope and unshed tears.

Elena sat on the edge of the kitchen chair she'd pulled over. "You still like my son, don't you?"

Sarah nodded as if involuntarily. "He is the kindest, best man I've ever met; and I blew it all because I was hooked on dope. What a fool I was."

"But you're trying to make up for that now." In fact, she was doing a good job with Isabel. Not so much with Rafael.

Sarah nodded. "Do you think there's any hope that Rafael and I could ever, you know, get back together?"

Sympathy constricted Elena's chest. She liked Sarah. But Rafael was her son. She owed her loyalty to him. Yet her prayers were for both of them.

"It's hard to say. But neither of us can control Rafael's heart. Whatever happens between you two is up to him. And God."

Sarah's chin quivered, and she wiped the back of her hand across her eyes. "Can I try another seam?"

"You bet you can." Standing, Elena placed her hand on Sarah's shoulder and gave her an encouraging squeeze. "This time you can speed up the machine if you'd like."

A moment of terror flashed in Sarah's eyes. She shook her head. "I think I'll keep it on slow until I master that. Then maybe . . ."

James came into the house from playing H-O-R-S-E with Gideon and Nelson on the half basketball court in the backyard. The boys had been so determined to play that they had shoveled and salted the court. James shrugged out of his jacket and hung it in the mudroom.

"Man, it's cold out there," he said to Fern, who was sitting in the family room reading a large-print book of daily meditations.

"Did the boys beat you again?"

He harrumphed. "What makes you think those kids can beat their old man?"

"Because they're still out there playing and you came inside."

"You're too perceptive by far," he grumbled, dropping onto the couch and putting his feet up on the coffee table. "I can't remember the last time I beat either one of them." Not that he didn't still enjoy playing with the boys on a Sunday afternoon. He did. But he wasn't anywhere as fast on his feet as he used to be and sure couldn't jump as high.

"You taught them everything they know about basketball."

"I think they've been getting some coaching at school. Gideon can drop those three pointers in the basket every time."

He leaned his head back and thought about all he should be doing. Like cleaning the garage. Finding some wallpaper for the family room.

Doing his Christmas shopping.

"I'm going to visit the video store next week," he said.

Fern looked away from her book. "To buy that Chicago Underground game?"

"No, I don't think so. I'm hoping a clerk can suggest an alternative or convince me it's not as violent as I think it is."

"If Gideon doesn't get the game he wants, he'll play it at his friend's house."

"Yeah, probably." He combed his fingers through his hair. "But at least he'll understand where we're coming from. We don't approve of violent games in our family. If he wants to choose otherwise . . ." He left the thought hanging in the air.

"Gideon never used to like violent video games," Fern said. "Do you suppose that being in Junior ROTC has changed him? Made him like the idea of weapons and killing people?"

"I suppose it's possible. But more likely the change is because he's getting older, trying to separate himself from his parents—"

"I don't like the idea of that at all."

He patted her hand. "I suspect the biggest influence is peer pressure. He wants to be like his buddies."

"I suppose you're right, James. But he's a good boy. If he doesn't get the game he wants, he might be disappointed and upset initially; but given a little time, he'll be okay with it."

James hoped his wife was as right about Gideon as she always was about him.

Dear Lord, it wasn't easy to be a father.

Elena slid into bed beside Cesar and sighed.

"Sounds like you had a long day," he said, reaching for her hand and lacing his fingers through hers.

"Not really. Sarah and I worked on Izzy's Christmas costume." She spoke softly so her voice didn't carry into Rafael's room or Izzy's. "I think Sarah's going to be a good seamstress once she gets the hang of it. She's very careful."

"She has a good teacher."

"Maybe." A teacher who was conflicted about her son's relationship with the mother of his child. "Have you talked to Rafael about Sarah recently?"

"Talked? About Sarah? Why would I?"

Mentally, Elena rolled her eyes. The good Lord hadn't given men an ounce of intuition except about how a car engine works. "I think Sarah would like to get back together with him. I thought maybe he'd talked to you about his feelings for her."

"He was as mad as a burglar getting caught in the act when she walked out on him."

"I know that. And I understand how he felt. But he doesn't seem quite so angry anymore."

"That's good, isn't it?"

"True. Anger isn't healthy for anyone." She turned onto her side to face Cesar. "Now he mostly ignores her."

"Sounds like an improvement to me."

She supposed that was true. Not very satisfying, however, at least from Sarah's perspective.

"I don't know what to wish for," she said. "Do you think it would be better if they all got back together again? Became a real family?"

Cesar didn't respond. Instead she heard his soft snores as his breathing slowed and he slipped into sleep.

His snoring rarely bothered her. Instead she found comfort in knowing her husband was beside her and his presence soothed her. Tonight, however, the noise annoyed her. She'd been looking for answers. Apparently she'd been looking in the wrong place.

Chapter Eleven

TWELVE DAYS AFTER IT HAD DISAPPEARED, SIMPLY walking through the hospital lobby and seeing the vacant spot where the Christmas tree should have been gave Anabelle a bad case of heartburn—the kind no medication could relieve. She'd made absolutely no progress determining why Varner had made such a strange, uncharacteristic decision.

A little after twelve, she went downstairs to the cafeteria. Picking up a tray, she found herself standing next to Candace at the salad bar.

"How's the baby business?" she asked.

"The happiest place in town, at the moment." Candace piled some fresh spinach on her plate, adding a topping of sliced hard-boiled eggs and bacon bits. "The closer we get to Christmas, though, the busier it will get. All the OB/GYN doctors like to go on vacation during the holidays."

Anabelle followed Candace's lead, using the tongs to serve herself a helping of spinach. She added tomatoes and sunflower seeds plus some raisins and then filled a small bowl with clam chowder.

When they had both paid for their lunches, Anabelle turned to survey the room for an empty table. Crowded with employees on their lunch breaks and visitors, few tables were available.

"Look!" She nudged Candace. "Penny Risser is sitting alone in the corner. Let's gang up on her."

"Gang up on her?" Candace questioned.

"We're going to find out why Varner took down our tree."

Anabelle marched directly toward Penny's table. "May we join you?" Without waiting for a response, Anabelle sat down next to Penny, effectively blocking her escape.

Candace sat down opposite the CEO's administrative assistant. She cut Anabelle a glance that suggested she wasn't thrilled about trapping Penny while she was eating her lunch.

Anabelle didn't care. The tree situation was growing more urgent by the day. Less than three weeks until Christmas and just a week and a half until the Hope Haven Kids' party, and still there was no Christmas tree in the hospital lobby. Shameful!

Making no pretense of eating her lunch, Anabelle turned toward Penny. "I'm sure you know who demanded Varner take down the tree in the lobby."

Penny scooted her chair a few inches away from Anabelle's. "I've already told you."

"Varner wouldn't deviate from tradition without a powerful reason. Someone influential made a fuss, didn't they? If you give me the name, I won't tell anyone I got it from you."

Penny's eyes darted around in search of a quick exit. "I can't, Anabelle. I don't know who it is."

"Of course you do. There's nothing Varner does that you don't know about."

Penny started to stand but she was wedged between Anabelle, the table, and the wall.

Frowning, Candace said, "Anabelle, if she doesn't know—"

"If you could just tell us who that person is," Anabelle persisted, "we'd have a chance to convince him or her there isn't a good reason to not have our tree where it belongs in the lobby. I promise I won't mention your name or involve you in any way."

The muscle in Penny's always stern jaw flexed. "Anabelle Scott, I have to get back to work." Her voice was as taut as a steel spring. "Let. Me. Out."

Defeat weighed heavily on Anabelle's shoulders. Making Penny angry was not a good professional move. Besides, pressing her wasn't working.

She stood and pushed in her chair so Penny could get past.

The woman narrowed her eyes. "Don't ever try to force me to reveal confidential information again or I shall have to discuss your behavior with Mr. Varner." With that, Penny stalked across the room, deposited her dirty dishes and tray on the conveyor belt to the kitchen, and left the cafeteria.

With a heavy sigh, Anabelle sat down.

"Maybe you shouldn't have pushed her so hard," Candace suggested.

"It didn't do me much good, did it?" Studying her untouched bowl of soup, Anabelle wondered what her next step should be. Giving up entirely wasn't an option.

Not when it involved a tried-and-true tradition, a tradition she loved. Yet she couldn't seem to make any progress on her short list of suspects: Emmaline Palmer and Regis Tanner, the fire marshal.

It seemed, actually, that her attempts to thoroughly enjoy the Christmas season were being thwarted at every turn. First the tree and then Ainslee's planned trip. She didn't want to be a whiner, but she couldn't help but feel as if Hope Haven wasn't the only victim of the Grinch this year.

Before going back upstairs, Anabelle stopped in at Janice's office. "Any news on the missing presents?"

"Not a word. I think I've determined which presents are missing, so I'm going to replace those with money out of my office's budget. And your husband called this morning. He's going to bring in the plywood tree he's making tomorrow, so I'll get the gift tags back up and on display again. And security is going to make sure someone is on duty in the lobby all of the time."

"Well, that's something. At least there will be a party."

"I'm going to get a few extra presents in case I've miscalculated. I wouldn't want any child to go home from the party without some sort of a gift from Santa."

Anabelle was all in favor of that.

Midafternoon, a discouraged Anabelle was checking supplies when she heard a male voice raised in anger.

"I want to see his doctor and see him now!"

Stepping out of the supply room, she followed the sound of the belligerent voice. She found a middle-aged man towering over Becky Tyler and yelling at her. He wore a tailored suit and a white shirt open at the collar.

She walked up to the pair and spoke directly to the man. "Excuse me. I'm Anabelle Scott, the nursing supervisor. Is there a problem I can help you with?"

"I certainly hope so," he grumbled. "This dimwit"—he pointed an accusing finger at Becky—"is both deaf and dumb. She won't listen—"

"If you could keep your voice down, sir. You're disturbing our patients." Trying for all the patience she could muster, Anabelle gestured toward the nurses' station. She hoped he'd step away from the occupied room.

The stranger puffed out his chest and stood up straighter to make himself more intimidating. "I'm not going anywhere until I find out why you quacks haven't fixed my father yet."

Becky spoke up. "This is Jefferson Randall, the son of Mr. Randall, the patient in 201. From Springfield," she added.

Anabelle nodded her thanks and silently indicated that Becky could go back to work. She'd take it from here.

"Mr. Randall, your father is quite ill. Shouting will not help his condition." Anabelle was familiar with the case: The senior Mr. Randall was in his late seventies and suffered from chronic congestive heart failure complicated by hypertension and the onset of Alzheimer's. His prognosis was not good.

Jefferson leaned close to Anabelle's face. "Why isn't the doctor around? I want to talk to him. I want to know if he's as incompetent as you two are."

Getting a whiff of alcohol on Jefferson's breath, Anabelle took a step back. The insult meant nothing to her. Only the patient's well-being. "Have you tried to call his doctor's office?"

"I called, all right. Told the receptionist I'd be here at two o'clock and I wanted to meet him right here. Find out what was wrong with my father. So where is he?"

As far away from you as he can manage, Anabelle imagined.

A technician with a portable cardiogram on a cart tried to get past Jefferson Randall, but the man wouldn't budge.

"Mr. Randall, I'm going to have to ask you to either wait in the waiting room or go downstairs," Anabelle said. "You're disrupting patient care."

"Don't you try to get rid of me, you ol' bat." Spittle sprayed from his mouth. "I'll stay here as long as I want. I'm a close friend of the governor, and he'll hear about Hope Haven and the treatment my father and I have received at your hands."

Anabelle stood her ground. "If you don't leave right now, I'm going to call security and ask them to remove you."

His face turned red. The vein in his forehead puckered; broken capillaries webbed his cheeks. "If my father dies, I'll hold you accountable."

Knowing it wouldn't do any good to argue, Anabelle turned toward the nurses' station.

"Did you hear me?" he shouted after her. "I'll sue the hospital and you personally if my father dies."

Wincing, she picked up the phone and dialed security. In less than three minutes, two burly security guards were escorting a loudly protesting Jefferson Randall down the hallway and out of the building.

Her adrenaline still pumping through her system, Anabelle sat down at the computer and tried to calm herself.

Becky cruised by the station. "Thanks for rescuing me from that guy."

"All part of a day's work." She smiled weakly.

"They don't come any more obnoxious than that man. He ought to take some anger management classes."

"He ought to stop drinking too." It was one thing for family members of a patient to become upset about the care their relative was receiving or to be concerned about their recovery. But Jefferson Randall had been over the top with his anger and threats.

Becky gave her a brief wave and went back to work. Anabelle stared at the blinking cursor on the computer, wondering if it were possible . . .

James came by to get an IV setup for one of his patients.

Anabelle gestured him over. "Do you think it's possible someone who lost a loved one here at Hope Haven threatened to sue the hospital if Varner didn't take down the Christmas tree?"

"A disgruntled member of a patient's family?"

"That's what I'm thinking."

"He'd have to be more than a little upset about the care the patient had gotten. If that were the case, wouldn't the family sue for malpractice? Not take out their anger and grief on a Christmas tree?"

"It does seem odd." But the whole thing, including Penny's secrecy, was decidedly out of sync with the usual holiday spirit around the hospital.

She plucked a hard candy from a Santa Claus jar that had been left on the counter. The peppermint flavor exploded in her mouth.

"Have you had any unhappy families lately?" she asked James.

"Not that I can remember. I've got to change a patient's IV, or I'll have one unhappy dude in about a minute."

"Well, think about it. Let me know if you recall any incidents where family members became hysterical about losing someone. Maybe we can get together early tomorrow morning at Cuppa Coffee to compare notes. I'll ask Candace and Elena to meet us there too." A small coffee shop, Cuppa Coffee had vanilla lattes Anabelle enjoyed on cold winter mornings.

The phone rang at the nurses' station. Anabelle picked up.

"Anabelle, you won't believe what just happened." Janice's voice telegraphed her excitement. "We've found the missing presents!"

Anabelle gasped and her hand flew to her chest. "Where? Who took them? Have they caught the thief?"

"It's nothing like that. One of our own security guards had put them in a locked closet downstairs for safekeeping," she hurriedly announced. "He'd been worried that someone might help themselves when no guard was around to watch them. That same night, he came down with that awful flu that's been going around. This is his first day back to work."

"For goodness' sake! I'm sure you or the police questioned the staff, particularly security. I wish he'd told someone."

"I do too, but everything's fine now. The gifts are right here in my office. I have no intention of letting them get away from me again. I thought you'd want to know."

With a feeling of relief, Anabelle thanked her for calling. After all the angst over the missing tree, this bit of good news felt like a small miracle.

Instead of going directly home after work, James went into town to the video-game store.

The windows were covered with garishly bright game posters, most of them featuring outlandish weapons and ridiculous bionic fighters. The whole idea gave James flashbacks to Desert Storm. He assumed the game designers had never been in an actual battle.

Maybe that was Gideon's problem. With only Junior ROTC as a reference, he'd begun to think of war as a game. The reality was quite different.

Inside, adolescents and young adult males crowded the store vying for a turn to try out a new game. Most of them had so many body piercings they looked like refugees from an acupuncture clinic. Battle sounds screamed through the air.

James felt as though he'd stepped into an alternate universe. This wasn't the Deerford he knew.

The store clerk, a guy in his late twenties, had his share of piercings, and tattoos covered his arms.

"What'aya need?" the clerk asked.

"I was thinking about Chicago Underground. My son—"

"Great game. I'll get one for you and ring it up." He turned to open one of the locked display cases behind the counter. Shoplifting had to be a major problem in the game business.

"Actually, I wanted to ask some questions before I bought it."

That seemed to puzzle the clerk. "Questions?"

"I did some research online. It's rated M for Mature. It's supposed to be for people over seventeen."

"So?" The clerk shrugged. "You're older than seventeen, aren't you?"

James laughed. "My son asked for Chicago Underground for Christmas. He's sixteen."

"Oh man, don't let those ratings bother you. Every kid in town's playing Chicago. He's plenty old enough."

James wasn't so sure. "I was hoping you could suggest an alternate game that was just as challenging but not as violent and without the bad language."

The clerk gaped at him blankly for a moment and then shifted his attention to the young customers waiting to buy something. "Naw, I can't think of any. You wanna buy Chicago or not?"

He hesitated. He hated to disappoint Gideon. "No, I think I'll keep looking for something else."

The clerk had stopped listening to James before he finished the sentence.

During dinner, Howie and Brooke related their day's activities, a special time for Candace to catch up with her children.

"At recess, Nathan Storm fell off the climbing equipment and cracked his skull," Howie announced with considerable glee. He kept right on eating his favorite meatloaf. His small serving of carrots had been pushed to the side.

"Oh dear," Candace gasped. "Was Nathan all right?" She recalled the playground surface had been changed years ago to prevent serious injuries.

"I dunno. He got some blood on his shirt and his mom came and got him."

"Well, I hope he'll be back in school tomorrow." She glanced at her daughter.

Brooke gave a toss of her head. "I got an A on my math test. The paper's in my backpack."

"Good job!" Candace raised her hand to give Brooke a high five. A perfectionist, her daughter's grades were top-notch. "You can show me after dinner."

After eating a few bites of her dinner, Candace turned to her mother. "This was your day at Cavendish House, wasn't it?"

"It was." Her eyes lit up with pleasure. A former school librarian, Janet had recently started volunteering as a docent one or two mornings a week at the historic home in Deerford. "We had a fourth-grade class field trip today. They were adorable. We have some old wooden skis and poles we let the students try on the back hill. The skis must be ten feet long. I don't know how anyone ever skied on them."

Candace laughed at the image it conjured in her mind.

"I could probably ski on 'em, Grammy," Howie said.

"I'll have to take you over on a Saturday and let you try," Janet said. "The boys today didn't do so well. They thought their snow boards were a lot better than those old skis."

"I suspect they're right," Candace agreed, thinking Janet's volunteer activities provided a good outlet for her mother's long-held interest in history as well as working with children.

After cleaning up the dinner dishes, Candace sat down at the computer in the family room. She had to figure out what kind of present to give Heath, and time was running out to make the decision.

After poking around at various Web sites, she found one with gift ideas for men.

Item number one on the list turned out to be tickets to sporting events or concerts. Deerford didn't have a major league team in any sport, and the only concerts held in the area were church choirs and the high school band. That didn't sound like what the author of the list had in mind.

Second on the list came footwear. Footwear? What was she supposed to do, give Heath a new pair of snow boots?

She shook her head.

Still reading the list, Brooke came to stand beside her.

"What are you doing, Mom?"

"I'm trying to figure out what to give Heath for Christmas."

"Really? Can I give him a present too?"

Surprised, Candace glanced at her daughter. "Would you like to?"

"Sure. He's been real nice to me and Howie."

"Yes, he has." She studied her daughter for a moment. "Do you have an idea of what you'd like to give him?"

"Well . . ." Tilting her head to the side, she contemplated her ideas. "I know. Remember that store that has ceramic things you can paint yourself and then they glaze and fire them for you?"

"I remember." Her mother had taken both Howie and Brooke to the store where they each made Mother's Day picture frames for Candace. She adored them.

"Well, they had coffee mugs, and Heath likes coffee, doesn't he?"

"Yes."

"Then it's simple. I'll paint some birds and flowers on a mug, and he'll like that a lot."

Candace gave her daughter a hug. "I think that will be a perfect gift for Heath. How smart of you to think of that idea." Candace wished she could come up with something equally appropriate.

Having overheard the conversation, Howie popped up and ran over to Candace. "Can I give him a present too? Can I?"

"Of course you may, assuming it doesn't cost too much. Do you have any ideas?"

His smooth forehead furrowed and he touched one fingertip to his chin as he mentally searched for a gift idea.

"I know. I can give him an autographed baseball," he announced.

"That is a good idea, honey. Whose autograph do you think he'd like? A White Sox player?"

"No, Mommy! He'd want my autograph on the baseball."

Candace's jaw dropped.

"Why would he want your autograph, silly?" Brooke asked. "You're just a little kid."

Raising his chin in defiance, Howie said, "Heath thinks I'm gonna be a great baseball player. That's why he'd want my autograph. My autograph's gonna be worth lots of money someday. So there!"

Across the room, Candace's mother made a choking noise.

Candace struggled to keep a straight face. "You know, sweetie, I think a baseball autographed by you would please Heath very much."

By the time she turned back to resume her search for ideas on the Internet, the muscles in Candace's cheeks hurt from grinning. Her two children were the most imaginative kids in the world, and she never knew what either one of them was going to come up with next.

Dean would have been so very proud of them.

Giving up on the general gift list for men, she went to the Audubon Society's Web site. Maybe she'd find something special there to mark their first Christmas as a couple.

She looked first at the books the society had available. There were several how-to titles, but Heath had been involved in birding for a long time. He could probably write every how-to book they offered.

There were some lovely coffee-table books about various species of birds or ranges where specific birds were generally found. Unfortunately, Candace had no idea what kind of books of this sort Heath might already own.

Not knowing what else to do, she browsed through the entire society catalog in the hope that something would strike her fancy.

Chapter Twelve

THURSDAY MORNING, ANABELLE EYED THE DANISH pastries in the display case at Cuppa Coffee. Their cream cheese Danish was absolutely melt-in-the-mouth delicious. And about a thousand calories.

Demonstrating astounding self-control, she ordered a vanilla latte and let it go at that.

Elena had already found a table and was enjoying an apricot tart. A little extra vitamin C wouldn't hurt her, she insisted, ignoring the gobs of butter that made the pastry extra flaky.

Feeling self-righteous about denying herself a Danish, Anabelle took a seat at the round table beside Elena.

"So did you think of any irate family members?" she asked.

"Some, I suppose. Grief comes in a lot of different guises, and we do lose a few patients in ICU. There's no getting around that."

Often patients arrived at the hospital too sick or too frail or too badly injured to be saved. The Emergency Room saw most of those cases, but the Cardiac Care Unit handled their share of terminal patients too. Anabelle grieved for every one they lost. Every nurse and doctor did the same. Love and loss were both a part of the Lord's plan.

However, handling verbally abusive members of a patient's family shouldn't be part of anyone's job description.

She pulled a notepad out of her purse. "I came up with a few names, but none of them seemed so upset that they wouldn't want a Christmas tree in the lobby. And so far as I know, none is all that influential in the community."

James breezed in the door, admitting a rush of cold air and a storm of snowflakes. He ordered a regular coffee and quickly joined them at the table.

"If this snow keeps up, we'll have a white Christmas for sure," he said.

"I hope we do," Elena said. "Isabel loves to play in the snow."

Little Lindsay was too young to play in the snow yet, but Anabelle was sure she'd love it in another year or two.

Candace arrived a moment later. She carried her foamy latte to the table. "Sorry I'm late. Howie decided to hibernate like a bear this morning. Mother had to practically drag him out of bed."

James chuckled. "Smart kid."

Knowing they couldn't be late to work, Anabelle got directly to the point of their meeting. "Well, did any of you come up with likely suspects responsible for our missing tree?"

"The Birthing Unit hasn't lost a mother or baby for almost a year," Candace said. "I don't think I'm going to be any help."

"Without checking the records," Elena said, "I can only think of two patients who have died in ICU. Both of them were elderly and quite frail. The families weren't wild about their loved ones dying, but they knew from the start that was the likely outcome."

Anabelle looked at James, who was holding his coffee between both of his hands, warming them.

"I came up with one possibility, although it would still surprise me. We had a cancer patient a month or two ago. She'd been doing fine at home, or so she and her husband thought. She fell and broke her hip. That's when Dr. Prelutski discovered her cancer had spread to her liver, kidneys, and bones." James sipped his coffee then set the cup down again. "Her husband was terribly upset. He felt either the doctor had done something wrong or we had at the hospital."

"How sad," Candace commented, visibly troubled by the talk of death.

"What was the patient's name?" Anabelle asked.

"Barbara Fontaine."

Anabelle gasped. "Her husband's Bill Fontaine? The owner of the car dealership that folded?"

James nodded. "He's the one. Under normal circumstances, I suspect he's a really nice guy. Loving father, good husband. His wife's imminent death made him a little crazy. His kids came all the way from Florida to visit at the end. They couldn't seem to comfort him at all."

"Grief can make you crazy," Candace said. "Your brain gets so fuzzy, you can't think straight."

Anabelle knew Candace was speaking from personal experience, and her heart went out to the young widow. The first year or two after her husband had passed away had been very hard on Candace. Understandably.

"As it happens, I was talking to a friend of mine— Dr. Hamilton's wife—at a quilting guild meeting. She mentioned Barbara Fontaine and how difficult it's been for Bill to adjust to her death." Remembering her conversation with Genna Hamilton, Anabelle jotted Fontaine's name down on her notepad. "Bill was a big donor to the hospital, wasn't he?"

"That was probably before his dealership folded," Elena said. "Apparently he still has some vehicle maintenance contracts with the hospital. I saw him in the lobby a week or so ago. He seemed distracted, not himself, and a little scruffy."

"That's so sad," Anabelle said, recalling Genna mentioning how hard it was on Bill to lose his wife.

"Fontaine might know Varner well enough to ask him to do a personal favor for him," James suggested.

"Like not celebrate Christmas?" Candace shook her head. "That's a bit extreme."

"Hard to believe he's our Grinch," Elena said.

It was hard to picture that, particularly since Anabelle had known Barbara, although they hadn't been close. The fact that she'd generously helped a military widow in the community spoke volumes about her character. Her husband too, it would seem.

"I think I should at least follow up on the possibility Bill is our man," she said. "Barbara and Bill are, or were, members of my church. I can have a word with Rev. Masterson. Hopefully he can provide some insight about Bill Fontaine."

James glanced at his watch. "Gotta go, ladies. The world awaits us. And so do the night-shift nurses who want to go home."

"Before you go," Anabelle said, "does anyone know anything about the new fire marshal in town, Regis Tanner? It's possible he decided the tree was a fire hazard."

Candace and Elena shook their heads.

James said, "Actually, Regis is working with my Scout troop on disaster preparedness. I can ask him if he had a problem with the tree's being a fire hazard in the lobby."

"Good. That would help. Thanks for coming, everyone."

Pushing back their chairs, they all stood. Anabelle had one last martyr's glimpse of the exquisite cheese Danish in the display case before she went outside into the blowing snow.

During her morning break, Anabelle called Rev. Masterson and arranged to meet him after work at the church.

The vestry and office were located on the west side of the main building between the social hall and the sanctuary.

Anabelle parked her car and had to walk through six inches of snow that had already fallen, with still more coming down. As beautiful and pristine as the church grounds looked, like a Christmas postcard, she didn't take the time to enjoy the scenery.

She knocked once and then stepped inside the warmth of the office. A large white poinsettia sat on the corner of the secretary's desk, although she wasn't in the office at the moment. Soft music played from unseen speakers.

"Anabelle?" the reverend called from his adjacent office. "Is that you?"

"Yes, it's me." She walked past the secretary's desk into Rev. Phil Masterson's spacious private office. "Thank you for seeing me this afternoon, Phil."

A tall man in his midfifties, his hair graying at the temples, he came around his desk to greet her. He wore a dark shirt with a clerical collar and black slacks. His jacket hung on a nearby coat tree.

"You're welcome anytime, Anabelle." He helped her with her coat and then gestured toward the arrangement of several comfortable chairs by the window. A ceramic Christmas tree sat on a table between two of the chairs. "Come tell me what brings you out on such a blustery day."

"We've had a bit of a controversy at the hospital," she began, telling the pastor about Varner's ordering the tree removed from the lobby. "Some of us have been trying to determine who initiated the request and why. We've considered several possibilities, and there's one individual I wanted to discuss with you."

Sitting with his hands tented beneath his chin, the pastor gazed at her thoughtfully. "Are you suggesting a member of our congregation demanded that a Christmas tree be removed from a public place?"

"As I said, we've considered several individuals. I don't want to falsely accuse someone, but if we can find out who's behind the action, perhaps we can change his or her mind and get our tree back. It has been a very long tradition that is worth continuing."

"I would agree with that. But a member of our church? That would be quite remarkable. Just who are you talking about?"

Uncomfortable about pointing a finger at a man who could be totally innocent, Anabelle took a deep breath. "When Barbara Fontaine passed away, her husband Bill was quite distraught. He felt either the doctor or the hospital were at fault, which wasn't the case. I understand he's still suffering grief. Loss of a loved one can make people act in ways they never would have under normal circumstances."

For a moment, the pastor didn't move or speak. Slowly he stood and walked to his desk where he straightened the papers in his In basket.

"You're right. Losing Barbara was very hard for Bill. Particularly on top of his financial problems and the slowing economy."

"I don't want you to break confidentiality, if that's what's bothering you, Phil. But whatever insight you can provide would be helpful if you think Bill could be behind banishing the tree."

He turned and leaned back on the edge of his desk, his arms braced on either side of his hips. "I've called on Bill twice since his wife's funeral. He hasn't been receptive to my visits or to the idea of joining a grief-counseling group. Which I believe would benefit him."

"I do too." From what Candace had told her, group counseling had been a godsend for her when she was struggling with her loss. "Men are often more reticent than women to share their emotions."

The pastor's lips lifted with the hint of a smile. "Yes, I fear we men are often far too macho for our own good."

"If Bill is the man behind the tree business, what would be the best way to approach him?"

"Not head-on, I wouldn't think." He paused, glancing out the window at the falling snow. "I suspect he's withdrawn from all of his social contacts. We certainly haven't seen him in church recently. That's not like the Bill I've known over the years."

"His wife was active in the community too."

Phil pushed away from his desk. "I don't know if Bill is the person you're looking for, but I can tell you that you'd be doing him a service if you could re-engage him in the community. He needs a reason to reach out. The best way to do that is to make him feel that he is needed. Then maybe . . ."

He left the thought unfinished, but Anabelle knew what he meant. If Bill Fontaine felt needed, his anger at the hospital, probably his anger at God as well, would ease. If he was behind removing the tree from the lobby, just maybe he would put things back to right again.

To Anabelle's delight, the Lord had provided the perfect project to engage Bill's interest again and honor his late wife in the process.

As soon as Anabelle got home, she called Genna Hamilton. After they finished the preliminaries, Anabelle asked, "Have you remembered the name of the military widow Barbara was helping?"

"Oh, I did. I meant to call you. Then I forgot that too." She laughed at her own forgetfulness. "Her name is Dawn Cassidy. She lives in a little place near the high school."

"How would you like to call on Mrs. Cassidy with me this Sunday afternoon?"

"Whatever are you up to, Anabelle?"

"I'm going to restore a longtime hospital tradition and, at the same time, help two people who are grieving for the loss of their loved ones." She explained to her friend about the banished Christmas tree and how she hoped to rectify the situation.

As she hung up, she prayed the Lord would help her achieve both goals.

By Sunday, the storm had left marshmallow caps on fence posts, and cars parked at the curb were hemmed in where plows had pushed snow up against them to clear the roads.

Anabelle picked up Genna at her house. Together they drove to the neighborhood where Dawn Cassidy and her family lived. They found the address, a small brick house set back from the street on a narrow lot, an attic window tucked in beneath the snow-covered roof. Someone had shoveled the driveway. Anabelle pulled her car in behind an older sedan.

"What are you going to say to Mrs. Cassidy?" Genna asked.

"First I want to get a feel for how she's getting along and if she still needs help, which I imagine she does. Then I'll try to figure out how Bill Fontaine could provide that help."

They walked up to the porch and rang the bell.

A moment later, a petite woman with dark hair pulled back into a braid opened the door. She wore tiny round glasses and looked them over with a skeptical eye.

"If you two ladies are looking for a donation for something, you've come to the wrong house. Sorry." She started to close the door.

Hastily Anabelle said, "Oh no, we aren't soliciting anything, Mrs. Cassidy. We're friends of Barbara Fontaine, or we were before she passed away. We've come by to see how you and your children are getting along."

Dawn's eyelids fluttered behind her glasses. "Oh, I'm sorry. I thought—" She opened the door wider. "Please come in. I didn't mean to be so rude."

"You weren't rude," Genna said. "I'm not fond of door-to-door salesmen or solicitors either."

Anabelle stepped inside, noticing immediately that it was quite chilly in the house. That explained why Dawn Cassidy was wearing a heavy cable-knit sweater over a sweatshirt. She was probably trying to save money on her heating bill.

Dawn led them into a tiny living room. Although the furniture was old and worn, the room was neat. A photograph of Dawn's late husband hung in a place of honor above an upright piano, the folded American flag that had covered his casket framed beside the picture.

A small Christmas tree decorated with colorful paper chains and strings of popcorn sat on an end table, a few small wrapped presents beneath it.

Anabelle introduced herself and Genna.

Dawn said, "May I get you some coffee or tea? It wouldn't take but a minute to fix."

"Please don't bother," Anabelle said. "We won't stay long. We felt we'd been remiss in not contacting you after Barbara passed away. She'd mentioned you to Genna several times, and I know she would have wanted us to look in on you."

Indicating they should sit on the couch, Dawn sat down in an overstuffed chair that practically swallowed her whole.

"Mrs. Fontaine was exceptionally kind to us," Dawn said. "She paid for Roseanne's piano lessons. She's my eight-year-old and loves to play. Her teacher said she has a good ear for music." She glanced at the piano and smiled. "Like her father. Of course, I had to stop her lessons after Barbara passed, but Roseanne still plays sometimes."

A wave of sympathy made Anabelle's heart constrict and reminded her of the many blessings she had in her life.

"You have a son, too, don't you?" Genna asked.

"Russell. He's sixteen." Her gaze skittered to the aging carpet as though she didn't want to talk about her son.

"What does Russell like to do?" Anabelle prodded.

"Get into trouble, I'm afraid. It started when Dan went to Afghanistan and I moved here because it was cheaper than living in Chicago where we're from. Russ couldn't seem to get his bearings in the new school." She looked up, her cheeks flushed. "I don't mean to lay all my troubles on you. We're managing, really we are."

Anabelle wasn't that confident. It had to be hard on a teenage boy to lose his father, first by his going off to war and then by being killed in action.

"Have you ever had any contact with Barbara's husband?"

"He came by once with Barbara. She'd found a set of white bedroom furniture someone was giving away that was perfect for Roseanne. Mr. Fontaine helped carry everything in and set it up for us. Roseanne was thrilled."

"I'm sure she was."

As they chatted, Anabelle discovered Dawn worked as a clerk at the mall, which meant she earned little more than minimum wage. And Russell, typical teenager, spent more time away from home than he did with his family.

"Do you think Russell would be interested in some sort of a part-time job?" Anabelle asked.

"I don't know, but I'd certainly like him to be earning a little money of his own. He spends most of his time tinkering with his friends' cars and complaining that I haven't bought a car for him."

Perfect! With a little luck, and the Lord's help, Anabelle knew just the place where Russell Cassidy could land a job.

Chapter Thirteen

A S SCHEDULED, MONDAY MORNING JAMES reported to surgery to assist Dr. Drew Hamilton, an opportunity he enjoyed and one that provided variety in his workweek.

James stood next to the doctor at the sink scrubbing his hands and forearms. "Looks like we've got three lap choleys this morning." He used the medical shorthand for laparoscopic cholecystectomy, or gallbladder surgery.

Not looking up, Dr. Drew continued vigorously scrubbing his hands. His surgical cap covered most of his silver hair, and he wore a green gown over his scrubs. "Seems like everybody wants their gallbladders out of the way before Christmas so they can eat holiday goodies to their heart's content."

"That may be fine for their digestion, but their hearts may catch up with them later," James said.

The doctor shot James a grin. "Then I can hand them over to Dr. Hildebrand. Let her take care of them."

A highly rated cardiologist, Dr. Hildebrand probably wouldn't appreciate Dr. Drew's jest.

Still smiling, their hands held high and away from their bodies to avoid contamination, James and the doctor backed their way through a pair of swinging doors into the operating room. Recently upgraded, the facility had all of the bells and whistles any surgeon could want. With increasing frequency, laparoscopic procedures employing a minute telescope were used to resolve a variety of surgical problems. Three little external holes instead of a long incision made for a better and faster recovery.

Unless something went wrong.

The patient, a slightly overweight thirty-five-year-old woman, was already prepped and waiting on the operating table. The anesthesiologist, Dr. Ethan Moore, was seated behind the patient ready to sedate her.

"Good morning, Jackie. How are you feeling this morning?" Dr. Drew asked.

"I'm fine, but my husband's a nervous wreck."

"Yes, you told me he might be a little anxious about your surgery."

"More than a little, I'm afraid. I'm not sure if it's because he's nervous about my surgery or because he's going to have to take care of our three children all by himself tonight." Looking relaxed, she smiled up at the doctor.

"Unfortunately, I don't have any spare babysitters waiting in my office, but I can promise your surgery will go fine. I'll be sure to talk to your husband right after I finish here and reassure him."

He gestured for the anesthesiologist to begin. Within moments, Jackie Yankura's eyes fluttered closed. While the patient slipped deeper into unconsciousness, the circulating nurse gloved Dr. Hamilton and adjusted the mask over his face. She did the same for James.

Dr. Hamilton began the laparoscopic procedure using remote-control tools.

Within minutes, he could see the inflamed gallbladder on the monitor. "Yep, there she is, just like it looked on the MRI. That's a bag of solid concrete, folks. No wonder she was having indigestion."

He manipulated the robotic arms to tie off the gallbladder and was about to remove it when Dr. Moore said, "Doctor, she's getting tachy. Heart rate abnormally rapid."

Dr. Hamilton continued to work. "Why? What's going on?"

"I'm not sure, doctor."

His own heart rate accelerating, James moved in closer. He'd assisted on any number of gallbladder surgeries, and he'd never seen this happen.

"Heart rate accelerating. Blood pressure up to 210/110."

Dr. Hamilton raised his head to check the heart and lung monitor above the patient.

"Patient is sweating. Oxygen saturation dropping," the anesthesiologist announced.

"This whole thing's going south," Dr. Hamilton mumbled under his breath. "I'm almost clear. James, get a crash cart over here. She's having a heart attack."

"Patient's in V-fib." The erratic heartbeat made the line on the monitor flutter, stealing the blood from the patient's heart.

The room came alive with action. Epinephrine was ordered stat and inserted into the IV. James shoved the crash cart into place next to the patient.

Dr. Drew withdrew the robotic arms from inside the patient and backed out of the way.

"Two hundred joules," the doctor ordered.

James put the paddles in place. "Clear!" He jolted the patient and her body jumped reflexively.

Holding his breath, James kept his eyes on the heart monitor. Nothing happened. The line continued to flutter. *Dear Lord, help her. She has three children.*

"Again," Dr. Drew ordered. "Three hundred joules."

"Clear!" The paddles made contact. The patient convulsed. No change.

"Again!"

Before James could shock her again, the heart monitor above the bed shrieked a warning. The moving line on the screen went flat.

"Start CPR," Dr. Drew ordered. "Push more epinephrine. We aren't going to lose this woman."

"She must've thrown a clot," the anesthesiologist said.

James leaned over the patient and started chest compressions. He'd done this before. Brought patients back from the dead. *Come on, Jackie. Your children need you.*

The green line on the heart monitor hiccuped, settled and began beating a normal sinus rhythm.

"Thank God," Dr. Drew whispered.

James echoed the sentiment, his own heartbeat slowing to a more normal pace. His legs a little shaky, he stepped back from the operating table.

The circulating nurse wiped the sweat from his forehead, but he could still feel the adrenaline coursing through his veins and the creep of sweat down his spine.

Dr. Drew ripped off his mask. Lines of worry etched his pale face. "Somebody call Dr. Hildebrand stat. This woman's gallbladder was the least of her troubles."

By noon, Jackie Yankura had been moved into the Cardiac Care Unit and Dr. Harriet Hildebrand—often referred to as Dr. Hildie by both patients and staff—had taken over the case.

Anabelle stood by while Dr. Hildie examined the young woman. In her midthirties, Jackie had a sweet face, big blue eyes the color of cornflowers, and short blonde hair.

"Why would I have a heart attack?" Worry creased two vertical lines between Jackie's blonde eyebrows. "I've been having indigestion, that's all. Dr. Drew said it was gallstones."

"We're going to find out what's going on, Mrs. Yankura," Dr. Hildebrand said. "I'm going to order a series of tests. Chances are good the gallbladder symptoms masked a more serious problem."

Jackie turned toward Anabelle. "Could you go talk to my husband? He must be going crazy by now. George is such a worrier."

"I'm sure Dr. Drew has spoken to him by now," Anabelle said. "As soon as Dr. Hildebrand orders the tests, she'll speak to him as well."

"Of course," the doctor said.

"It's almost time for my husband to pick up the children from the sitter. She had something else to do this afternoon and couldn't keep them but a few hours."

"I'll make sure he remembers to fetch them," Anabelle said.

Jackie looked back at the doctor. Her fingers worked the edge of the sheet like a worry stone. "Am I going to have another attack?"

"We're going to do everything we can to prevent that, Mrs. Yankura."

"My babies. They're two, four, and six. They need me." Tears sprang to Jackie's eyes. A typical wife and mother, her first worry was for her family.

Anabelle's throat tightened on the fear she saw in the woman's eyes. She took Jackie's hand. "The best thing for you and your children is to stay calm and try to relax. I'll go talk to your husband so he won't worry unnecessarily."

Glancing at the doctor, Anabelle silently asked for her permission to leave. She received a quick nod of approval.

Three people were in the waiting room. Two were seated in the pale green upholstered chairs reading magazines and sipping vending machine coffee. One was pacing near the doorway, checking up and down the hall with every pass.

"Mr. Yankura?" she asked the pacer.

As slender as a fence post with a nose that rivaled Cyrano's, George Yankura nearly jumped out of his skin. "Is my wife all right? Can I see her now?"

"It will be just a few more minutes." Anabelle introduced herself and urged him to sit down. "The doctor is with her and will come out to see you when she's finished her exam."

"How could Jackie have a heart attack? She's never had any problem before." His fingers trembled as he swiped his palm over his face. "I can't lose her. She's my life. She and the kids. I wouldn't know what to do without her."

Wishing she could ease his distress, Anabelle patted his shoulder. So many times, a strong husband would come apart when his wife was ill, yet they could be stoic when they were the one who was sick. Amazing how dependent a man could be despite being macho. She wondered if under the same circumstances Cam would fall apart. She didn't think so.

In fact, he was still upset with her for interfering with Ainslee's holiday plans. Anabelle hadn't heard from Ainslee since her birthday dinner and hadn't yet felt brave enough to call her after their tense conversation, even though today was her actual birthday.

"No one is talking about losing your wife," Anabelle said. "Dr. Hildebrand is an excellent cardiologist. She'll find out what's wrong. Your wife doesn't want you to worry too much."

He fidgeted, shifting in his chair and tugging at his lower lip. "We've got three kids—George Junior, Bobby, and Betsy. She's just two."

"Your wife mentioned your children are at a sitter's. What time do you have to pick them up?" Anabelle asked.

He glanced at his watch. His eyes went wide. "Five minutes ago." He leaped to his feet but seemed indecisive about where he should go. "The doctor . . ."

"Why don't you go pick the children up now? You can talk with the doctor when you get back."

"Can I bring the kids here?"

A hospital waiting room clearly wasn't a good place for young children. Anabelle could scrounge some toys from the Pediatric Unit, but that might not hold their attention for long.

"Go ahead and bring them with you until you can make some other arrangement."

"Okay. Right. I won't be long. Tell Jackie I'll be right back." He dashed off down the hallway, nearly crashing into a food cart in the process.

Grimacing and squeezing her eyes shut, Anabelle sent up a quick prayer that George wouldn't be so rattled and rushed that he'd get into an accident. Poor man.

Anabelle returned to the nurses' station just as Dr. Hildebrand exited Jackie Yankura's room.

"I'm ordering an ECG, blood tests, and a chest X-ray for Mrs. Yankura and scheduling her for a nuclear scan tomorrow morning. Is her husband still here?"

"No, he went to pick up the children. He'll be back shortly."

"Fine. Page me when he returns."

"Yes, doctor." Anabelle made her own notes on her clipboard. She had confidence Dr. Hildebrand would determine what was causing the patient's heart problem, but that meant Jackie Yankura would remain in the hospital, possibly for several days. George was going to have to cope on his own.

True to his word, he was back in the waiting room within a half hour, his stair-step children in tow, all of them wearing heavy winter jackets. The six-year-old tried to keep the two-year-old corralled while George talked to the doctor, but the little one kept escaping down the hallway.

Anabelle caught baby Betsy and led her by the hand back to the waiting room. "Mr. Yankura, would you like me to take the children down to the cafeteria while you talk to the doctor?

Perhaps they'd like a dish of ice cream." She was due for a break anyway, and the youngsters were adorable.

Anabelle didn't know who looked the more relieved by her suggestion, George or the doctor.

She didn't anticipate any problems as she ushered the children into the elevator. She'd raised three children, although they weren't quite as close in age as these three. Still, the promise of ice cream ought to keep them on their best behavior.

Each of the children wanted chocolate ice cream. "Okay, children, let's sit at this table over here in the corner." Anabelle carried the tray with the three dishes of ice cream, spoons, and a generous handful of napkins.

George Junior and Bobby dutifully hopped up onto their chairs. Anabelle turned around to help Betsy.

The baby was gone again.

"She headed for the elevator," a nearby stranger said.

Why didn't you stop her? Behind her smile of thanks, Anabelle gritted her teeth. "You boys stay right here. I'll get Betsy."

She reached the elevator just as the doors were closing with Betsy inside. Alone.

Anabelle jammed the button. The doors opened.

"Come on, honey." She scooped the baby up into her arms. "Let's go have your ice cream."

"Daddy, Daddy!" The child pointed skyward.

"Daddy will come get you in a minute." Or so Anabelle hoped.

Grabbing a booster chair for Betsy, Anabelle returned the child to her siblings.

Anabelle realized that managing three young children had seemed much easier when she was in her thirties than now.

Wherever had she found the strength?

How would Jackie Yankura manage if her apparent heart disease worsened?

How much worse would it have been if Jackie had died on the operating table, leaving her husband caring for their three adorable, and very quick-footed, youngsters?

Please, Lord, watch over Jackie. Give Dr. Hildebrand the knowledge and skills to make her well again.

After she finished her shift, Anabelle drove to the car dealership Bill Fontaine had lost to bankruptcy. She hoped to catch him at his office in the former service department, the only part of the dealership that had survived the downturn in the economy.

She parked her Ford Fusion off to the side, out of the way of customers picking up their cars. Inside, the receptionist directed her to Bill's office.

Sitting at his desk, Bill had his feet propped on an open drawer, his chin on his chest, snoozing. He looked thinner than she remembered, and he hadn't shaved in a day or two. His shaggy gray hair was in need of an emergency visit to his barber. Everything about his appearance shouted the depression Genna had suspected.

Not a single Christmas decoration was apparent anywhere in the building, which lent credence to her suspicions that Bill Fontaine was behind the removal of the hospital Christmas tree.

Emmaline Palmer and the fire marshal slipped to the bottom of her suspect list.

She knocked on the open door.

Bill snorted, jerked upright, and swiveled around to look at her.

"Hello, Bill. It's Anabelle Scott from Barbara's quilting guild."

It took him a moment to process what she'd said and then he stood. "Anabelle, of course. Come in, come in. Sit down. What can I do for you?" He gestured to one of the leather chairs in front of his desk, which was piled high with papers and car magazines.

She hoped she'd be able to do something for Bill, as well as for Barbara's memory and for Dawn Cassidy. Plus, she wanted him to rescind whatever he'd said to Varner about the Christmas tree that got it banished from the lobby.

"Yesterday I met a friend of Barbara's," she said, sitting down. "Dawn Cassidy. Your wife had mentioned her often at our quilting group."

His bushy, unkempt eyebrows pulled together in thought. "Her daughter's that little girl who got the white bedroom furniture, right?"

"Dawn tells me Roseanne still adores the bed. Did you know Barbara was paying for the child's piano lessons?"

"She mentioned it a time or two." His eyes welling, he blinked and cleared his throat. His shoulders hunched, collapsing his chest. "Barbara was a saint, always looking for ways to help others."

"You've always been generous too. I know in the past you've donated to Hope Haven Hospital."

He lifted one shoulder uneasily. "I hope you're not here looking for a donation. I've already talked to Varner. He knows my position."

Aha! Chances were Bill and Varner had discussed more than his maintenance contracts the day before Thanksgiving. "Your position on contributions to the hospital? Or your feelings about Christmas?" she probed.

He narrowed his eyes and hid them beneath his lowered eyebrows. "As far as I'm concerned, with Barbara gone, there isn't going to be a Christmas ever again."

"I see." She saw his grief clearly, and it was disheartening. For the moment, she'd leave the topic of Christmas alone. "I do wish Roseanne could resume her music lessons. Her mother can't afford to keep them up."

He harrumphed noncommittally.

"Dawn has a son too. Russell's sixteen and loves to tinker with cars. It sounds to me like he has the makings of a good mechanic."

"I don't have any job openings, if that's what you're getting at." His mouth barely opened as he spoke. "I'm doing my best to keep my men employed so they can feed their families. It's not easy these days." His lips looked as though a child had drawn a sad face, the corners turned downward.

"No, I'm sure it's not." Bill wasn't exactly jumping at Anabelle's ideas. "I was only thinking the boy would benefit by having a part-time job, something that would encourage him to stay in school long enough to graduate."

"He'd better graduate, or he won't ever be able to land a decent job." His words had a bite to them reflecting his underlying anger at the world. Even God, she suspected.

"I agree," Anabelle said. "So does his mother. But the young man has been having trouble ever since his father went to Afghanistan. And then when he was killed . . ." She paused hoping Bill would take the bait. "You were in Vietnam, weren't you?" It wasn't a guess. A photo on the wall showing Bill in camouflage and helmet standing with his buddies in front of an armored troop carrier made it obvious he'd served in the army.

His gaze slid toward the photo. "Yeah, I was in 'Nam. Half of those guys didn't come back." He shook his head as though trying to dislodge the memory. "I'm sorry, Anabelle. I can't help the lady or her kids out. Or the hospital. I'm not in any shape to handle much of anything these days."

"I understand, Bill. It's been difficult for you since you lost Barbara." Anabelle stood, the taste of failure bitter in her mouth. "I thought Barbara would want me to ask. But I'm sure she'd understand too. Thank you for taking the time to see me."

When he didn't respond, she said, "As for the hospital, I think we all miss seeing the Christmas tree in the lobby. It's been a hospital tradition for a very long time and the children love seeing it at the Christmas party."

Bill didn't rise to say good-bye. Instead he continued to stare at the photo on the wall, deep in the past with his lost buddies.

Sick at heart for his loss and the hospital's, Anabelle left his office.

Chapter Fourteen

ASED ON JACKIE YANKURA'S EARLY MORNING nuclear scan Tuesday, Dr. Hildebrand scheduled a stent to be inserted the next day. The young woman had a severely blocked artery. A stent would open up the artery to let the blood flow to her heart as it should.

"It's a very common procedure," Anabelle assured her patient when she resettled Jackie in her room. "There's very little pain involved and recovery time is quite short. You'll start feeling better right away."

"How long will I have to stay in the hospital?"

"I imagine Dr. Hildebrand will keep you overnight after the procedure tomorrow to be sure everything is fine."

Closing her eyes, Jackie exhaled a worried sigh. "Then I won't go home until Thursday?"

"Probably not." Anabelle checked the site of the gallbladder surgery for swelling or inflammation. Everything looked fine.

"But I'm sure you'd rather be safe than leave us too soon and have a problem at home."

Jackie looked up and her eyes glistened with unshed tears. "I haven't finished my Christmas shopping yet. I've been so tired lately, and I was waiting for a really good sale, you know? Everything is half price or better just before Christmas."

"The best present you can give your family is to be healthy." The memory of Anabelle's mother not being at home on Christmas still had the power to tighten a band of regret around her chest.

"I know. But having me in the hospital is hard on George. He already took yesterday off work and is taking today off too. He's keeping the kids."

Anabelle hoped he had them on a short leash, for his sake as well as theirs. "They'll do fine without you for a couple of days."

"I hope so."

Giving Jackie an encouraging smile, Anabelle continued on her rounds. A young mother had every right to be concerned about her family under the circumstances. She'd effectively died on the operating table. Only the skill of the doctor and medical staff had saved her. No one would want to go through that twice.

She knew Dr. Hildie would do her very best not to let that happen again.

At lunchtime, Anabelle went downstairs to the cafeteria. She spotted Elena and joined her.

"How's your day going?" Anabelle asked.

"Relatively quiet, which is a good thing for ICU. How about you?"

"We have a young mother of three who coded on the operating table yesterday." She tasted a spoonful of her beef-and-barley soup and savored the rich flavor. "A very scary situation for her and her family. I've been praying for her."

"I'll say a prayer for her too. She must be very frightened." Elena finished the last bite of her pastrami sandwich on rye. "I think I may have a problem too, and I need your advice."

"Not a problem with your heart, I hope."

"Oh no, nothing like that." She shook her head. "It does involve matters of the heart, however."

Anabelle arched her brows. "Oh?"

"It's Isabel's mother, Sarah. She's been helping me to make Izzy's angel costume for the Christmas Eve service at Holy Trinity. I'm teaching her to sew."

"That's nice of you. I can't imagine a better teacher." Anabelle suspected that wasn't the problem that concerned Elena.

"I really like Sarah. She's worked so hard to turn her life around and be a good mother for Isabel." Thoughtfully, Elena forked a bite of cottage cheese and canned pineapple into her mouth. "She'd also like to get back together with Rafael."

"And that's a problem?"

"Not for me. But I think it is for Rafael. First of all, he was very hurt when she left him. I think he's gotten past his anger, but he's dating other girls and is barely polite to Sarah."

"That must be hard on her."

"It is. But she knows that she and her addiction caused the problem. She accepts the responsibility for abandoning him and Isabel. Having Rafael ignore her hurts, though."

Anabelle set her empty soup bowl aside and picked up her half turkey sandwich on whole wheat. "What do you need from me?"

"I'm not sure what to do. Obviously, I love Rafael and don't want to go against him. But I like Sarah too. Should I talk to Rafael, get him to pay attention to Sarah? I mean, if they could get back together, which is Izzy's dream, that would be good for their family. But I'm not sure how much I should interfere in my son's life or Sarah's."

Anabelle thought about how Ainslee objected loudly every time she got overly involved with her daughter's life. "If Rafael is anything like my Ainslee or Kirstie for that matter or"—she laughed—"Evan, I'd say he wouldn't listen to you if you tried to push him in Sarah's direction. In fact, he might do just the opposite."

Her dark brows pulling together, Elena sipped her diet soda. "But what if he doesn't realize how much Sarah cares for him? Shouldn't I at least mention—"

"If the attraction is gone, there isn't anything you can do about it. What is he, almost twenty-eight now? I think he's old enough to make his own decision about whom to date."

"I suppose you're right," she said with a sigh. "But I do feel sorry for Sarah. Unrequited love and all that."

Anabelle chuckled. "Most women go through that one time or another and survive." Although she'd been fortunate. Cameron had been her high school sweetheart and was still the love of her life.

Elena checked her pager. "Oops, gotta go. ICU has a new customer." She started to pick up her tray.

"Go ahead. I'll bus your dishes for you." She waved her friend away and watched Elena hurry out of the cafeteria.

It's true that a mother can't make decisions about her adult child's life. That's why children grow up, move away, start their own—

Anabelle's thought came to a screeching halt.

Ainslee's trip to Disney World!

Anabelle had an epiphany, of sorts. She had been trying to influence her daughter not to go. To stay home for Lindsay's first Christmas.

With more clarity than she'd had before, she realized just whose well-being she'd been looking out for. Not Lindsay's. Certainly not Ainslee's. It was her own interests she'd been attending to.

She put her head down in her hand and rubbed her forehead. *What an old fool you are*, she chided herself. She'd tried to interfere in her daughter's life. Again. No wonder Cam was upset with her.

She'd rectify the problem as soon as she got home this afternoon.

She still believed that it was a mistake to take a young baby on a long, crowded flight during the holidays; and more importantly, her desire to share Christmas with her daughter and granddaughter went deep. But Ainslee had a right to make her own decisions.

When Anabelle finished her lunch, she carried the dishes to the conveyor belt, sending the dirty dishes into the kitchen to be washed.

Rather than going back upstairs, she headed for Penny Risser's office. Anabelle was 99 percent sure that Bill Fontaine was the impetus for removing the Christmas tree from the lobby. She wanted Varner's executive assistant to confirm that for her.

She found Penny talking on the phone, Varner's office door closed. She stepped inside to wait. Two healthy, bright red poinsettias had made an appearance in Penny's office and were displayed on top of a filing cabinet.

When Penny hung up, Anabelle said, "Hi, Penny. I wanted to tell you I stopped by to talk with Bill Fontaine yesterday."

"Oh?" Her eyebrows shot up.

"Yes, we had a nice chat. I think he's on the verge of changing his mind about the Christmas tree in the lobby. Poor man has been so upset about losing Barbara."

"Yes, he has been grieving. Although I didn't think he'd change his—" She snapped her mouth shut in sync with her eyebrows scrolling downward. "You didn't really talk to him, did you?"

"Oh yes. I visited him at his office." And now she knew for sure that Bill was the local Grinch who had stolen their Christmas tree. Not Emmaline or the fire marshal. She had less confidence he'd actually retract his demand for the tree's removal. "With any luck, he'll let you and Varner know soon about his change of heart."

She prayed that would be the case. With only ten days left until Christmas Eve, he'd have to recant his demand soon or there wouldn't be time for anyone to enjoy the tree.

Despite her bravado and efforts to convince Bill he was wrong, she feared changing his mind might take a miracle.

When James got home from work, he found Fern in the family room sitting in front of her easel, painting. Her friend Elyse Larson had encouraged her to try watercolors as an outlet for her creative energy. It was something Fern could do despite poor fine motor skills, a result of her MS. Having a hobby and something new to learn had bolstered Fern's spirits. She also enjoyed getting together with the other women in Elyse's painting class.

"Hi, sweetheart. How're you doing?" He bent to kiss her on the cheek. She had on an old blouse and sweater she didn't mind getting dirty and one sleeve was streaked with white paint.

"I'm fine. This stupid tree I'm trying to paint isn't so good though. It looks like it has warts or something for him."

James eyed the winter scene she'd drawn, the red maple tree she could see out the window the focus of her painting. "It looks all right to me."

"It's easier to paint a tree with its leaves on. You can kind of smear the paint around and fake it."

"So put some leaves on the tree."

She looked up at him with a frown. "It's a snow scene. Maples don't have leaves in the winter."

"So paint the snow green. It'll be great."

"Oh, you . . ." Laughing, she took a halfhearted swipe at him with the back of her hand.

He shrugged out of his jacket. "Where're the boys?"

"They're both shoveling the neighbor's driveway. They're so anxious to make extra money for Christmas, I think they've been praying for snow for the past two weeks."

"Well, God certainly answered their prayers this time. Maybe you and I can expect some pretty fancy Christmas presents."

"Unlikely. I think they have in mind about two thousand downloads for their iPods."

"Entirely possible." Slinging his jacket over his shoulder, he said, "I'm going to use Nelson's computer for a bit. I'm still troubled by that video game Gideon wants. There has to be something else that he'd like that isn't so violent."

"I'm as concerned as you are, so I hope you can find something for him."

"Good luck with your tree." Giving her another peck on her cheek, James went down the hall to Nelson's room.

It wasn't as neat as he would have liked. The bed hadn't been made, and yesterday's dirty clothes were on the floor instead of in the hamper. He'd have to remind Nelson he was still subject to periodic inspections, snow shoveling job notwithstanding.

Sitting down at the computer, he logged on and brought up the Internet to do a search. A whole raft of possibilities appeared. Slowly he started to work his way through the Web sites.

He searched through videos rated T for Teen, which included some violence and strong language but not as foul as the vocabulary in Chicago Underground. But nothing struck his fancy. Or more importantly, he didn't see anything that he thought Gideon would be thrilled to play.

It appeared being sixteen was an odd niche for video games: not quite old enough to handle mature subject matter, but plenty old enough to understand exactly what they were talking about.

He finally came across a Web site called Ask Mr. Gamer. The site had a bunch of game trailers, like movie previews, and James could view and get an idea of what the game was all about. He watched several. The fact that he knew little about video games and what kids liked left him feeling uneasy making a decision. So he decided to ask Mr. Gamer himself for advice.

He typed in his question and sat back to wait for an answer, which might take hours or even days to receive.

As he waited, he recalled the days when the boys were little and got excited about Santa's arrival. When Gideon was about six, he insisted he was going to stay up and hide behind the couch until Santa Claus showed up to eat the cookies they had left out for him. No amount of persuasion could change Gideon's mind. No threat that Santa wouldn't come if Gideon was waiting to ambush him.

Finally, Fern and James put Nelson to bed, leaving Gideon downstairs with a pillow and blanket, the Christmas tree lights glowing in the dark room.

Less than an hour later, James sneaked downstairs. Curled up on the floor, Gideon was sound asleep. James carried his son upstairs and put him to bed while Fern hurriedly put out the gifts Santa had hidden in the utility room.

Smiling at the memory, James remembered how stunned Gideon had been the next morning. Santa had delivered his gifts without Gideon catching him.

That had been a great Christmas for all of them.

Glancing back at the computer screen, James discovered he'd received an answer from Ask Mr. Gamer with suggestions for several possible video games Gideon might like. Some were produced especially for the Christian market and featured biblical tales. Others were for the general market. All of the suggestions included games requiring real-time strategy and adventure.

"That's great!" James said aloud before he typed in his thanks.

With the names of suitable games, he could check out each one and make his decision.

Whew! Thank You, Lord!

Now he could relax and get ready for this evening's Scout troop meeting. With Regis Tanner, the fire marshal, planning to set a few real fires, the kids ought to be excited about the meeting. Attendance should be 100 percent.

Crossing his fingers, James said a little prayer that nothing would go wrong with the demonstration. It would set a very bad precedent if they managed to burn down the Church of the Good Shepherd.

Anabelle went upstairs to use the phone in the master bedroom.

She sat down on the edge of the bed and tried to compose her thoughts. Yes, she had tried to interfere in Ainslee's life. Her intentions had been, well, mixed. Her heart simply ached knowing she wouldn't see little Lindsay on Christmas Day.

So be it.

Taking a deep breath, she picked up the phone and dialed her daughter's number.

"Hello, Mother," Ainslee answered, her voice cautious.

"Hello, dear. Am I interrupting anything?"

Ainslee hesitated. "Not really. Lindsay's napping, and I was starting to think about dinner."

"Oh, good. I wanted to talk to you about Christmas."

"Mother, we've already gone over—"

"I was thinking," Anabelle interrupted, "that since you'll be gone on Christmas, that maybe you and Doug and the baby would like to come over for dinner this Sunday. We could have our part of the family Christmas together before you leave for Florida."

"Oh." Another pause. "That might be a good idea."

Anabelle's chin quivered. "I'm glad you think it's a good idea." *I'm trying so hard to be a good mother and grandma, but I don't always get it right. Please forgive me.*

"I'll have to check with Doug, but it sounds fine to me."

"Wonderful. You'll let me know?"

"Sure. And, Mother . . . thanks."

"You're welcome, sweetheart." Very gently, her vision blurred with unshed tears, Anabelle cradled the phone. She pursed her lips to stop her chin from quivering.

"*Ach*, Annie, my luv, sure 'n' you've done a good thing, you have," Cameron said in his mock Scottish accent.

She turned to find her husband standing in the bedroom doorway where he had apparently overheard her phone conversation.

She gulped and swallowed a sob. "Cam, why am I such an awful mother?"

In a few quick strides, he crossed the room and pulled her to her feet. "You're a great mother. You always have been. The girls and Evan know that." He wrapped his arms around her and held her close.

She cherished the feel of his solid chest and his strong arms, the warmth of his old sweater and the special outdoorsy scent that was his alone. "I do love them so much."

"And they love you, Annie. They always will. And so will I, 'til death do us part and beyond."

Chapter Fifteen

WHEN CANDACE ARRIVED AT WORK WEDNESDAY morning, she knew she couldn't put off inviting Heath to Christmas dinner any longer. She'd barely had a chance to talk to him since their dinner date almost two weeks ago, their kiss on the porch, and their mutual declaration of love.

She wanted him to come to Christmas dinner, but the thought of asking him, of having him feel like he was being paraded in front of her family, made her palms sweat and a knot form in her stomach.

He'd said he loves me. And I love him.

It was only her own insecurities that made her nervous about asking him to dinner.

When there was a break in the action in the Birthing Unit, she hurried upstairs to Radiology in the hope of catching Heath when he wasn't busy.

She found him outside an examining room consulting with Dr. Omar Hashimi, the staff radiologist. He was listening intently to the doctor, nodding occasionally, his forehead furrowed in concentration. Even so, he seemed completely at ease dealing with a more experienced colleague.

Not wanting to interrupt them, she lingered at the end of the hallway. She could always return later if necessary.

But Heath spotted her and smiled, holding up one finger to signal he'd only be a minute longer. His welcoming expression and the memory of their kiss eased the knot in her stomach and sent a wave of heat to her cheeks. Their growing romance was making her as giddy as a teenager, her emotional reactions spiking anytime she saw him.

Heath and the doctor finished their conversation, and Heath strolled toward Candace. Beneath his white lab coat, he had broad shoulders and walked with the comfortable stride of an athlete. His grin creased both of his cheeks.

"Hey. What brings you upstairs to my world, my little chickadee?" His blue-eyed gaze skimmed over her in appreciation, warming her cheeks all over again.

"I . . . I wanted to ask you something," she stammered like a silly goose.

"Ask away."

She could ask a lot easier if he wasn't looking at her with such a teasing gleam in his eyes.

She broke eye contact to gather her thoughts.

"Christmas. I wanted to invite you, and your father, if he'd like, to my house for Christmas dinner. My sister and her family are coming. It's my and Mom's year to cook the dinner."

"Oh. *Uh*, I'm sorry. I already promised my dad that I'd take him to Shaun's house for Christmas. You know, visit his grandson kind of thing."

"Of course." Her mood deflated like the air leaking out of an old tire. She'd been there to help with the delivery of Heath's nephew Michael more than a year ago. In fact, that was the first time she'd met Heath. "I should've asked you sooner."

"Wouldn't have mattered. Since my mother died and Dad moved in with me, he's been happiest hanging out with little Mikey."

Understandable. But she still had to find a time to get together with Heath to exchange presents.

"As an alternative," she said, thinking on her feet, "would you and your father like to come to Christmas Eve service with us? You could both come to our house afterwards for a light supper."

"Yeah, I could do that. I'll have to ask Dad if he wants to come." Heath looked pleased at the idea.

"I should warn you, my great-grandmother was Polish, so Mom and I do a modified traditional Polish supper for Christmas Eve. That means smoked salmon, cucumbers and cream cheese, veggie pizza squares, and beet soup."

He shrugged. "Sounds fine to me."

"Also apple dumplings for dessert. They go over bigger with Howie and Brooke than the soup does."

"I'm sure your beet soup will be great." His dimpled grin warmed her heart.

"Brooke and Howie both have something they'd like to give to you." Earlier in the week, Janet had taken Brooke to the ceramic store to decorate a coffee mug for Heath. It should be glazed and ready to pick up by the weekend.

"Presents too? Wow! Pretty special."

"Not anything huge, I promise. More like a thank-you for being so nice to them. They thought up the ideas by themselves." Now that she'd decided what to give Heath, she'd have a gift for him too. Actually, two small presents.

"That sounds great." He glanced around then lowered his voice. "I'd kiss you but there are too many eyes around here."

She flushed again. "Like Mrs. K.?"

"Exactly, only several just like her." He gave her another dimpled grin and winked. "Gotta go, chickadee. I'll give you a call."

Feeling lighter in spirit, Candace headed downstairs to the Birthing Unit. Christmas Eve would be perfect. Heath had already met her mother, so that would be comfortable for him. And her kids adored him.

She was sorry she hadn't thought of that alternative earlier.

Now, if the presents she'd ordered online arrived in time, she'd be set for the holidays.

Anabelle heard George Yankura and his children in the waiting room before she saw them.

"Betsy, come back here. George Junior, go get her."

"Mommy, Mommy, Mommy," a tiny voice chirped.

Anabelle ducked past the nurses' station to waylay Betsy in the hallway.

"Whoa." She snared Betsy by the hand, which was sticky. The red ring around her mouth indicated a sucker had been on the child's breakfast menu. "Are you looking for your mommy?"

"My mommy!" She pointed in the direction of the elevator.

"Let's go see your daddy. Maybe he knows where your mommy is." Anabelle knew Jackie Yankura had not yet returned from the stent procedure. That wasn't necessarily a bad omen. There could've been a delay in starting the procedure. *Or*, she thought with dread, *there could have been a problem with Mrs. Yankura's heart.*

George Junior met them before they reached the waiting room.

"You're not supposed to run off like that, Betsy." He took the baby's free hand and dragged her back to where she belonged.

Anabelle followed.

She found George Yankura sitting on the floor with Bobby constructing a racetrack for his Hot Wheels cars. George noticed Anabelle and pushed himself to his feet. "Is Jackie back in her room yet?"

"Not yet. I imagine she will be soon."

Betsy tugged on her father's pants leg. "I want Mommy."

"I know, sweetie." George cupped the back of his daughter's head. "Sorry I had to bring the kids along. I couldn't get a sitter."

That much was obvious. "You'll have to keep the children here in the waiting room. It's dangerous for them to be wandering the halls on their own."

"Yeah, I know. But what's taking so long with Jackie?"

"I don't know. If you'd like, I can check for you."

"Please. I'm worried sick about her. Didn't hardly sleep at all last night."

The dark circles under his eyes confirmed the tale of his lack of sleep. Poor guy.

"I'll see what I can find out. But please keep your children under control."

"Yes, ma'am." He sank to the floor again and tugged Betsy into his lap, hooking his arm around her middle.

Before Anabelle had a chance to walk upstairs, she ran into Winona Stouffer, an LPN in the Cardiac Unit and a bundle of energy in a package less than five feet tall.

"Winona, have you had an update on Jackie Yankura?"

"She's coming down right now. Somebody overbooked day surgery this morning, and they got backed up."

"Good. Her husband's been waiting and is worried."

Winona's dark eyes flashed with amusement and she smiled. "Those are some energetic little kids."

"Hopefully, I can get them in to see the patient and encourage the father not to stay long."

Anabelle returned to the waiting room. "Your wife will be in her room soon. You'll be able to see her, but please don't stay long. Your wife will need her rest."

"Hear that kids?" George said. "Let's get the toys picked up so we can go see your mom."

"I wanna play with my cars," Bobby complained.

"You can do that at home," his father said. "Put them away now."

He'd taken his eye off of Betsy. The child took advantage of the lax supervision and was out the door in a nanosecond.

Anabelle dashed after her. Surely babysitting wasn't a part of her job description.

She caught Betsy again. The two-year-old giggled as though this was the most fun game in the world, her high spirits infectious.

"Mommy! Mommy! Mommy!" She patted Anabelle's cheek and bounced in her arms.

"You'll see your mommy in a minute, little mischief maker." She carried the toddler back to the waiting room with little hope her father could keep her there.

On what had to be a foolish impulse born of Anabelle's bleak Christmas when her mother was ill, she invited George to bring the children to the Hope Haven Kids' party on Saturday.

"There'll be ice cream and presents for the children."

George's eyes lit up and so did those of his sons.

"That's very nice of you to invite us. I'm sure the kids would love to come."

About fifteen minutes later, George and his children were allowed into Jackie Yankura's room. The tearful reunion was one of the sweetest things Anabelle had ever seen. The children were extra careful not to hurt their mother as she hugged and kissed them one by one. George's whispered, "I love you" could not have been more deeply felt.

The sight of this young family together nearly brought tears to Anabelle's eyes.

Thank You, Lord, for bringing Jackie to Hope Haven where Dr. Hildebrand and the operating room staff could use their skills to save her life. Watch over her now as she recovers and take care of her family as the children grow and flourish in Your loving embrace. Amen.

Thursday morning, Dr. Hildebrand signed discharge papers for Jackie.

Anabelle was trying to explain the posthospital regimen Jackie should follow when Phyllis Getty, a longtime hospital volunteer, arrived with a wheelchair. A dozen or more Volunteer of the Year pins decorated Phyllis's kelly-green hospital jacket.

At the doorway, Phyllis pulled the wheelchair to an abrupt halt and looked in stunned disbelief at the children, who were using Jackie's hospital bed as a jungle gym.

"Whoa!" she said, her voice cutting through the childish squeals like a Marine drill sergeant's. "Looks like I'm going to have a load of passengers for this trip." She spun the wheelchair around, almost making it do a wheely. "Patients have first priority, young 'uns. Let your mama get on board first."

Grinning all the time, George helped his wife into the chair and then sorted out his children. Betsy got first place on one side of Jackie's lap, Bobby on the other. Phyllis balanced George Junior on a crosspiece at the back of the wheelchair and told him he could help her drive.

Shaking her head, Anabelle handed all the paperwork to George. "Take good care of her, Mr. Yankura. Those children need her."

"So do I," he responded, following Phyllis and her entourage out the door toward the elevator.

Anabelle headed back to the nurses' station. James had just gotten some supplies out of the storeroom and was watching as the elevator door closed behind Phyllis and the Yankura family.

"Was that the gallbladder patient who coded?" he asked.

"It was. Dr. Hildebrand put in a stent. She's stable now."

"The way that surgery went south was really strange." His brows were pulled together in concentration, and he rotated his head as though he had a crick in his neck. "Even when we managed to resuscitate her, something seemed to be off."

"Off? Like what?" She sat down at the computer and put her glasses on to read the screen.

"I'm not sure. She was still a little blue around her lips like she wasn't getting enough oxygen. And lethargic."

She looked up at him over the top of her glasses. "The stent should fix that."

"Yeah, I know. It's just that I had this feeling. . . ." He left the rest of the thought unsaid.

An icy finger of unease raised the hairs on the back of Anabelle's neck. "If you know something, James, you have to tell Dr. Hildebrand."

He studied the IV bag in his hand as though it were a fortune-teller's crystal ball.

"It's nothing specific, just a feeling. Sometimes in Iraq I'd get this, I don't know, intuition maybe, that we'd missed something. Whatever we were treating, like a bullet in a guy's shoulder, wasn't the whole story, and if we didn't explore a little more deeply, we'd lose the patient."

"Dr. Hildebrand is always very thorough."

"I know. So were the army docs." He shrugged. "I'm probably hallucinating. Ignore me."

That was hard to do. James had years of experience as a nurse. He wasn't someone who exaggerated or cried wolf. His instincts were good. "Did you ever find out if your intuition was right?"

He gazed off into the distance as though remembering another time, another place.

"Most of the time the docs listened to me and took another look at the patient. Even those who were Iraqis who'd been shooting at us. But this one time . . ." He glanced down at Anabelle. "An Iraqi woman had been shot. We were busy, treated the gunshot wound, and wheeled her out of the way. She was pregnant. She miscarried without us knowing and bled to death twenty feet away from us. We never knew until a medic checked on her a couple of hours later."

Anabelle's breath caught and her hand flew to her mouth. "I'm so sorry."

"Me too. She shouldn't have died." Turning away, he strode purposefully down the hall toward the General Medicine and Surgery Unit.

Dear heaven, what an awful thing to have happened. Still, she couldn't believe Dr. Hildebrand or any of the nurses on the cardiac staff, including herself, could have missed an obvious medical problem.

She'd have to pray that James's intuition had failed him in Jackie Yankura's case.

Please, God.

Chapter Sixteen

EARLY FRIDAY MORNING, ANABELLE CAME DOWN to put the coffee on and let Sarge out. She stood outside by the back door watching the dog sniff his way around the yard to determine if intruders—animal or human—had invaded his private territory during the night. The sun wasn't up yet, and the moon cast a shadow of the barn across the yard. Her breath clouded in front of her face.

She smiled as Sarge dived into a patch of snow and dug furiously at the remnants of the last storm. Failing to uncover anything of interest, he bounded across the yard to make a new attempt.

She shivered in her robe. "Come on, Sarge. It's cold out here."

He ignored her in favor of exploring a way to get out under the fence, a trick he hadn't yet accomplished. Not that his failure had deterred his continuing efforts.

"Sarge. Come." She spoke more sternly trying to imitate Cam's tone of voice.

Sarge stopped. Tilting his head, he looked at her as if to say, "You're not the boss of me."

"You heard me. Come. Now." She stared back at him. "If you want your breakfast this morning, you'd better get in here or I'll leave you outside. I'm going upstairs to get dressed."

He appeared to consider her threat. Breakfast won out. He galloped toward her, leaped up onto the porch and scooted in the door, his tail wagging furiously.

However much Sarge might annoy her and stretch her patience, Anabelle couldn't help but laugh at his antics.

She poured a generous portion of dry food into his dish and then went upstairs to shower and dress.

She'd lost all hope that Bill Fontaine would rescind his demand to have the Christmas tree removed from the hospital lobby. With just a week left until Christmas Eve, Bill's getting past his grief and coming to his senses seemed unlikely.

While Cam's plywood tree now stood proudly in the lobby, it wasn't a very satisfactory substitute for the real thing.

Maybe by next year, Varner would develop enough spine to restore the holiday tradition no matter what Bill demanded.

She dressed, ate breakfast, then went back upstairs to kiss Cameron good-bye. Since his retirement, he'd relished the opportunity to sleep later than he used to.

In downtown Deerford, artificial holly branches with bright red berries circled light poles. High above the center of the street, large wreaths had been hung, and most of the store windows were decorated for the holidays. Red-suited Santas and hardworking elves vied with traditional nativity scenes for attention.

As Anabelle pulled into the hospital parking lot, there wasn't a single sign that Hope Haven acknowledged or celebrated the birth of Christ.

Shameful!

In the employee lounge, she poured herself a cup of coffee. Someone had brought in hot cross buns from the bakery and set them out for everyone to enjoy. Forget watching her weight. She decided to indulge herself.

Elena arrived and got herself a Styrofoam cup. "Hey, you're looking a little down in the dumps this morning." Picking up the pot, she poured herself some coffee. "Is something wrong?"

"I've got the Christmas blues, I'm afraid."

"Because there's no tree in the lobby?"

"That and the fact that Ainslee is taking the baby to Florida for Christmas and they'll be with her in-laws, not here at home where she belongs."

"Oh, I'm sorry, Anabelle. I know you'll especially miss Lindsay."

"Too true." She finished her hot cross bun and coffee, washed her hands at the sink, and dried them on a paper towel. "Well, I'd best get to work. If I stay busy maybe I won't wallow in self-pity."

"Hope you find a way to cheer up."

Anabelle waved her thanks and headed downstairs. It wasn't as if the world was coming to an end without a tree in the lobby or Lindsay to cuddle on Christmas Day. She had the rest of her family nearby and her own tree in her living room with all of its happy memories.

She settled down in front of her computer to complete the weekly report and work out the staff duty roster for the following week. Schedules during the holiday season were always complicated. Most of her nurses wanted the holidays off so she had to juggle days off, taking into account those who had had Thanksgiving off and those who had volunteered to work on Christmas.

She was still working on it when Elena came racing into the nurses' station.

"The tree's back!" she announced.

Anabelle's head snapped up, and she looked at Elena over the top of her glasses. "What tree?"

"The one in the lobby, of course. Mr. Fontaine just brought in the most humongous tree you've ever seen. Eddie Blaine and Hap Winston have gotten out all the decorations again, and they're putting the lights on the tree now."

Excitement and hope propelled Anabelle to her feet. She took her glasses off and let them dangle on a chain around her neck. "I have to see this for myself."

She rushed out of the nurses' station and down the stairs to the lobby, where she stopped abruptly. The tree was glorious. More than fourteen feet tall, it was beautifully shaped, each branch tapering down to the next. Eddie Blaine stood halfway up on the ladder draping a string of lights around the tree.

Standing at the bottom of the ladder helping him was Bill Fontaine.

Anabelle exhaled a prayer. *Thank You, Lord.*

Slowly, taking in every beautiful inch of the tree, she walked toward Bill. The scent of freshly cut fir filled the lobby. Visitors glanced up at the tree and smiled. Children pointed.

Tears burned at the back of Anabelle's eyes as though she were eight years old again. *This one's for you, Mother.*

"Hello, Bill."

Holding the string of lights, he turned at the sound of her voice. A half smile curved his lips, and his color was no longer gray but rosy with renewed purpose. "It's bigger than the first one."

"I know. It's gorgeous. I've never seen a nicer tree."

"It cost a bundle, but I decided I needed to make up for coercing Varner into taking down the first tree."

Like the Grinch who stole Christmas returning the gifts to the townspeople. "I'm glad you changed your mind."

Eddie climbed down the ladder and moved it a few feet to his left. Bill moved with him.

"I dropped by the Cassidy house the other day." Speaking in a casual voice that lacked the bitterness of grief, Bill played out more lights for Eddie. "Nice lady. I told her I'd keep paying for Roseanne's piano lessons as long as she practiced every day."

"That was generous of you. Dawn told me Roseanne enjoyed playing."

"The boy, Russell. He's going to start next week at the shop. I can't pay him a whole lot, but I'm going to put him with one of my best mechanics so he can learn. If he messes up or his grades drop, he's gone."

"That sounds fair to me. I hope he works out."

Hap attached another string of lights to those Bill was holding. He winked at Anabelle. "Too bad Eddie and me don't get double pay for doing the same job twice."

"You'll have to take that up with Mr. Varner," Anabelle said with a laugh.

"I hope the kid works out too," Bill said. "Mrs. Cassidy invited me to Christmas dinner. I told her I'd bring one of those ready-made dinners that Ripley's Diner boxes up for Thanksgiving and Christmas. All she'll have to do is heat it up, and it'll be ready to eat."

Anabelle was so proud of what Bill had done. Despite his grief, he'd stepped forward to help someone less fortunate. She knew it had been hard for him. Perhaps the Lord had known what Bill needed even when Bill didn't know himself, and the Lord had used her to plant the seed that would ease the grief of two of His children.

Eddie finished stringing the lights. All three men started hanging ornaments on the tree.

"Would you gentlemen allow me to hang one of the ornaments?" Anabelle picked up one of the gold glass balls. "My mother always favored gold ornaments on our Christmas trees."

With their approval, and love in her heart, Anabelle hung the ornament at eye level where every visitor to the hospital could see and enjoy it.

As she stepped back to admire the shiny bauble, it caught the light like the sparkle of love she remembered seeing in her mother's eyes.

Dear Lord, You've given me so many blessings over the years, and this is yet another blessing You've revealed to me—how love and caring can heal the deepest grief. How memories of those we have loved enrich our lives long after they are gone. How, every day, we need to create new memories that others can carry with them throughout their lives until You call them to Your side.

Thank You, Lord, for these gifts. Amen.

At the end of his shift, James logged out of the computer and went upstairs to change into his street clothes. He was going to make a run by the video-game store to buy Gideon's present before going home. Mentally, he crossed his fingers that his son would like the game he'd selected. Ask Mr. Gamer said it was highly rated.

He was retrieving his jacket from his locker when Candace walked into the employee lounge.

"Hey, Candace. You ever decide what to give Heath?"

Her lips curved into a smile. "I did. Your suggestion helped."

"It did?" That surprised James. He thought she hadn't liked the idea.

"I'm not actually giving him a photo of myself—well, sort of." She opened her locker and pulled out her winter coat. "Heath's been super good with Brooke and Howie, and I've been taking snapshots of some of the things they've done together. I ordered a photo cube online that he can use as a pencil holder or something, and I'm putting their pictures in it."

"Hey, that sounds great. He'll like it. But you'd better include a picture of yourself, or he'll be disappointed."

Her cheeks turned a soft shade of pink. "Are you sure?"

"I'm a guy, right? I know these things."

She laughed and said, "I'll think about it, okay?"

Laughing with her, he tugged on his jacket and headed downstairs. He hoped things worked out between Candace and Heath. They were both good people. James wanted everyone to be as happily married as he and Fern were.

When he reached the lobby, he gawked at the huge Christmas tree and felt a moment of awe. He'd heard talk among the nurses that a tree had been put up again, but he hadn't realized how tall it was.

He wasn't sure how Anabelle had managed it, but this was the best-looking tree he'd ever seen.

With a happy heart, he strode out to his car. He hoped his efforts to buy the perfect video game for Gideon went as well as Anabelle's efforts to restore the Christmas tree to the lobby.

With heavy holiday traffic in the downtown area, it took him almost twenty minutes to get to the video-game store. The same bored tattooed salesclerk was behind the counter at the cash register. Working every day in the racket made by a dozen video games pinging and exploding, and even more adolescents shouting, had to drain a man's energy.

"What can I get ya?" the clerk asked in a lazy, uninterested voice.

"I'd like to buy Galactica IV: Conquest." James pulled out his credit card.

The clerk stared at him blankly. "Not many people ask for that one."

"It's highly rated by Ask Mr. Gamer." The expert had told James the game required several different strategies in order for the player to win or reach the highest intergalactic level.

Sometimes the player had to negotiate with strange alien beings, sometimes they had to battle them, but only when the aliens attacked the Galactica spaceship first. Even then the player had to know when to offer the aliens new technological tools in exchange for safe passage. The game sounded like a training course for the next US secretary of state.

Shrugging noncommittally, the clerk vanished into a back room. Apparently Galactica games weren't very popular, which sent James's spirits plummeting. Maybe if the game was awful, he would give in and allow Gideon to exchange it for Chicago Underground.

He grimaced at the thought.

The clerk reappeared. "I only had two left." He dropped the game on the glass-topped counter. "I'm going to buy the other one. Ask Mr. Gamer is the main man when it comes to games. Really knows his stuff."

The clerk rang up the sale. With great relief, James swiped his credit card. Minutes later he was out of the store into the hubbub of holiday shopping and shaking his head. Lucky for the clerk James had checked with Ask Mr. Gamer.

Anabelle arrived home tired but jubilant. As she was hanging up her coat, Sarge came racing out from Cam's office. He hippity-hopped around her, his tail slicing through the air like a metronome in overdrive. Then he plunked down as though not wanting her to get away.

"My goodness, you're being a wild little puppy today." She petted his head and scratched around his floppy ear.

"Is that you, luv?" Cam called from his office.

"It is. Were you expecting someone else?" She patted the side of her leg to encourage Sarge to follow her.

"Only the loveliest lass in Deerford," he said, leaning back in his swivel desk chair. His gray hair was slightly mussed as though he'd run his fingers through it recently. Scribbled numbers covered a yellow notepad on the desk as if he'd been working up a proposal for a new landscaping job. "And my wish has been granted."

Smiling, she bent to kiss him. "Sounds like you're about as spry as Sarge is today."

"I suppose I am. Evan is considering taking on some indoor accounts, maintaining potted plants and whatnot for offices and such, in order to even out his yearly income. He's asked me to work up some cost estimates and figure the break-even point."

"What a good idea for both of you." Pride in the two men in her life filled her heart. "I had a good day too."

He lifted his brows.

"Hope Haven Hospital once again has a glorious Christmas tree in its main lobby."

"Really? So there was no need to worry after all."

"Plenty of reason, but somehow the good Lord worked it out." With a little help from her, she thought in a moment of conceit. "Furthermore, Janice tells me almost all the gift tags that were displayed on the tree you made have been selected, and wrapped presents for the children have been arriving by the dozens."

The phone rang, and Cam answered it.

"Hello, Ainslee," he said. "How's my girl today?" He listened a moment then said, "She's right here. I'll put her on."

Anabelle waved him off. "She probably wants to tell me what time they'll be here on Sunday. I'll take the call in the kitchen."

The chicken she'd put in the slow cooker that morning scented the air in the kitchen as she picked up the extension. "Hello, dear, how was your day?"

"The usual, I suppose. The store was a madhouse this morning, and Lindsay didn't want to go down for her nap this afternoon."

"Oh, I'm sorry, dear. Babies can be like that." Anabelle heard Cam hang up his extension.

"Actually, I called to talk about this Sunday."

Anabelle's heart sank. Surely her daughter wasn't going to cancel their early Christmas celebration. Lindsay's first Christmas.

"Doug had to take another trip, this time to Kansas City," Ainslee continued. "He flew down and back today, and tells me the holiday travelers are already out in force. The planes are overbooked and a lot of flights were cancelled because of the weather in New York City."

"I'm glad he got home safely."

"Yes, so am I. But the thing is, on both of his flights he had crying babies either in the seat in front of him or in his same row. He says the babies were miserable and so were the mothers."

"That's a shame. It couldn't have made the trip pleasant for Doug." She glanced out the kitchen window. A few flakes of snow drifted past the glass.

"Doug wasn't worried about himself. The flights weren't long. But he has decided that we'd be foolish to fly to Florida over the holidays and risk flight delays and a miserable trip for Lindsay."

Anabelle straightened. Anticipation sped up her heart rate.

"So if it's all right with you, Mother," Ainslee continued, "we'd like to come to Christmas dinner at your house."

Anabelle squeezed her eyes closed. She felt bad for Louise and the rest of the Giffen family—but she couldn't help but be overjoyed for her own.

"That will be wonderful, dear. I can't think of anything nicer than to have you all here on Christmas Day."

"I knew you'd be okay with us coming."

"Of course. I'm sure Doug's parents will miss having you with them, but staying home will be the best thing for Lindsay."

"I think so too, Mother. Oh, Lindsay's awake. I've got to go get her."

They ended the call, promising to talk again soon about Christmas dinner.

Back straight, head held high, a grin on her face, Anabelle strolled back to tell Cam about the change in plans. Had she been a few years younger, she might have skipped instead of walked. She felt as though something of a miracle had just happened.

"Good news," she announced. "Ainslee, Doug, and the baby are coming to our house for Christmas dinner."

He looked up from his work sheet. "What happened to Disney World?"

She explained Doug's flight problems and the decision not to fly during the holidays with Lindsay.

"Well, there you see, all your worries about Christmas traditions have been solved inside of twelve hours."

She felt pretty smug about the turnabout both Bill Fontaine and Ainslee had made. She vowed Lindsay's first Christmas would be her best ever.

Starting to go upstairs to change, she reversed course back to Cam's office. Troubled, she said, "Cam, do you really think I've overdone it with all the presents I bought for Lindsay? I could still take some of them back if you think Ainslee will be upset with me."

Cam gaped at her a moment and then broke into laughter. "Annie, my luv, I'm glad you still have something left to worry about. Without you fussing over something, life wouldn't be the same."

She planted a fist on her hip and scowled at him. "Cameron Scott, I do not fuss over things. I'm simply trying to do what's best for my family."

"Yes, luv." His agreement would've been much more convincing if he hadn't had to wipe the tears of laughter from his eyes.

Chapter Seventeen

IDMORNING ON SATURDAY, SARAH ARRIVED at Elena's house to help finish Isabel's angel costume.

Izzy beat Elena to the front door to let her in. "Mommy's here!" she screamed in her high-pitched voice.

Elena winced at the piercing sound. "Yes, Izzy, I can see that she's here."

Elena recalled Jesus' words from Matthew 19:14: "Let the little children come to me, and do not hinder them, for the kingdom of heaven belongs to such as these." She wasn't sure that meant He wanted the little ones screaming at the top of their lungs.

Squatting down, Sarah held out her arms. "Good morning, my little angel."

Izzy flew into her mother's arms. "Buela says angels are supposed to be very good because they help God."

"Yes, I believe that's true," Sarah said.

"Come in, Sarah." Elena opened the door wider. "It's cold and blustery out there." A new storm was blowing in, dark clouds tumbling across the sky like scorched marshmallows.

Sarah picked up Izzy and carried her inside, pushing the door closed behind her. "I've been excited all week thinking that we'd finish the costume today."

"When it's done, can I wear it, Buela?"

"You may try it on so we're sure it fits." Elena led them into the family room for the final touches. The sewing machine was all set up and the costume ready. "Just put your jacket over on the recliner and we'll get started."

Sarah shrugged out of her jacket, which seemed barely adequate for the weather, and took her place at the machine. Wearing a pair of cute jeans with a white sweater tucked in at the waist, she looked up at Elena expectantly.

"We're going to start by gathering the neckline so the dress doesn't fall off of Isabel's shoulders," Elena said.

Izzy giggled. "Dresses aren't supposed to fall off."

"No, they're not." Sarah winked at her daughter.

"Isabel, sweetie, your mother is going to be learning something new and she needs to concentrate. You either have to be very quiet, or you need to go play in your room."

The child puffed out her lower lip. "I want to watch."

"All right. But remember you have to be quiet."

Isabel's expression darkened, but she remained silent.

Elena showed Sarah how to place the fabric on the machine and set the stitch. "Start slowly, and ease the fabric around as you go."

The young woman's forehead pleated and the tip of her tongue appeared as she set the machine in motion.

Elena suppressed a grin. The poor dear was as tense as a proverbial board but just as determined. If she worked this hard at her job in the hospital kitchen, she'd be promoted to a supervisory position in no time.

As Elena had suspected, sewing didn't hold Isabel's attention for long. She wandered off, perhaps in search of her father, who hadn't appeared as yet for breakfast. His band had played in Peoria last night and had another gig there this evening. Rafael had gotten home quite late, close to four o'clock in the morning. She worried about him driving so far on icy roads in the dead of night, but all she could do was pray that he would be safe.

Working with care, Sarah completed gathering the neckline, backed up the stitches, and snipped the thread.

"I hope it's all right." She held up the costume to examine her work. "It's hard to keep the stitches the same distance from the edge all the way around."

"It looks fine to me. As they say, this isn't rocket science."

"It might as well be for me," Sarah said grimly, making Elena laugh. The young woman had a good sense of humor, which made her pleasant to be around.

The next and final step was to hem the skirt with a blind stitch. Elena had already pinned it to what she hoped was the proper length, which was never a sure thing with just-couldn't-stand-still Isabel.

With just a little instruction, Sarah seemed comfortable with the hemming task, so Elena decided to straighten the magazines that had been left scattered about the room. She didn't want to over-supervise Sarah but wanted to be nearby to help if needed.

A few minutes later, Rafael strolled into the room. He'd pulled on some old jeans. His shirt hung open and his hair was mussed from sleep, his jaw shadowed by dark whiskers.

"Morning." His voice sounded rough from disuse.

Sarah abruptly stopped sewing and looked up. She smiled tentatively. "Good morning."

His head swiveled toward her. "Oh. I didn't know you were here."

Elena wondered if he would've buttoned his shirt if he'd been aware of Sarah's presence. Or if he would have simply stayed in his room in order to avoid her.

"You got in late last night," Elena said.

Barefooted, he walked to the refrigerator and got out a gallon of milk. He started to drink directly from the container.

"Excuse me." The sharp tone of Elena's voice stopped him in midmotion. "Somebody else might want to have some milk later and won't want your germs all over the jug."

He frowned at her, but got himself a glass. "A gang of us hung out for a while after the gig. Sorry if I woke you."

"I always hear you come in, son. That's what mothers do."

"Have you worked any new songs into your routines lately?" Sarah asked.

He slanted her a look. "Sure. All the time. Reggie's always working on new stuff."

"Maybe I'll try to come hear you sometime."

"Up to you." He turned away from Sarah to get some eggs from the refrigerator for his breakfast.

Feeling sorry for her son's offhand dismissal of Sarah, and somehow protective of the young woman, Elena stepped over beside her.

Isabel came skipping into the room dragging Dorie, her stuffed elephant, with her. "Hi, Daddy. You're awake now."

"I am, mi bonita." He scooped her up with one arm and kissed her on the cheek. "Have you been good for Buela this morning?"

"I've been very good 'cause Mommy has to concentrate on my angel costume. She's almost done."

"Is that so?"

As if in response, Sarah started the sewing machine going again, focusing hard on her work. Her bright red cheeks made it obvious she was self-conscious with Rafael around.

"She's doing a wonderful job," Elena said. "She's going to be a fine seamstress someday."

"Great." Putting Isabel down, Rafael got out a small frying pan, added some butter, and put it on the burner. When the butter started to sizzle, he broke two eggs into the pan and then dropped a couple of slices of bread into the toaster.

His disinterest in Sarah and anything she was doing was like erecting a six-foot block wall between two neighbors: not exactly rude, but not cordial either.

"There." Sarah snipped the threads. "The hem is done."

"Wonderful. Let's see how it looks," Elena said.

Sarah shook out the gown and held it up.

"It's bea-u-tiful!" Izzy raced over to Sarah and wrapped her arms around the costume. "Can I try it on now? Can I?"

Elena nodded to Sarah.

"Of course you may, angel. Let's take off your shirt so it won't show." She helped Izzy take off her long-sleeved T-shirt and then slipped the costume over the child's head. Adjusting the fit, she slipped the gold-braid rope around her waist and helped her put on her shimmering wings.

"Now, let me see how you look." Elena stepped back.

Isabel stood in the middle of the room and twirled around, flapping her arms. "I'm an angel! I can fly!"

Sarah laughed and so did Elena. Rafael's grin was that of a proud papa.

"Looks like it's a perfect fit," Elena declared.

Isabel stopped her spinning. "Want me to sing the song we're gonna sing in church? I know the words."

"Please do, angel."

Puffing out her chest, Isabel stood up straight and took a deep breath. "Hark and Harold were angels singing. Glory be the king . . ." Her shrill voice pierced the room.

Elena nearly swallowed her tongue trying so hard not to laugh. She covered her mouth with her hand.

". . . Peace on earth and mercury mild. God a sinner recognized . . ."

Elena thought sure her sides were going to burst. One look at Sarah and Rafael—who had lost all interest in his fried eggs—and she knew they were all in the same boat.

By the time Isabel finished her creative rendition of "Hark! The Herald Angels Sing," there were tears in Elena's eyes. She clapped her hands. "Bravo!"

"That was great, Izzy," Rafael said, chuckling. "You're going to be singing with my band any day now."

For Sarah's part, she was quiet but the tears streaming down her cheeks expressed her feelings more powerfully than any words could have achieved.

Shortly after lunch, Sarah left to do her weekly grocery shopping.

Rafael came into the family room where Elena was reading her daily Bible lesson. He was going over to a friend's house before leaving for the evening's gig in Peoria.

Rafael sat down next to her. "Mama, I'm worried that you're getting too close to Sarah."

Elena marked her place in her book and closed it. "Why would you worry about that? She's a nice girl."

"Maybe. But that doesn't make any difference. She won't be sticking around."

Elena shook her head in confusion. "She's Isabel's mother. She has a job here. Of course, she'll stick around."

"Mama, I'm seeing other women. There's a girl who's coming to hear me play tonight. I've moved on with my life, and there's no place in it for Sarah."

Sadness pressed in on her chest. "I think she knows that, Rafael."

"I don't think so." He leaned forward, his elbows on his knees. "Earlier she talked about coming to see the band play. That's a bad idea, Mama. Seeing me around Alicia was one thing," Rafael said in reference to his ex-girlfriend, "because Sarah had just come back around, and surely she expected me to be dating someone. But now that she's really here, actually sticking around, I don't want her to expect that I won't date people. I'm worried it'll hurt her feelings now."

At least her son was concerned about Sarah's response to all this. Elena could be grateful for that.

"She's a grown woman, son. She'll figure out she has no future with you, and eventually she'll find someone else." He frowned at her words. "But nothing will change the fact that she's Isabel's mother. I'm sure of that."

"Yeah, well, it's definitely awkward with her around all the time."

"Then you should try to make it less awkward, son. Remember, it took two of you to create Isabel. You are not blameless in this matter. You have to help resolve whatever difficulties you have with Sarah. For Isabel's sake."

"I'm not going to marry her, if that's what you're talking about."

"Lots of children have two parents who aren't married and don't live together, yet they get along. It's your duty to make it work."

Rafael didn't appear convinced, which saddened Elena. She'd so hoped her son would find a woman he could love and start a family with. That could still happen, of course, with or without Sarah. Either way, Sarah would always be in the picture.

With the Lord's help, Elena would see to that.

Feeling a responsibility for the Yankura children's behavior at the Hope Haven Kids' party, Anabelle decided she needed to attend. She'd lend a hand to Janice, as needed, and keep an eye on

George Junior, Bobby, and—especially—Betsy. Anabelle had warned Janice she'd have three unexpected guests.

Every square inch of the lobby was filled with children and their parents, the crowd overflowing into the cafeteria. The Christmas tree towered over the gathering like a benevolent giant, its limbs heavy with ornaments that sparkled in the reflected lights.

In one corner of the room, a trio of musicians played carols. Phyllis Getty, standing on a box with a mike in her hand, led the crowd in singing, bellowing out the songs in a surprisingly strong alto for her small size.

Working their way through the crowd, other hospital volunteers in their green jackets delivered bowls of ice cream to the children.

Anabelle caught the excitement, enthusiasm, and eager anticipation in the room; and her heart echoed the rhythmic thump-thump-thump beat of the bass.

Smiling, she looked around, trying to spot the Yankura children somewhere in the mob.

From the corner of her eye, she caught the flash of a small red sweater bursting out of the crowd and making a dash for the piano. Before Anabelle could react, Betsy was playing her own tinkling song on the piano.

Hurrying, Anabelle wove her way through the crowd, stepping over and around children seated cross-legged on the floor.

"Excuse me. Excuse me. Sorry." She didn't know where George Yankura was or if he was in pursuit of his youngest.

The young woman playing the piano looked up and smiled as Anabelle reached Betsy.

"No one told me I'd be playing a four-handed duet," the pianist said with good humor.

"Sorry about that." Anabelle scooped up the wayward Yankura. "We have to let the nice lady play the song, Betsy."

"No, no, no!" She stretched in Anabelle's arms to reach the piano again.

"It's all right. Let her stay," the pianist said. "My three-year-old loves to play with me."

Rather than leave Betsy on her own, Anabelle sat down on the end of the piano bench and held the child on her lap. Her hair smelled of baby shampoo, and there was a dribble of chocolate ice cream on her pretty red sweater.

"The nice lady says you can play with her," Anabelle said. "But let's use just one finger, okay?" She gripped Betsy's tiny hand, helping her to strike a key.

It wasn't long before Betsy was hitting every note in the top two octaves on the piano, one finger at a time. Loudly.

"Ho, ho, ho!" The arrival of Santa Claus in his red suit and white beard started the children shrieking his name. Right behind him were two security guards wearing green elf hats pushing wheeled trolleys heavily laden with presents.

"Merry Christmas, children!" Santa shouted. "Ho, ho, ho!"

As Santa began calling out children's names to come get their present, Anabelle began to realize his voice was somehow familiar. For a moment she couldn't place it, thinking Santa might be Albert Varner. Then she caught a glimpse of gray hair beneath Santa's red hat and it came to her. She gasped.

Bill Fontaine! Provider of the gigantic Christmas tree, a grieving husband, and a man who had rediscovered the gift of giving. And now, a man who joyfully played Santa Claus.

Thank You, Lord.

Sunday morning, Anabelle climbed into Cam's truck for the drive to church. Six inches of snow had fallen overnight, topping houses and cars with white, fluffy blankets, and more snow was expected later in the day. As long as the temperature remained seasonably cold, the snow would make for a white Christmas. Perfect for Lindsay's first yuletide season.

She sat back and exhaled a relieved sigh.

"What was the sigh for?" Cam backed out of the driveway and turned onto the street.

"I'm just so grateful Ainslee and the baby will be here for Christmas. Doug too, of course."

"Kirstie and Evan are coming, aren't they?"

"Oh yes. I let them know about the change in plans yesterday and told them if they wanted to invite someone, they'd be welcome. Neither did. Kirstie didn't invite Mark—she said she's still not ready for that kind of step in their relationship."

"Christmas is the most important time of the year, isn't it?" Cam tapped her knee. "I'm glad you got your way, Annie."

She glanced at him sharply. "If you're talking about Ainslee and Doug deciding not to take the trip to Florida with the baby, that was their decision, not mine. I had adjusted to the idea that they wouldn't be here for Christmas." Reluctantly adjusted, she admitted. But she had proposed an alternative and deserved some credit for that. The final decision had been in Ainslee and Doug's hands. And the Lord's.

One of the older churches in town, Good Shepherd's red brick structure stood out against the gray sky. The aluminum cross on the sharply slanted, snow-covered roof and clarion bells beckoned the congregation to morning worship.

As Cam and Anabelle walked toward the main entrance, they overtook James Bell and his family. Moving slowly, Fern was using her walker, which was a good sign that the symptoms of her multiple sclerosis were being well controlled. Her two boys were walking ahead of her almost as though creating a safe path for their mother to travel.

"Good morning," Anabelle said as she reached Fern.

"Oh, good morning." Fern stopped and smiled. "Happy holidays to you both."

"And to you. I imagine your boys are glad to be off on Christmas break."

"Oh yes. They're even more excited about it snowing," Fern said. "They've got quite a little business going shoveling sidewalks and driveways in our new neighborhood and the old one."

"Ah, entrepreneurial spirit," Cam said. "Good for them."

Fern started walking again. Cam and Anabelle edged around them so they wouldn't hold up the line of parishioners filing into the church.

Inside, the end of each wooden pew was decorated with a bright blue bow for Advent, and at the front of the nave, purple candles stood on a table covered in the same blue velvet.

As Anabelle sat down in a pew, she recalled how she had bought an Advent calendar each year when the children were young. She and the children would faithfully open a new door each morning and she'd relate the meaning of the symbol they'd find inside. The closer to Christmas, the more eager the children were to unveil the day's surprise.

The memory of those days brought tears to her eyes. She prayed she'd have the chance to share the story of Advent with her precious granddaughter.

Glancing across the aisle, she discovered Bill Fontaine sitting with Dawn Cassidy and her children.

Delighted, Anabelle smiled. The Lord had placed His hand on that poor grieving man and the young widow and had created a miracle for them both.

She looked up at the stained-glass window at the front of the nave and smiled, remembering the words of Psalm 105:5: "Remember the wonders he has done, his miracles, and the judgments he pronounced."

Chapter Eighteen

S THE NEW WEEK BEGAN, THE PATIENT CENSUS in the CCU tapered off. People tended to put off elective procedures until after Christmas. Anabelle didn't blame them. A lot of doctors wanted to clear their calendars for the week following Christmas as well.

She also knew that holiday stress, and the overeating that was so common this time of year, could bring on a heart attack. Her unit would remain ready to handle the critical patients who were sure to be admitted during the next couple of weeks.

For now, though, there were few pages for doctors or technicians heard over the loudspeaker. Even the meal carts seemed to roll up and down the hallway on silent wheels.

As she tidied up the counter at the nurses' station and watered the two poinsettias that were gifts from patients' families, she smiled in anticipation of her Christmas celebration. The gifts she'd purchased were all wrapped and under the tree. She'd do her last-minute grocery shopping on Wednesday. Kirstie was bringing homemade date muffins; Ainslee volunteered to make two pies, a pecan and a traditional mincemeat. Evan, bless him, was going to toss a spinach, pecan, dried cranberry, and goat cheese salad together with a raspberry dressing.

Anabelle would provide the ham and scalloped potatoes. An easy day in the kitchen for her, which would allow her more time to play with Lindsay.

This was going to be a very good Christmas.

By Wednesday morning, the Cardiac Care Unit felt like a ghost town. One stent patient would be discharged later in the day. A pacemaker patient had already gone home this morning to celebrate the holiday in good health. A third patient would likely be discharged tomorrow.

Elena, wearing scrubs printed with bright red candy canes, strolled up to the nurses' station. "I think the whole town of Deerford has been abducted by aliens. I don't have a single patient in ICU."

"In that case, we should be counting our blessings," Anabelle said.

"The only unit that's really busy is the Birthing Unit. I saw Candace fly by a few minutes ago. She said she had six women in labor, all of them ready to pop. She had to call down to the kitchen to get more chipped ice."

Anabelle chuckled. "Sounds like there'll be lots of little bundles of joy this Christmas."

In the uncommon quiet of the nurses' station, Anabelle heard the faint sound of a siren outside announcing the arrival of an ambulance. The Emergency Room was getting some action. Anabelle prayed the patient's condition was not serious. That he or she would be back home for Christmas.

James arrived and went into the supply room. "You two look like you don't have anything to do."

"I don't," Elena said. "How busy are you down in Med/Surg?"

He reappeared with a package of gauze. "It's so slow, Lorraine is thinking about leaving early."

Anabelle knew Lorraine Wilder, her fellow nurse supervisor, wouldn't leave early, nor would she. But on a day like this, it was tempting.

"I certainly plan to be out of here on time," she said. "I've got to go by the grocery store before I go home, and it will be extra busy today with people doing their last-minute shopping."

"Are you having the whole family for Christmas dinner?" Elena asked.

"Every one of them." Her anticipation of Christmas Day sped a smile to her lips. "But most importantly, this is Lindsay's first Christmas. Her presents are already under the tree."

James seemed to be in no hurry to get back to his unit. "We're going to Fern's parents' house, as usual. How about you, Elena?"

"My mother and grandmother are coming. We'll make our traditional sweet tamales for supper."

"Oh, I love those. Brown sugar and raisins. Yum," Anabelle said. "What about Sarah? Did you invite her to dinner?"

Elena's dark eyes shifted to the left and she focused on the blank computer screen. "We'll see her at church on Christmas

Eve. Isabel's singing with her kindergarten Sunday school group. Rafael didn't want me to invite Sarah to Christmas dinner."

"So that relationship isn't—"

The loudspeaker sputtered to life and a harsh female voice announced, "Dr. Harriet Hildebrand to ER. Dr. David Weller to ER." The disembodied voice repeated the request three times, urgency in her tone.

Anabelle sucked in a painful breath. The siren she'd heard. The patient was in serious trouble. Members of the hospital staff were girding to save a life.

As though they'd had the same thought—that they might be called upon to act quickly to save a sick or injured patient—both James and Elena excused themselves and hurried back to their respective posts.

Anabelle picked up her clipboard. She'd check on her remaining patients now in case she had to deal with a new patient transferred from ER.

As many times as she'd heard an ambulance arrive at Hope Haven, she still wondered if the patient was someone she knew. A family member. A close friend. A relatively small town, Deerford had been her birthplace. She'd grown up here and knew many others who had spent their whole lives right here. Between church and her quilting guild, she'd made even more friends as an adult.

A good many of her acquaintances had been patients at Hope Haven over the years, including her daughter Kirstie when she'd lost her leg, and Ainslee when she gave birth to Lindsay. A few friends had died here.

After she finished her rounds, she returned to the nurses' station and checked the computer for new admissions.

She stared at the computer screen, stunned. Dread snaked across her skin and burrowed into the pit of her stomach. She wanted to deny the words that appeared on the screen.

Jackie Yankura had been admitted to ER. Heart attack.

"It couldn't be," she said aloud, unable to take her eyes off the screen. The stent Dr. Hildie had installed in the young mother of three should have corrected the problem, opened the artery to allow blood to flow freely through her heart. She was on medication to prevent a clot.

She should not have had another heart attack.

Except that James's intuition had told him the young woman was still at risk.

Dear God, the doctors are going to need Your help to treat Mrs. Yankura and restore her health. She's so young. Her babies and her husband need her. Please, Lord . . .

James's pager vibrated at his waist. He checked the message. Dr. Hamilton wanted him in surgery stat. A spurt of adrenaline kicked in.

He found Lorraine Wilder, his supervising nurse, and told her that he was needed for an emergency surgery.

"Go," she said. "It's not a problem. I'll cover the floor for you."

He hurried upstairs to the operating room. Dr. Drew was already scrubbing for surgery. James joined him at the sink.

"What happened?" he asked.

"The woman who came in on the thirteenth for gallbladder surgery and then had an MI on the operating table just had another heart attack. They brought her in to the ER a half hour ago. She was unconscious and not breathing. The EMTs got her breathing again and her heart going. It was touch and go."

"That doesn't sound good." Which was an understatement, to be sure. They'd barely saved Jackie Yankura when she'd coded during the first surgery. Coding again without immediate medical treatment could have meant the end for her.

"Apparently the patient passed out and fell," Dr. Drew continued. "Dr. Hildebrand is getting a chest X-ray now. We think there's blood in her lungs."

The scrub brush froze in James's hand, and his own heart stalled in his chest. The poor woman.

"We don't know yet if it was from the fall or if she ruptured something. I've ordered six units of blood to be ready."

James had almost finished scrubbing when Dr. Hildebrand arrived and joined them at the sink. The concern in her eyes contrasted with her usual bubbly personality.

"Her left lung is half full of blood." Dr. Hildie picked up a scrub brush and got to work. "I think there's a tear in the lining of her lung or her aorta. We'll put in a drain and see if we can get rid of the blood."

"Is the stent still working?" Dr. Drew asked.

"I can't tell, but I suspect the artery has collapsed below the stent. I quizzed her husband hard. Turns out her mother had similar heart problems and died young."

Dr. Drew audibly blew out a breath. "Would've helped to know that before I started the gallbladder procedure. Why don't patients tell us honestly about their medical history?"

"Fear," James said. "And denial."

"Fat lot of good that does them," Dr. Drew muttered.

"We'll do an angiography first so we know what we've got," Dr. Hildie said. "But I'm betting she's going to need a double bypass."

James wasn't a doctor, but that sounded right to him. Although bypass surgery was common these days, it was a serious operation that could take as long as six hours. Assuming the patient survived the procedure, she'd be in the CCU for several days.

Not the best way to spend Christmas.

It was a little after twelve noon when Anabelle saw Mr. Yankura and his three children trooping toward her nurses' station. The two youngest children held tightly to their father's hand. George Junior trudged along behind.

"Hello, Mr. Yankura. I'm sorry to hear your wife is back in the hospital."

His blue eyes held no spark and were red rimmed. He hung his head. "The doctors say it's very bad."

"I'm sure they're doing everything they can for her." Sometimes the words she had to say to patients or their families were little more than puff, something to help them keep their hopes up. In the case of Jackie Yankura, Anabelle didn't know enough facts to say more than that.

"Yes, I know. We were waiting upstairs to hear the news, if there was any. But we've been there for hours. My children are hungry." He cupped little Betsy's head. "You were so kind to my children. I wonder if you could—"

"Take them to lunch downstairs?"

"Yes, please. If it's not too much trouble. I want to stay upstairs near my wife."

She glanced at the three children, so subdued now they looked like strangers. How could she possibly say no to this young family?

"I'd love to take them to lunch, Mr. Yankura."

He made an effort to smile and reach for his wallet.

Anabelle held up her hand to stop him. "It's my treat. You go back upstairs to the waiting room. I'll find someone to bring you a sandwich or something."

"It's all right. I'm not hungry."

"We don't want you passing out, Mr. Yankura. You need to keep up your strength."

He nodded and thanked her, tugged on his ear as though that would somehow help him to clear his thinking and then walked back to the elevator. His hunched shoulders and shuffling feet were a picture of defeat.

"You children stay right here. I'll be just a minute." Anabelle hurried off to find Becky, the floor nurse on duty, to let her know she'd be in the cafeteria if she was needed. She expected it would be several hours before Jackie Yankura would be out of surgery. She and the children would be back by then.

Downstairs in the cafeteria, Anabelle gave the children a choice of grilled cheese or peanut butter and jelly sandwiches with milk and chips. She decided on a bowl of clam chowder for herself and asked the cook to arrange for someone to deliver a grilled cheese sandwich to Mr. Yankura in the surgical waiting room.

"Can we have ice cream again?" George Junior looked up at her with solemn eyes.

"After you eat your lunch," she promised.

For once, the cafeteria wasn't crowded during the lunch hour. She found a nice table in the corner and a booster chair for Betsy. The children settled down immediately.

"Mama fall down," Betsy said. "She gots an owie."

"I know," Anabelle said. "The doctors are trying to fix her owie right now. You eat your lunch, honey."

"Is our mom going to die?" George Junior asked.

Fear for their mother's life tangled with her reluctance to frighten the children. "I hope not, and I'm praying for her."

The six-year-old stared at her with eyes far older than his years. "Our grandma died before I was born."

"I'm sorry." Worried that Mrs. Yankura had a genetic problem that had contributed to her heart attack, Anabelle made a show of eating her soup. "Eat your sandwiches, children. Then we'll have ice cream."

"Want chocolate," Betsy announced.

"First, peanut butter." Anabelle pointed at the little one's sandwich.

Bobby's appetite seemed undiminished by his mother's illness. He gobbled up half his sandwich and ripped open his bag of chips, which sent them sailing all over the table.

"Uh-oh." Anabelle scooped up the chips she could reach. Sitting with these youngsters reminded her of the picnics at Bass Lake State Park she'd enjoyed when her children were young.

There'd been spills and messes then too and a much happier time. "We have to be careful, don't we?"

Pastor Tom strolled over to the table. As usual, he wore a navy shirt and white clerical collar. "Looks like you've acquired a triad of moppets."

George Junior looked up. "What's a moppet?"

"A moppet, young sir, is a darling child," Tom replied.

George Junior wrinkled his nose. "I'm a boy, not a child."

"My apologies, sir." With a smile threatening, Tom dipped his head in deference to the youngster.

"Their mother was readmitted this morning after a second heart attack," Anabelle told the pastor. "She's in surgery now. Her husband's in the waiting room upstairs. You might want to stop by to chat with him."

"I'll be sure to do that. Thanks for mentioning it."

Confident the pastor would sit with Mr. Yankura and comfort him, Anabelle encouraged the children to finish their lunches.

James passed Dr. Drew the instruments he needed to crack open the patient's chest. A respirator was helping her breathe, and a tube was drawing blood from her lungs. Several bags of medication hung from an IV pole delivering meds to her system. For the moment, her color looked good.

As Dr. Hildie had suspected, the angiography had shown Mrs. Yankura had two blocked arteries and needed bypass surgery.

"How's she doing, Ethan?" Dr. Hildie asked the anesthesiologist.

"Vitals are steady," he answered. "So far."

The two doctors synchronized their work. Dr. Hildie removed a vein from the patient's leg to be used to bypass the blocked arteries; Dr. Drew tied off the arteries while a heart-lung machine did the work of circulating the patient's blood. Because the doctors were so proficient at their jobs, the surgery was like a four-handed piano duet. No one hit a discordant note.

Even so, sweat beaded on James's forehead and trickled down his spine. Concern for the patient made his mouth go dry. The life of a wife and mother rested in the skilled hands of those who hovered around the young woman on the operating table.

The circulating nurse wiped the sweat from his brow, and he nodded his thanks.

Please, Lord, give us all the wisdom and skill to make this woman well.

Anabelle herded her well-fed young charges to the third floor waiting room where their father was talking with Pastor Tom. The hospital chaplain had apparently come directly upstairs after she'd told him about Mr. Yankura.

Little Betsy went directly to her father and climbed up into his lap.

"Hi, squirt," he said. "Did you have a good lunch?"

"Chocolate ice cream."

"Lucky girl." Her father rubbed at the telltale bit of chocolate around her mouth that Anabelle had missed when she washed the child's face.

"She also had half a peanut butter sandwich." Anabelle didn't want him to think she hadn't fed them something nutritious for lunch.

Mr. Yankura looked up at her, the lines of worry crisscrossing his face deeper now than they had been earlier. "Thank you. You've been very kind."

"No one's come out to talk to you yet?" she asked.

He shook his head. "Not yet."

Pastor Tom stood. "I'll go see what I can find out."

"If you'll be all right for a minute, I'll run down to pediatrics, see what kind of toys I can round up to entertain the children."

"We'll be fine. Thank you."

By the time she returned with a couple of coloring books, crayons, an Etch A Sketch, and a jigsaw puzzle, the chaplain was talking with Mr. Yankura.

"They're closing her up now," he said. "Your wife made it through the surgery fine. She'll be moved to the Cardiac Care Unit in about a half hour. The doctor will come out to speak with you then, George."

Knowing that the surgery had gone well, George's shoulders relaxed and lips curved with the hint of a smile. Anabelle handed the toys to the children. "I have to go get things ready for your wife, Mr. Yankura. I'll see you later."

Without waiting for his thanks, she hurried downstairs to the CCU. The patient wasn't out of the woods yet. She'd be on heavy-duty pain meds and antibiotics to ward off infection. She'd remain on a respirator until they were sure she could breathe on her own, and she'd probably be kept under sedation for at least twenty-four hours.

And that was if she remained stable.

It was after five o'clock, well after her shift ended, when she was able to call Cam to let him know why she was late and that she still had to stop at the grocery store. The patient's blood pressure had spiked, and they were still drawing blood from her lung. It had taken a cadre of nurses and doctors to keep her vitals steady.

"I'll be here, Annie, and your dinner will be ready whenever you are," Cam said.

She suspected she'd be too tired to eat.

As she walked through the lobby en route to her car, she looked up at the Christmas tree with its twinkling lights.

"She's in Your hands, Lord. Keep her well."

Chapter Nineteen

EATH IS GONNA LIKE MY PRESENT BEST!" HOWIE held up the baseball he had spent several minutes laboriously autographing, printing his name with a black felt pen.

Candace stifled an amused smile. Nothing wrong with Howie's confidence gene. "I'm sure he'll love the presents both of you are giving him." She and her children had cleared the kitchen table after dinner and were going to wrap Heath's presents together.

"I think he'll like my present because he likes to drink coffee." Brooke had found a gift box in the cupboard that was the perfect size for the ceramic coffee mug. She'd painted a robin on one side and a hummingbird on the other with a Christmas wreath in between. After glazing, the mug looked almost professionally done.

"He'll love it because you did such a beautiful job of painting the birds," Candace assured her daughter.

"But mine's better," Howie insisted.

Ignoring his comment, Candace said, "Do you want to find a box for the ball or a gift bag or wrap it as is?"

Howie pondered his answer for a moment. "I'll go look."

He hopped down from his chair and raced downstairs to the laundry room where Candace kept her supply of gift wrap and ribbons.

Brooke wrapped a sheet of red tissue paper around the mug and put it in the box. "Howie's silly. What makes him think Heath wants his autograph?"

"I'm sure Heath will be pleased. It's really a sweet idea Howie had. And please don't call your brother names."

Making a face, Brooke selected a foil sheet of gift wrap with blue and silver stripes.

Howie came stomping up the stairs from the lower floor of their split-level house. Somehow he never walked anywhere quietly, more like a one-man army storming the castle.

He produced a medium-sized gift bag he'd found.

"Howie!" Brooke said. "That's a Halloween trick-or-treat bag."

Howie dropped the baseball into the bag. "I like black and orange. It's pretty."

Candace resisted the urge to correct his taste in Christmas gift wrapping. "It'll be fine, Howie. Maybe you could nest the ball in red tissue paper and tape a red bow on the bag to make it look more like Christmas."

With great glee, he wadded up several sheets of tissue and stuffed them on top of the ball and then found a red self-sticking bow to press on the bag. Color coordinated it wasn't, but the gift did look festive.

Brooke worked with much more care, aligning the striped wrapping paper with the edge of the box and folding the ends in place.

"Good job, both of you. Now for the name tags." Candace let them choose which tag to use. She spelled Heath's name for Howie, who wrote the letters as carefully as he could. He'd sometimes struggled at school, his ADD making it hard for him to concentrate and sit still. But his first-grade teacher said she was pleased with his progress, assuring her that Howie was not lacking in intelligence. Only patience.

"Okay, we're done." Candace shoved her chair back from the table. "Now you may put the presents under the tree and then it's up to bed."

Howie made a dash for the tree, which was in the living room in front of their picture window.

"I don't want to go to bed yet," Brooke complained. "I don't have to get up in the morning for school. It's vacation."

"I know that, honey. Why don't you read for a half hour. Then I'll come tuck you in and say prayers with you."

Brooke's halfhearted shrug indicated her agreement with Candace's decision.

Sighing with a combination of relief and fatigue, Candace cleaned up the kitchen table and put away the wrapping supplies. Her mother was down in the family room watching a show on the Discovery channel.

"Did they get their presents wrapped?" Janet asked.

Candace went to stand beside her mother and rested her hand on the back of her mother's recliner. "They did, with only a small amount of bloodshed."

"Yours or theirs?"

Candace chuckled. "Neither, I guess. I'm so tired, I don't think it matters."

Her mother muted the program on the Serengeti desert. "Long day?"

"We had so many births today, at one point all the labor rooms were filled, and we had a woman in labor out in the hallway. Her husband didn't seem to mind, but her mother was having a fit."

"Mothers are like that." Janet patted Candace's hand.

"You would've been much more understanding and not nearly as loud and pushy." She kissed her mother on the cheek. "I've got to get Howie to bed. Brooke is going to read for a while."

"Come back when you've got Howie down, and I'll tell you all about the Serengeti and desert lizards."

"I can hardly wait." Laughing, Candace climbed the stairs and went up to Howie's room.

This Christmas, especially Christmas Eve, would be much different than the ones she had experienced in the past few years since Dean died. For the first time in four years, she'd share the holiday with a man she cared for, a man she loved. She'd bought him presents and so had her children. She suspected he'd have something for her and the children as well.

Excitement and anticipation pumped adrenaline through her veins. Worry about what Dean would think tempered her enthusiasm.

She wished that she'd get a sign, an indication that it was all right for her to have found someone else. That it wasn't too soon.

She wanted Dean's blessing on her relationship with Heath.

But how could she get that from a dead man, whom she had deeply loved?

Standing in front of the Christmas tree in her living room, Anabelle fingered the ornament she'd purchased the year Evan started taking trumpet lessons. She wished he'd continued with his music. But other activities and sports had lured him in different directions.

A Barbie holiday ornament purchased in Kirstie's honor hung near the miniature trumpet. Higher still on the tree was Ainslee's favorite Cinderella coach.

As she had every Christmas season, she'd gotten Ainslee and Kirstie's dollhouse down from the attic. It, too, was decorated for the holidays, a miniature tree in the living room, poinsettias on the kitchen counter and a wreath on the front door. A tiny sprig of mistletoe hung between the living room and the kitchen.

"Is there something wrong, lass?" Cam said from behind her.

Still scanning the ornaments that brought back so many memories, she said, "What would you have done if I had died when the children were young?"

"I probably would've gone mad." He slid his arms around her waist and pulled her back against him. "What makes you ask that now?"

"A patient in Cardiac Care. She's a young mother of three. Her condition is critical after a double bypass operation. If she doesn't make it . . ."

"She will. She has the doctors of Hope Haven and you taking care of her, doesn't she?"

"But is that enough?"

"I suspect you're praying for her too."

"And her husband. He seems so lost already with those three little children." She turned so she could look up at Cam. She smoothed a few wayward strands of his gray hair. "If I had died while the children were little, would you have remarried?"

"I never could've found a girl as lovely as you. Still couldn't."

She smiled and brushed a kiss to his lips. His mustache always tickled a little, but she'd grown to love the feeling. "Nor could I have ever found a better man."

"Guess that makes us a perfect couple then, lass."

Her heart filled with love for this man who had held her so often, both in sorrow and celebration. She was incredibly lucky to have married Cameron and raise three children with him. While they'd had a few arguments over the years, they'd settled them quickly, kissed, and made up.

Kirstie's bicycle accident where she'd lost her leg had been the only real tragedy that had struck their family. Not only had they survived that, they'd grown closer as a couple and family, supporting Kirstie during her rehabilitation in every way they could.

Now they were moving through the next stage of life, grandparents to an adorable baby girl.

She prayed that Jackie Yankura would live long enough to experience the joy, and sometimes the exasperation, of being a grandmother.

Anabelle got to the hospital early the next morning and didn't linger over a cup of coffee in the staff lounge as she sometimes did. Instead, she went downstairs to check on her critical patient.

She found Mrs. Yankura's chart and quickly scanned the entries. She was still under sedation, breathing with the help of a respirator, and had received two additional units of blood. She was running a slight fever, so additional antibiotics were ordered, and her blood pressure had spiked a couple of times. While that wasn't the best possible news, her situation wasn't unusual for a patient recovering from bypass surgery.

Debbie Vaughn, the Cardiac Care night-shift nurse, was still on duty. Anabelle found her in Jackie Yankura's room.

"How'd she do overnight?" she asked in a low voice.

"Hanging on," Debbie told her. The worry in her eyes and her furrowed forehead spoke more loudly than her words. Mrs. Yankura's condition hadn't improved as much as Debbie would have liked.

Anabelle shared her concern. "Have either Dr. Hildie or Dr. Drew come in yet?"

"Not yet. I think they'll try to wake her up this morning and see where she is."

Among other things, the patient had been deprived of oxygen for a time, which could have starved her brain cells. The doctors would check for brain damage by asking the patient to comply with a few simple commands.

"How about the patient's husband? Is he still here?"

"No, he left with the children about nine o'clock last night. I'm sure he'll be here soon. Poor guy is really stressed out."

"Aren't we all?" Anabelle hoped he could find someone to care for the children. It simply wasn't healthy for them to spend their entire day in a hospital waiting room.

Anabelle returned to the nurses' station to check on the status of the other patients in the unit. Fortunately, there weren't many. The staff could concentrate most of their efforts on monitoring Mrs. Yankura.

A few minutes later, both Elena and James stopped by to see how Mrs. Yankura was doing.

Anabelle brought them up to date. "It seems your intuition after the stent procedure was prescient."

"She just looked a little off to me, like her circulation wasn't all that it should be," he said.

"Prescient." Elena repeated the word carefully. "That's a great word. It means you know things before they happen, right? Bet you can spell it too."

Half smiling, Anabelle knew James had studied root languages like Latin and Greek just for the fun of it. Elena was always testing him with new words that she had learned.

Without hesitation, James spelled the word. "That was too easy."

"That was perfect," Elena said. "Now, since you're *prescient*"—she emphasized the word—"maybe you can tell me what Cesar's going to give me for Christmas. I've been hinting around, but he hasn't given me a clue."

"I'm sure whatever he gives you, you'll love it and will give him a big thank-you kiss."

"*Humph!* You don't have to be prescient to know that." She turned to Anabelle. "Keep us posted on your patient. I'll pray for her."

"I think the entire staff is praying for her," James said. "They've all seen her children and don't want them to be motherless."

"I'm certainly praying for her and her family." Anabelle hoped the power of prayer would give the Yankura family a Christmas miracle.

Shortly after eight o'clock, Mr. Yankura arrived without his children.

"How is she?" he asked immediately. His eyes were bloodshot and his face drawn with worry. His shirt looked as though he'd slept in it.

"She made it through the night, so we're all remaining hopeful. You found someone to care for the children?"

"Yes. A very nice neighbor offered to keep them." His gaze darted toward his wife's room. "May I see her?"

"Of course. She's still sedated, although the doctor may let her wake up later today."

"I want to tell her I love her. The children love her. We need her."

Anabelle walked with him into Mrs. Yankura's room. Becky had taken over monitoring the patient's vitals. In a quick glance,

Anabelle checked the monitor above the bed. Everything looked within normal parameters.

"Mr. Yankura, you're welcome to talk to your wife," Anabelle told him. "Sometimes when patients are sedated, they can still hear their loved ones talking to them. It may reassure her to know you're here."

"Yes, I will. Thank you."

Nodding to Becky, Anabelle slipped out of the room. The doctors would be making rounds soon. Meanwhile, if Mrs. Yankura developed a problem, Becky would let her know.

At this point, Anabelle would be the most useful by praying for the young woman.

Chapter Twenty

BY MIDMORNING, THE DOCTORS DECIDED TO STOP sedating Mrs. Yankura and allow her to wake up slowly. She began to stir a little after noon.

Since this was a critical juncture in a patient's recovery, Anabelle paged Dr. Hildebrand and Dr. Hamilton and joined Becky in the patient's room. She told George Yankura he could stay in the room but he needed to step back away from the bed so the doctors could have easy access to his wife.

Anabelle took Jackie's hand and leaned close to her. "It's all right to wake up now, Mrs. Yankura. You've had surgery, and you're in a hospital."

The patient's eyes fluttered open but remained unfocused.

"You're doing fine, Mrs. Yankura. Don't be frightened. Your husband is right here."

Moaning, Jackie Yankura tried to pull away from Anabelle.

"Just be still, Mrs. Yankura. You have a breathing tube down your throat and you're on a respirator, so you can't talk. I know it may hurt, but try not to fight it. Do you know where you are?"

She nodded.

"Good. I'm Anabelle Scott, one of your nurses. Can you squeeze my hand?" Anabelle felt a slight pressure on her fingers and wanted to give a cheer. Jackie's response was a good sign that at least part of her brain and body were still in working order.

The patient moaned again and thrashed her free arm around.

Anabelle held her arm steady for fear she would pull out her IV. "Easy does it, Mrs. Yankura."

"Is she in pain?" her husband asked. In jerky motions, he rubbed his right hand against the back of his left so hard he all but removed the light brush of hair that grew there.

"Probably," Becky told him. "The doctors will administer more pain killers as necessary."

Dr. Drew arrived with Dr. Hildie right behind him.

Anabelle stepped away from the patient.

"I'm Dr. Hamilton, Mrs. Yankura. You're going to be all right."

She struggled more forcefully, her eyes wide and frantic. The low, animal sound she made tore at Anabelle's heart. The patient was in more than ordinary pain. She was in agony.

Dr. Hamilton ordered an increase in the pain meds. Becky adjusted the IV drip.

When that didn't appear to help, the doctor increased the dosage again.

"Please." Mr. Yankura's lower lip trembled. "Can't you do something?"

Dr. Hildie tried to console him. "We're helping her as best we can. Try not to worry."

Easier said than done, Anabelle thought.

The patient continued to thrash around. Dr. Drew ordered her restrained so she wouldn't hurt herself.

"Can't you take the breathing tube out of her mouth?" Mr. Yankura pleaded. "It's hurting her."

"We want to be sure she's able to breathe on her own," Dr. Hildie responded. She asked him to talk to his wife and try to calm her.

He leaped at the chance. "Jackie, sweetie, they're trying to help you. Be still. Let them do their work. Please, sweetie, I know it hurts; but you're going to get better. I know you are."

Simply watching the man talk to his wife brought a lump to Anabelle's throat. He stroked her hand over and over trying to communicate his love through touch as well as words.

"Let's sedate her again," Dr. Drew said. His gaze met Becky's. She nodded and increased the medication that would put Mrs. Yankura back to sleep.

When she slipped back into a near coma, Anabelle and the two doctors left the room, leaving Mr. Yankura still stroking his wife's hand and arm and talking to her while Becky continued to monitor her vital signs.

Dr. Drew shook his head and ran his palm over his face. "There's still blood draining from her lungs."

Looking off in the distance, Dr. Hildie folded her arms across her chest. "She's so young to be in this much cardiac distress. The bypass should've improved her condition by now."

"What do you suggest?" Dr. Drew asked.

"We can't open her up again. She's too weak."

"I agree."

Anabelle had faith these two doctors would find the answer to help Mrs. Yankura's condition improve. The fact that they didn't have a ready answer troubled her. Medicine was 90 percent skill and experience and 10 percent luck. Mrs. Yankura needed a basketful of luck right about now. Or rather, providence.

The monitor in the patient's room squealed a warning. Becky stuck her head out the door.

"She's going into V-fib, and her oxygen saturation is dropping." The woman's heart was pumping too hard, too erratically, to circulate the oxygen the patient needed in her bloodstream.

Spurred by the news, both doctors hurried back to Mrs. Yankura's bedside.

As the doctor ordered a change in meds, Anabelle ushered Mr. Yankura, who looked on the verge of collapse or hysteria, out of the room. She'd had more than one patient's spouse faint during a crisis, which didn't help the doctors do their work.

She escorted him to the waiting room down the hall, sat him down, and told him to put his head between his legs. Suspecting he had eaten little all day and his blood sugar was probably low, she retrieved a soda from the nurses' station and made him drink it.

By the time she returned to the patient's room, they were preparing Jackie Yankura for transfer back to the operating room to install a pacemaker.

Anabelle prayed that would stabilize the patient.

She returned to the waiting room to tell Mr. Yankura what was happening.

"A pacemaker?" Agitated, he kept rubbing his hands together, and he didn't seem to understand what was happening. "Why now? Why didn't the bypass make her better? Why do the doctors keep changing what she needs? It's almost Christmas. What are my children going to do?"

Anabelle remembered the desperation in her father's face the Christmas her mother had been so ill. How he must have prayed that year, pleading with God and the doctors to make her mother well again. The fear of losing her had weighed heavily on her father's spirit, so much so he hadn't had time for his children.

Another dreadful thought crossed her mind. Jackie Yankura was only a few years older than Ainslee. What would Anabelle be doing if her child were in such critical condition? The thought of losing Ainslee or any of her children caused sweat to break out on her forehead and her hands go clammy.

"Mr. Yankura, would you mind if I sat with you for a time?" With Mrs. Yankura en route to surgery, Becky could handle the few other patients in the unit.

"Sure, I guess."

Anabelle sat down on the mint-green couch. In order to calm him, she wanted him to think about something other than his wife having another surgery, albeit a generally routine one.

"How did you and your wife meet?"

"*Um*, I was working at a 7-Eleven. She started coming in every morning for coffee on her way to work and we got acquainted. I finally got up enough nerve to ask her out." At the sound of a laundry cart rolling past, his gaze darted toward the hallway.

"That's a nice story. I bet you still make coffee for her."

"Yeah, I do. We moved up here to Deerford when they offered me a job as manager of the local 7-Eleven. I'm hoping someday to buy the franchise."

"You're ambitious. Good for you."

As he began to relax, she asked him more questions about his wife and children, his wife's family, and where they lived. She wished they had a larger support group locally, but they hadn't lived here long enough to have put down solid roots yet.

Finally the gurney returning his wife to her room rolled past.

Mr. Yankura was on his feet in an instant ready to go to his wife.

Anabelle held him back. "Let them get her settled again. The doctor will come out to talk to you in a few minutes."

As Anabelle had promised, soon Dr. Drew appeared, his face drawn with fatigue. "The pacemaker is working and your wife is stable for now, Mr. Yankura."

Mr. Yankura sank back down on the couch and sighed with relief.

Hearing the troubled tone of Dr. Drew's voice and recognizing the nervous flex of his jaw for what it was, Anabelle felt no relief at all. Jackie Yankura's life remained on a razor's edge.

When Anabelle arrived at work Christmas Eve day, Jackie's condition had barely changed.

Mr. Yankura looked like he had spent the night in the chair beside his wife's bed. Anabelle brought him some coffee and a breakfast tray, though she noticed later he had eaten little.

Mentally, she railed at the unfairness of the situation. A mother should be with her children on Christmas Eve. Should be sharing the excitement of Santa Claus's imminent arrival and preparing for the celebration of Christ's birth tomorrow. She should be enjoying a joyous time of year.

And so should a father.

By midafternoon, she called Cameron. "I'm going to stay late tonight. I can't leave Mr. Yankura all alone. He seems so adrift. Do you mind terribly?"

"I mind, but I understand. Do what you have to do, luv."

"I promise I'll come home in time to go to the eleven o'clock church service. I don't want to miss that." For years, she and her family had celebrated the culmination of Christmas Eve at Church of the Good Shepherd. This year, more than ever, she needed her spirits lifted by the joyous music of the season and the promise of God's love.

Chapter Twenty-One

WHEN ELENA GOT HOME FROM WORK ON CHRISTMAS Eve, she found Isabel jumping up and down on the couch in the living room singing "Hark and Harold" at the top of her lungs.

Elena caught her on the next bounce. "Whoa, young lady. I know you're excited about tonight, but we don't jump on the couch at our house."

"But I like to jump, Buela."

Kissing her granddaughter, Elena lowered her to the floor. "You may jump on the floor or outside, but not on the furniture."

Izzy started to jump, but clearly it wasn't as much fun hopping on the floor as on a makeshift trampoline. "Where's your father?" And why wasn't he supervising his daughter?

"He's talking on the phone to a girl." She wrinkled her nose.

Elena wondered which girl Rafael was currently dating. She'd have to remind him that talking to a girlfriend did not excuse him from his parental duties. Isabel could have fallen off the couch and cracked her head on the coffee table.

"Can I put on my angel costume now? Can I?"

"Not quite yet. I want you to eat a little something before we go to church, and I have to change clothes too."

"I'm not hungry." Arms held wide, she twirled around, pirouetting in imitation of what she'd learned in her ballet class.

"You will be later if you don't eat something now."

"Nuh-uh." She spun a little faster.

Suspecting the best way to stop the child from spinning and making herself dizzy was to eliminate her audience, Elena headed for her bedroom. She would wash up and put on her bright red sweater with the white snowflake on it, a reflection of her holiday spirit.

Before she'd left the hospital, she'd stopped by the nurses' station to wish Anabelle a merry Christmas. To her surprise, her friend intended to stay with the husband of a critically ill patient for a time. For Anabelle to sacrifice a part of her own Christmas Eve was so like her. Beneath her professional demeanor, she had a truly giving heart.

She heard Rafael come out of his bedroom. Apparently his conversation with this girl, whoever she was, had been completed.

"Rafael, would you please heat up some of the leftover chicken casserole for Izzy to eat?"

"Aren't we going to have supper after church?"

Elena rolled her eyes. Men didn't seem to have any concept that allowing a child to become hungry and overtired invited a temper tantrum. "Yes, but she'll be too hungry if she waits that long."

He mumbled a response, which Elena assumed meant he'd feed Izzy.

At about four, an hour before the church service, Elena helped Isabel dress in her angel costume. For once the child stood still while she brushed Izzy's long, dark curls and pinned her hair back from her angelic face.

"You're beautiful, angel."

"What about my halo?" she asked.

"When we get to the church you may put that on."

Mrs. Joiner, the chorus director, had asked that the children arrive a little early and meet in the kindergarten classroom.

Rafael, who had dressed in dark slacks, green pullover sweater, and leather jacket, drove them to church in his aging white Chevy van. He had a couple of stickers on the back bumper touting his favorite bands and a local radio station that played the kind of music he liked.

Elena felt a sense of pride and joy to have her son with her as he pulled into the parking lot. It wasn't often he crossed the church's threshold. For his daughter, he made the effort.

She wished Cesar would do the same for his granddaughter, if not for Elena.

They walked Izzy to the classroom. Sarah was waiting for them. Shedding her warm coat, Isabel went running into her mother's open arms.

"There's my beautiful girl." Sarah hugged her daughter. "Where's your halo?"

"Buela has it."

Elena picked up the coat Isabel had dropped and started to hand Sarah the halo.

"Mama, I'll do that." Rafael took the halo from her. "Come here, mi bonita. Let me put this on for you."

The joyous expression on Sarah's face faltered and the sparkle in her eyes faded as Isabel turned to her father.

Frowning, Elena pursed her lips. She didn't know if Rafael was being intentionally rude to Sarah, or if he simply didn't realize how much Sarah wanted to share in this moment with her daughter.

Rafael carefully set the headband on Isabel's head and straightened the halo. "There you go. You look perfect now."

"Yes, she is perfect." Sarah's whispered words of praise spoke of a heart filled with motherly love.

Quickly, before the moment passed, Elena pulled her camera from her jacket pocket, knelt and took Isabel's picture—*my little angel saved for posterity*, she thought, smiling.

Holy Trinity Church wasn't large, but they did have a vibrant youth program that attracted young people from all around the town as well as their parents. On this festive Christmas Eve, teenagers dressed in their best acted as greeters at the door, passing out programs to the members of the congregation.

The young people had been in charge of the decorations as well. Red and green paper chains and popcorn strings made by the youngest children decorated a Christmas tree near the church organ.

Other children had made ornaments of cookie dough, which they'd cut out, baked, and painted and then hung on the tree branches.

The tweens had created imitation stained-glass windows mounted on the walls that depicted various moments in the Christmas story: Mary and Joseph arriving in Bethlehem; the couple being turned away from the inn; the birth of Jesus and the joyous announcement by angels; the arrival of the shepherds and the three wise men.

Combined, the pictures recreated the powerful story of God's love first told two thousand years ago: "For unto you is born this day in the city of David a Saviour, which is Christ the Lord."

Finding seats in a pew as close to the front as they could, Elena sat between Rafael and Sarah.

As the organist played "Ave Maria," Elena bent her head in prayer. She prayed for Rafael and Sarah to find some accommodation that would allow them to raise Isabel cooperatively. She prayed for Cesar, that he would find his way back to the church.

She prayed for Anabelle and her heart patient and the patient's young children and husband. She prayed that God would watch over them all on this eve of Christ's birth.

As the final chords of "Ave Maria" faded, the members of a contemporary musical group—two guitars, an electric keyboard, a drummer, and a female vocalist—took their places on the stage. The group played regularly for the Saturday evening services that attracted so many young people. Sunday services were more traditional in nature.

In an explosion of sound, they opened with an energetic version of "Joy to the World," and the congregation stood.

The volume of the music made Elena wince, but she noticed Rafael smiling. It was his kind of music. Maybe that was the lure he needed to get back to attending church, assuming he wasn't playing a gig himself on a Saturday night. Perhaps, once he became a police officer, he'd be able—and willing—to attend church more regularly.

The group played two more Christmas carols in a loud and up-tempo style. Then the minister made a few welcoming remarks. When he finished, the kindergarten chorus of angels paraded down the center aisle, Isabel and her friend Hayley holding hands, their sheer golden wings bouncing behind them. They lined up on the steps at the front of the church.

Unable to help herself and bursting with love as she watched Isabel take her place, Elena took both Sarah's hand and Rafael's, squeezing them.

Sarah leaned toward Elena. "Her halo's crooked," she whispered, grinning.

Elena smiled in response. "She's not always a perfect angel."

With a soft organ accompaniment, the kindergartners sang their hearts out, the words of "Hark! The Herald Angels Sing" as clear as could be. No one in the congregation would have guessed Hark and Harold were joining in the song.

When the song was over, the youngsters dutifully trooped back up the aisle. A huge grin on her face, her halo dipping to the right, Isabel waved to her parents and Elena.

When she'd passed by, Rafael looked past Elena to Sarah and winked. "She's a great kid, isn't she?"

A smile blossomed on Sarah's face. "Yes, she is."

Older children in elementary school came next, followed by those in middle school, the latter group singing an animated, urban-style version of "Good King Wenceslas" that had Rafael snapping his fingers in rhythm. *No wonder Holy Trinity attracts so many young people*, she thought.

As the service ended and they began making their way out of the church, Sarah said to Elena, "I brought a present for Isabel with me, and one for you as well. Would it be all right if I gave Isabel's present to her now?"

A splinter of guilt pricked Elena's conscience. Of course Sarah would want to see her daughter open her present and see her reaction. That was entirely understandable.

She also thought of the critically ill heart patient who wouldn't be with her children this Christmas Eve. Elena made an impromptu decision, even though she knew Rafael might object.

She hooked her arm through Sarah's. "Why don't you come to the house now and have a light supper with us? Then you can give Isabel her present and help her hang her stocking for Santa."

Sarah's eyes widened in pleasure. "Could I?"

"Of course you may. We'll pick up Izzy from her classroom and meet you at home."

Sarah thanked her and hurried off to her car.

With a dark look in his eyes, Rafael stopped Elena before they reached Isabel's classroom. "Why did you invite Sarah over? Christmas Eve is for family."

Although her son was two inches taller than she, Elena could stare him down. That's what she intended to do as she planted her fist on her hip.

"Sarah *is* family. You simply have to accept that. A mother should be with her child on Christmas Eve. And it's high time you got past your anger toward Sarah. It wouldn't hurt you one bit to forgive her for what she did and give her a little credit for what she's trying to do now, which is to be a good mother to the child you helped to create." Shaking on the inside, she drew a quick breath. "It's the Christian thing to do, Rafael. Forgive her."

He opened his mouth to argue, then thought better of it. Turning, he marched toward the kindergarten room to pick up Isabel.

A mother should be with her child on Christmas Day, as well, Elena thought. But she didn't want to anger her son more than she had already by inviting Sarah to join them again tomorrow.

She'd let Rafael think about what she'd said.

Perhaps next year . . .

After the early Christmas Eve service at Riverview Chapel, Heath followed Candace home in his Jeep. His father had elected to skip the Christmas Eve celebration and save his energy for Christmas Day with his grandson.

Candace let Heath in the front door.

"Hey, you've got a flocked tree." Carrying a paper grocery sack, he stepped into the living room.

"In Poland they often sprinkle their trees with some artificial snow. This is easier but it can still get messy."

"It's beautiful."

"Both my sister and I have a couple of ornaments—blown eggs that have been decorated—that came over with my great-grandmother when she immigrated in the early 1900s. Over the years, the children and I have made a few of the decorations too."

"Hey, Heath!" Howie came running across the room. "Come see all the presents under the tree. Santa's gonna come tonight and bring more presents. Then Aunt Susan's gonna come tomorrow and bring even more presents." He grabbed Heath's hand and dragged him closer to the tree.

"You're a lucky kid."

Howie squatted in front of the tree. "See all these presents? They're all for me. I put Brooke's presents over there," he said dismissively. "Grammy's and Mommy's too. I put yours right here in the middle."

"Hey, sounds like you've got it all organized. Want to put some more presents under the tree?"

"Sure!" His green eyes sparkled with heightened anticipation.

"Some of us get really excited about Christmas," Candace commented, amused by her son's enthusiasm.

Heath handed Howie one present at a time from the grocery sack. Howie carefully placed each one under the tree. With a frown, he noted that Brooke's present was larger than his.

"Size doesn't always matter, sport. It's what's inside that counts." He handed the boy two smaller boxes. "This one's for your mom, and the other one is for your grandmother."

"Aren't you sweet," Janet said, watching the action with the same amused expression as Candace.

Heath looked up. "A smart guy knows it's best to make points with his girl's mother."

Both Candace and Janet laughed.

"Can we open them now?" Howie asked, apparently unsatisfied by simply counting his presents one more time as he had a dozen times since the tree had gone up.

Janet said, "Let me put the soup on the stove to heat, and then we can open Heath's presents and he can open yours."

When Janet returned, Howie and Brooke sat on the floor in front of the tree. Candace and Heath took their seats on the love seat. Janet chose the matching chair opposite the baby grand piano.

"I get to go first," Howie announced.

"We can both go first," his big sister countered, picking up the larger package.

Both children ripped at the wrapping paper instantly turning it into confetti.

"So much for having the packages wrapped at the store," Heath whispered to Candace, taking her hand and closing his fingers around hers.

"A new baseball mitt!" Howie held up his prize to show everyone.

"Look, Mom, a painting easel," Brooke said. "I can put it on my desk or take it outside to paint."

"Perfect. Both presents are just perfect." Candace squeezed his hand. "Thank you."

Grabbing the presents for Janet and Candace, Howie delivered them with the same eagerness he'd used destroying the fancy wrapping paper on his own package. "Now you get to open yours."

Janet went first, unwrapping a beautiful silk scarf that went well with her silver hair and green eyes.

"Thank you, Heath. You have wonderful taste."

"You're next," Heath said to Candace.

Her stomach tightened and her hands were clumsy as she slowly unwrapped her present, drawing out the moment. It had been more than four years since a man she cared about had given her a gift.

Her fingers trembled as she opened the long, slender box.

She gasped. "Oh, Heath..." A necklace made of beautiful green stones lay on a bed of satin. "It's beautiful. You really shouldn't—"

"I thought they matched your eyes. Let me put it on for you."

She nearly melted as she turned for him to clasp the necklace in place, his fingers brushing gently against her nape. Longing curled into her midsection and her breath came in little gasps.

When she faced him again, his smile touched his eyes. "You're beautiful." Leaning forward, he kissed her.

"Grammy! Heath is kissing Mommy," Howie announced in a voice that could probably be heard by Mrs. Kowalski.

"Yes, I know he is, dear." The tremor in Janet's voice suggested there were tears in her eyes.

Tears welled in Candace's eyes too. Tears of love and gratitude.

"Now it's your turn," she whispered. "Don't expect too much."

Once again Howie became the delivery boy, carrying the gifts for Heath in his arms and dropping them in his lap.

"Open mine first," Howie ordered.

"You're doing a lot of me-firsts, young man," Candace warned. "Maybe you should let someone else go first for a change."

His lower lip pushed out.

"How about I open Brooke's present first," Heath suggested. "Then yours."

Although not pleased by the decision, Howie didn't object when Heath proceeded to unwrap the coffee mug.

"Hey, this is great. Did you paint this yourself?"

Nodding, Brooke beamed. "I knew you liked birds."

"I do indeed. And the Christmas wreath. It's awesome Brooke. Just perfect. Thank you so much." He then moved on to Howie's present, turning the Halloween package this way and that.

"It's an autographed baseball. I signed it myself."

Candace nearly choked.

Brooke said, "You're not supposed to tell him what it is. He's supposed to open it to find out."

Heath's grin cut deep slashes into his cheeks as he removed the red tissue paper to reveal Howie's present. "A baseball autographed by Howard Crenshaw. That's great. I bet in a few years, that'll be worth a lot." He pulled the ball out of the bag and held it up to the light.

"It just says Howie. I don't know how to spell Crenshaw yet."

"That's okay, buddy. It's still worth a bundle to me."

Turning his attention to the two packages from Candace, Heath raised a questioning brow. "Which do I open first?"

She indicated the one she bought from the Audubon Society, which he quickly opened. Shaking out the wrinkles in the rain hat that could be squished into a small, plastic container, he perched it on top of his head.

"How do I look?"

The children giggled.

"How does adventurous and very handsome sound?" Candace replied.

"I like that. Sort of Harrison Ford in *Raiders of the Lost Ark*?"

"Only better," she added with a grin that made his cheeks flush a dull red.

He opened the second package more slowly and took his time examining each side of the photo cube. "So this is what you've been doing taking all those pictures lately."

"I thought you could use it as a pencil holder or something." She couldn't quite read his expression and couldn't tell if he liked the gift or not.

Uninvited, Howie climbed up onto Heath's lap. "That one's a picture of me."

"I know, sport. And you know what I'm going to do? I'm going to put this right on top of my desk at the hospital. Then every day I'll see this and think of you and your sister and your mom. Pretty neat, huh?"

"Kinda like we were your family, right?"

Heath glanced at Candace, his expression serious, his eyes dilated with intensity. He cleared his throat. "Yeah, kinda like that."

Chapter Twenty-Two

WHEN JAMES AND HIS FAMILY HAD FINISHED dinner, the boys set up the card table in the living room for their traditional, and often extended, Christmas Eve game of Monopoly. There had been some years when they hadn't completed even one game by the time they had to leave for the eleven o'clock service at the Church of the Good Shepherd.

The lights of the Christmas tree were on and Christmas music played on the stereo. The flames from the fire in the fireplace licked upward, spreading warmth into the room. The boys' decorative stockings had been hung from the mantel with care. A perfect setting for their first Christmas in their new home.

The boys had spent much of the week, when they weren't shoveling snow from the neighbors' driveways, unpacking boxes and straightening out the mess in the garage. They'd pretty well gotten all the tools in order. James appreciated that and had told them so.

"All right!" Nelson cheered. "You owe me five hundred dollars. Double rent."

"It's not fair," Gideon complained. Frowning, he forked over the money without looking at his brother. "You own practically the whole board."

"Guess it's just my night." Nelson's gloating grin was so wide, squint lines appeared at the corners of his eyes.

Fern took her turn rolling the dice. "Don't get too smug, young man. I've been known to come from behind to wipe you out." She moved her piece five places and landed on a free space.

After a moment, she said, "James, it's your turn."

"What?" He jerked back into the present and realized he'd been thinking about the heart patient at the hospital. "Sorry." His roll of the dice took him to a space occupied by a hotel that Nelson owned. He groaned.

"This is a great game, isn't it?" Nelson scooped up his father's rent money.

"It's great if you think bankrupting everybody else is fun," Gideon grumbled.

Fern cocked her head toward her husband. "You seem to be preoccupied tonight. Is there something wrong?"

James shoved the dice to Nelson. "I was thinking about a patient. She's had two major surgeries and been in and out of the hospital for the past two weeks. She's still in critical condition."

"You're usually able to put your work aside when you get home," Fern said. "You must really be worried about her."

Nelson rolled the dice, landed on an unoccupied square, and bought another property.

"I guess I'm thinking about her because it's Christmas," James said. "She's a young mother with three children. Here we are, playing Monopoly together, and she's on a ventilator and may not make it." He knew that because Anabelle had insisted on staying with the patient's husband. James knew she was praying for the family but anticipating the worst.

"I'm sorry." Fern patted his hand.

"No, I'm sorry for being in such a dour mood on Christmas Eve."

"We'll pray for the family at church tonight," Fern promised.

Gideon rolled the dice and landed on another property his brother owned. "That's it. I'm broke." He pushed the remainder of his money toward Nelson's stash and shoved his chair back from the table.

"Hey, don't give up, man," Nelson said. "I'll loan you some money."

"Naw, it's all right. I'm bored with this game." He glanced at the presents under the tree. "I'd rather play a video game anyway. Monopoly is nothing but luck. Video games take more skill."

"So go play one of your games," Nelson said. "I'm about to wipe out Mom and Dad too."

"True enough." James had less than a thousand dollars left, and Nelson had bought up almost the entire board. Fern didn't have much more cash than he did.

"I've got an idea," Gideon said. "Why don't we each open one present tonight? That'll make things go faster in the morning."

"But we always wait until Santa has filled your stockings," Fern said.

"Mom, we aren't little kids anymore. We don't exactly believe in Santa Claus." Standing, Gideon tucked his fingertips into the front pockets of his jeans and walked over to the tree. "Just one present wouldn't be a big deal. Lots of families open all their presents on Christmas Eve."

James met Fern's gaze. They both knew what was going on. Gideon wanted to get his hands on his new video game, which he thought would be Chicago Underground. He was wrong about that. When he opened the game, thinking it would be the one he asked for, he might be very disappointed.

Fingering a hundred-dollar Monopoly bill, James wondered if it was better to let him be disappointed tonight and get over it by tomorrow. Or wait until morning when he might feel just as let down and spend the whole of Christmas Day in an adolescent funk.

James puffed out his cheeks. With teenagers, there were no good answers.

"What do you think, Fern?"

She lifted a shoulder. "I think you and I should concede the game. Let the boys open one present tonight. Then we'll all go to church and be reminded Christmas isn't about presents. It's about God's gift to us."

Gideon took about a millisecond to consider that thought and then dived for the package he had guessed was his video game.

Moving more slowly, Nelson sorted the Monopoly money and stacked it in the box.

"Go ahead, son," James said. "I'll do that."

The boy double-checked with his mother, who nodded her approval.

He walked to the tree and studied the pile of gifts while tugging on his earlobe. "So, philosophically speaking, is it better to save the best for last? Or just jump right into the deep end?"

"Come on, baby brother." Gideon grabbed up the present he'd been eyeing for days. "I'm sure not going to wait for you to make up your mind." He sat down cross-legged and began to unwrap the package.

James held his breath. He hated for his sons to be disappointed, whether it was by the gifts they received or failing to achieve a goal they'd established. But he knew he'd made the right decision. His palms began to sweat as Gideon whipped the last of the wrapping paper onto the floor.

He stared at the box. "This isn't—" He looked up, his forehead wrinkled, a puzzled look in eyes that were the same shade of blue as James's.

"It's a game Ask Mr. Gamer recommended. It's supposed to be action packed and require complicated strategy to achieve higher levels."

"*Galactica IV: Conquest.*" Gideon read the name of the game as though it were written in a foreign language. "Never heard of it."

"When I told the clerk at the video-game store that Ask Mr. Gamer had recommended it, he bought the last copy himself."

"Yeah?" He glanced once more at the box.

"Give it a try, son. If you don't like it, well, we'll work out something." James didn't think an opened game could be returned, but maybe he could talk the clerk into some kind of an exchange. They'd sort of bonded over Ask Mr. Gamer.

While James had been discussing the game with Gideon, Nelson had quietly gone about opening his present. Oblivious to anyone else in the room, he was already pouring over the instructions trying to learn how to use the new calculator.

"Is that the one you wanted?" Fern asked.

"Oh yeah, this is awesome." He grinned up at his mother. "This thing has so many functions, you can program a rocket to go to the moon."

"You might want to start with something a little simpler," James suggested, knowing full well that Nelson was so intelligent, he might figure out how to launch a rocket by morning.

The boy didn't respond. He was too involved in learning to calculate math problems James could barely understand.

Gideon had wandered down the hall to his room, presumably to try out Galactica IV, or maybe to pout. James couldn't be sure which.

An hour later, James called to the boys, reminding them they'd have to change clothes before they went to church.

Gideon yelled back, "I can't leave now! I finally made it to level two. This Galactica game is awesome. The guys are gonna freak out, it's so tough."

James shot a smile in Fern's direction and gave her a thumbs-up. Looked like this Christmas would be not only pout-free, but even happier than expected.

At the hospital, Anabelle continued to sit with George Yankura in the waiting room outside his wife's room. Some time ago, she'd gone down to the cafeteria to get sandwiches and chips before the staff closed up for the night.

Neither of them had eaten much.

He sat with his arms resting on his thighs, hunched over, hands clasped together. He stared at the floor, his head unmoving, shoulders taut. Sweat beaded his forehead. The heel of his shoe tapped a beat on the floor like a tom-tom, each stroke reverberating in the small waiting room.

He inhaled a quick breath that sounded like a sob.

"Dear God, I love her." The catch in his voice cut through the silence. A stubble of whiskers roughened his jaw, and his eyes were sunken and redrimmed.

Anabelle reached her hand out to him to give him some comfort. His pain was too deep. Too painful to bear. Yet she had little in the way of solace to give him.

She couldn't lie to him about his wife's critical condition.

Every hour or so, George went into his wife's room, sat with her, holding her hand and telling her how much he loved her. That the children missed her and needed her. When he became overwhelmed with his fear for her life, he'd step out of the room again and pace or sit staring off into space.

Seeing the sorrow in George's eyes, the desperation, nearly broke Anabelle's heart.

She checked her watch. She could stay another hour or so and then she'd have to leave if she was going to make it to church tonight. She hated to leave George alone.

There'd been few visitors in the hospital during the evening. One or two families had come by with miniature trees or a handful of balloons to brighten a patient's room.

For the most part, the hospital was working with a skeleton staff.

Debbie Vaughn, the night-shift nurse in Cardiac Care, spent most of her time with Jackie Yankura. She, too, looked strained and worried. Her many years as a nurse gave her an instinct about the eventual outcome of a difficult case.

Jackie Yankura's outlook wasn't good.

The scream of a heart-lung monitor shot razor blades of fear down Anabelle's spine. She was on her feet in a heartbeat.

So was George.

"No, you stay here," she ordered.

The call came over the loudspeaker. "Code blue. Room 215. Code blue. Room 215."

Debbie had called it in. Jackie Yankura had coded. Again.

Anabelle grabbed a crash cart and was in the room before the second call for the Code Blue team stopped echoing down the hallway.

Despite a surge of adrenaline, years of training kicked in and steadied Anabelle's hand. Airway check. Ventilate. Epinephrine.

She was barely aware of Debbie working in tandem with her. Or when Dr. Hildie arrived, quietly issuing orders. Requesting more meds. Changing meds. The choreographed protocol was second nature. She had been a part of this dance dozens, maybe hundreds, of times. Her heart pounded as though it wanted to do double duty, beating for both Anabelle and her patient.

Still the monitor screamed they were failing. The flat green line confirmed it.

Jackie Yankura had slipped away.

On Christmas Eve.

Dear God, help her!

Anabelle was unaware of how much time had passed when Dr. Hildie stopped issuing orders.

"That's it." The doctor's voice was hoarse with the grief they all shared. "I'm calling it. Time of death . . . 9:42 PM, December 24."

Instinctively, Anabelle reached up and switched off the monitor. Her arms felt weak as the adrenaline drained from her body. Her hands trembled.

All of those who had responded to the call for the code blue team stood in silence, out of respect for the deceased, and in acknowledgment that they had failed. Their grim expressions mirrored the pain of loss they all felt.

Tears burned in Anabelle's eyes.

Dr. Hildie cleared her throat. "I'll go talk to her husband. He'll want to come in to . . ."

"I'll take care of her." Anabelle knew George wouldn't want to see his wife with the breathing tube down her throat, with the IVs stuck into her arms. She couldn't do anything about Jackie's pale face or the fact that she'd never look at him again with love in her eyes.

Debbie cleared up the remnants of IV bags and meds they'd used and carried them out of the room while Anabelle removed the breathing tube and undid the wires that had been monitoring her heartbeat and oxygen consumption.

She took the time to smooth Jackie's blonde hair away from her face, tucking the longer strands behind her ears. There was so little she could do. So little consolation she could provide for George and his children.

Please, Lord, take this woman into Your loving embrace, and help this woman's family cope with her loss. Help them to understand she has been called back to—

Jackie gasped.

Shocked, Anabelle's hand flew to her chest and she stared at her patient. Her deceased patient.

What she'd heard had to be one of those last breaths a dead person exhales. Not a real breath. Only a body expelling air—

Jackie's eyes opened. She looked around. Eyes blinking. Alert.

"George?" It was the faintest of sounds. No more than the ripple of wind through the leaves of an aspen tree. More imagined than heard.

Anabelle's jaw dropped. "Jackie?" It couldn't be. She'd flat-lined. She'd been declared—

Jackie looked directly at her. Conscious. Comprehending. Definitely alive. "Where's my husband?" Though hoarse, her voice was stronger than a moment ago.

Anabelle placed her fingers on Jackie's carotid artery. Definitely a pulse. A strong one. This was crazy. Or a miracle.

"I'll, *um*, go find your husband." Not believing, certainly not understanding, Anabelle hurried out of the room to find Dr. Hildebrand.

She found the doctor talking with George and trying to console him. "Dr. Hildebrand, I need you to come here for a moment."

Dr. Hildebrand looked at her and shook her head.

"It's important." Anabelle gestured toward Jackie's room.

Still scowling, Dr. Hildebrand followed her out into the hall. "I was talking with—"

"The patient's alive, doctor. And talking."

Dr. Hildebrand took a step back as though she'd been struck, as dumbfounded as Anabelle had been.

At the patient's bedside, the doctor checked Jackie carefully, all the time shaking her head. There was no reasonable explanation that Anabelle could think of for Jackie's amazing resurrection. The doctor didn't seem to have an answer either.

When the doctor allowed George into the room, he and his wife fell into each other's arms. Anabelle didn't think there was a dry eye in the place. Hers certainly weren't.

When the doctor was sure Jackie was stable, Anabelle decided to go home. Or rather go to church, where she intended to thank the good Lord for His intervention tonight. She called Cam and told him she'd meet him at Good Shepherd.

As she walked downstairs to the first floor, she looked up at the shining Christmas tree—its lights winking, the star on top a beacon to the faithful.

This was the real miracle of Christmas, she realized. The birth of Jesus Christ and the promise of salvation and eternal life.

She smiled as she walked out of the hospital, the parking lot nearly empty. In the frigid winter air, she looked up at the sky where the stars twinkled as brightly as the joy in her heart.

Thank You, Lord, for the blessings You have given us.

With a determined step, she walked to her car. She'd have to remember to hug Ainslee and Lindsay Belle especially hard tomorrow as they celebrated Christmas together. And Evan and Kirstie. Cameron too.

Having her family together at any time of year, particularly to celebrate the birth of the Savior, was a gift from God.

She wouldn't soon forget that.

About the Author

Charlotte Carter has been telling stories since a very early age when she and a friend acted out *Bambi* stories. Her friend got to play the role of Bambi; Charlotte was Thumper. Now the author of fifty published novels, Charlotte's books have appeared on Waldenbooks best seller lists and been translated into a half dozen different languages. Her honors include a Career Achievement Award from *Romantic Times* and winner of both the National Readers' Choice Award and the Orange Rose contest.

A native Californian, Charlotte and her husband of forty-eight years have one spoiled cat, two married daughters, and five grandchildren, who they are occasionally allowed to babysit. In her spare time, Charlotte pursues her lifelong goal of performing stand-up comedy.

Charlotte Carter can be reached through her blog at www.CharlotteCarter.com.

Read on for a sneak peek of the next exciting and
heartfelt book in *Stories from Hope Haven*

The Healing Touch
by
Pam Hanson & Barbara Andrews

ELENA HURRIED INTO THE STAFF LOUNGE AT HOPE
Haven Hospital on Monday morning and was surprised to see a number of nurses milling around instead of reporting for work.

"Mrs. Rodriguez, what do you think they'll do about the
flu?" The question came from a young LPN who had recently
been assigned to Elena's shift in the Intensive Care Unit. The
query took her completely by surprise.

"Who has the flu?" Elena asked. Her first thought was that a
staff member had called in sick.

"No one yet," her friend and Cardiac Care Nurse Supervisor
Anabelle Scott assured her as she joined the group. Her voice was
calm, and Elena could tell it was meant to reassure those around
her. "There's no reason to panic."

"But what happens when we run out of vaccine and there aren't enough beds in the hospital for all the sick people?" the same LPN asked.

Elena arched her eyebrows and looked to Anabelle for an explanation.

"It seems," Anabelle answered, "that there's a serious shortage of flu vaccine in the county. All the available supplies have been allocated to the hospital, but there isn't enough for everyone who might be vulnerable. It remains to be seen whether there will be an epidemic this late in the winter, so I suggest everyone report for work as usual."

A few nurses grumbled, but Anabelle's practical explanation effectively broke up the crowd. In a few moments, she and Elena were the only ones left in the lounge.

"Is there something to worry about?" Elena slipped out of her winter jacket and patted her dark brown hair to be sure no strands had slipped out of the ponytail she wore for work.

Anabelle frowned and fiddled with the glasses she kept on a chain around her neck. She was as slender as Elena but considerably shorter, with neatly styled salt-and-pepper hair that was on its way to turning white. The fact that she hesitated to answer alarmed Elena more than the concerns of the other staff members.

"We could have a serious problem," Anabelle admitted. "Mr. Varner stopped me on the way in and asked me to reassure any staff members who might be worried."

Elena frowned, thinking of one of her mother's favorite sayings: *Where there's smoke, there's fire.* If the hospital CEO wanted to calm staff members, the flu scare must be more than rumor.

"Today's the last day of February," Elena said. "I thought the flu season was pretty much over."

"Apparently not," Anabelle said. "We could be hit by a really serious outbreak. Unfortunately, the vaccine has been unusually scarce this year. Far too many people waited too long to get their shots and found their doctors didn't have any vaccine left. It's so scarce that the county has asked Hope Haven to be in charge of all that remains. The physicians are all on board because it's a way to make sure the most vulnerable people receive shots."

"I guess it's good that all staff members were required to get shots last fall, but it doesn't solve the problem of a potential epidemic."

Elena couldn't help but think of her own family. Her husband Cesar had been the first to get his flu shot. As a police detective, he came into contact with too many people to neglect getting one, although he was none too crazy about shots of any kind. She was sure her granddaughter was protected. It had been strongly recommended by her school that the children have the mist so they wouldn't need shots. She couldn't remember whether her son Rafael had taken her advice and had his flu shot, but she doubted it.

"Unfortunately there's nothing we can do about it now except pray that Deerford doesn't have an epidemic," Anabelle said. "The whole state of Illinois is short on vaccine, so we can't look to the government for help. No one seems to know why there's a shortage." She glanced at her watch. "Guess it's time to get to work."

Elena was surprised to see that it was nearly seven. She took pride in never being late, but this morning it would be a near thing. "See you later then," she said, hurrying to the elevator that would take her down one floor to the Intensive Care Unit.

She tried not to think about Rafael as she began her duties for the day, but she was afraid he'd neglected to get his flu shot in spite of her reminders. He was, after all, twenty-eight years old, much too old for his mother to take him in for a shot even though he lived with them. He and his adorable six-year-old daughter had come home to Deerford after Isabel's mother, Sarah, had deserted them shortly after Isabel's birth. Sarah had recently come back into their lives, but Rafael and Izzy still lived with Elena. Elena loved having her son and granddaughter share their home, but she had to keep reminding herself that Rafael was an adult and not her little boy anymore.

The flu was on everyone's mind this morning. It was the main topic of conversation whenever two staff members had a moment to talk. Elena reminded the new LPN that this was only a rumor right now. The young nurse was beginning to remind Elena of the little chicken who thought the sky was falling.

When her lunch break came, Elena went down to the hospital cafeteria, looking forward to a few minutes of peace and quiet with no talk of epidemics. She chose a tuna salad on a croissant and hot tea, carrying her tray to an empty table on the far side of the busy room, but before she finished even half of her sandwich, one of her favorite people came up to her.

"Mind if I join you?" James Bell, an RN from the General Medicine and Surgery Unit, asked.

Elena smiled in welcome and nodded at an empty chair. At fifty-four, James was five and a half years older than she was and had been a friendly face when she first started working at Hope Haven. Besides being an outstanding nurse, he was a man of faith who had encouraged her to return to the church after years of neglect. He was a role model for faith-based, empathetic patient care, but he also had a great sense of humor. Since he was an avid reader and a lover of words, they'd made a game of testing his vocabulary. She loved to stump him with a word he couldn't define, but it wasn't easy to do.

"Well, is everyone in your unit panicking about a possible flu epidemic?" he asked as he settled down to his helping of shepherd's pie.

So much for getting away from disaster talk, Elena thought with an ironic smile, but she knew that James wasn't given to spreading rumors. If he was concerned, she certainly respected his opinion.

"That's putting it mildly. I even had to reprimand an LPN because she couldn't keep her mind on the day's work."

"I take it you've heard about the task force." He raised one eyebrow and looked at her with deep blue eyes.

"No. What is it?"

"Apparently the administration is taking the threat very seriously. They're putting together a task force to deal with all the demands for vaccine and the possible consequences if we do have an epidemic."

"Sounds like a good idea. Let me guess—you've been tapped for it."

"Yes. There was no way I could refuse, given how serious the situation could become. Candace has agreed to serve too," he said, mentioning another friend, Candace Crenshaw, an RN in the Birthing Unit.

"Who else will be on it?"

"The county health nurse, for sure. Not surprisingly, Penny Risser is co-coordinating the whole thing."

"Oh dear."

"She is efficient," James said with a knowing grin.

"Oh yes, she is that," Elena said sympathetically, knowing that the CEO's executive assistant wasn't easy to work with. In fact, her nickname with the staff was the Dragon because she zealously guarded access to her boss, Albert Varner.

"The first meeting is later today," James said.

"Is it going to take a lot of your time?" Elena knew James's plate was already full. His wife Fern had multiple sclerosis, and much of the responsibility for their home and two teenage sons fell on him. He was also active in church and a scoutmaster, and yet, he rarely said no to a worthy cause.

"How much time it will require remains to be seen," James said, "but I couldn't refuse. A flu epidemic would be really bad news. I would much rather work on preventive measures than be involved in a full-fledged epidemic."

James finished his lunch rather quickly and then excused himself to phone his wife. Elena slowly finished her own meal. She was usually refreshed by a few minutes of solitude; but today her mind was anything but tranquil. James was the last person to react to rumors or panic when things went wrong. As a veteran of the first Gulf War, he could handle almost any situation, including his wife's debilitating illness. If he was concerned, so was Elena.

Elena was standing to leave when she heard the sharp click of heels coming toward her. Medical staff members wore rubber-soled shoes or other quiet footwear, and Elena could think of only one person whose walk sounded like she was warming up for an Irish dance.

"Good morning, Penny," Elena was quick to say when the CEO's executive assistant reached her table.

"Closer to afternoon," Penny corrected her. "Can I have a minute of your time?"

Elena plopped back down on her chair, a bit surprised that she asked. Usually Penny assumed that her business took precedence over anyone else's.

"Sure, that's about how long I have before my lunch break is over." Some nurses shook in their shoes when Penny approached them, but Elena wasn't one of them. She'd been at Hope Haven for too many years.

The executive assistant didn't sit. Elena suspected that she liked towering over her. Although Penny was younger than Elena, whose hair had yet to start turning white, Penny had tight graying curls that did nothing to flatter her rather sallow complexion. The woman had one passion—growing plants and flowers—but her love of floral beauty hadn't carried over into her style choices. Today she was wearing a gunmetal-gray suit that made her look like a character in a sci-fi movie. Her mood wasn't any cheerier.

"You've probably heard about the flu scare," Penny said.

"I've heard a lot of rumors, yes, but I'm not sure what to believe."

"Believe." Penny cleared her throat as though preparing to make an important announcement. "There's not enough vaccine anywhere in the county, and Deerford may be vulnerable to an epidemic. Mr. Varner has given me the job of putting together a task force." Using her boss's name, she made it sound like a presidential appointment.

"So I've heard," Elena said.

"I'd like you to serve on the task force. Mr. Varner recommended you."

"I'm not sure what I have to contribute."

Penny waved away Elena's hesitation. "We're meeting in the conference room as soon as your shift is over. Please be there. I trust I can tell Mr. Varner that you're on board."

At least she said please, Elena thought. "I'll be there." Mentally, she rearranged her family situation as Penny nodded and walked away. She took her calling as a nurse and a Christian too seriously to refuse being of service in a potential crisis.

Rafael would have to get off work early to pick up Izzy from school, usually something Elena did on her way home from work. She was sure it would be all right, though, because he was working at Baldomero, her mother's Mexican restaurant in downtown Deerford. Certainly Camila Baldomero wouldn't object to letting her grandson leave early to fetch his daughter.

Izzy loved to sit on a stool in the restaurant kitchen and watch her great-grandmother cook, often sampling little tidbits. That would pretty much take care of her appetite for dinner, and Cesar could heat up the casserole left from yesterday if she was too late to fix anything else. Her husband sometimes grumbled at leftovers, but his detective work often kept him too busy for lunch, and he'd eat anything when he was hungry enough.

Heading back to work, she continued to mull over the flu scare. If there was a serious epidemic, the hospital's resources would be taxed sorely. There had been deaths in other states from the current strain of flu, and she could hardly imagine how the hospital would isolate an onslaught of flu cases and still provide services for other patients. The more she thought about it, the more important the task force seemed. She was a great believer in preparedness, and Hope Haven Hospital certainly wasn't ready for a major outbreak. Cesar's eating warmed-over casserole was a small price to pay if there was anything she could do to help get ready for a potential disaster.

To read *The Healing Touch* in its entirety,
you can order by mail:
Guideposts
PO Box 5815
Harlan, Iowa 51593
by phone: (800) 932-2145
or online: shopguideposts.com

A Note from the Editors

Guideposts, a nonprofit organization, touches millions of lives every day through products and services that inspire, encourage and uplift. Our magazines, books, prayer network, and outreach programs help people connect their faith-filled values to their daily lives.

Your purchase of *Stories from Hope Haven* does make a difference! To comfort hospitalized children, Guideposts Outreach has created Comfort Kits for free distribution. A hospital can be a very scary place for sick children. With all the hustle and bustle going on around them, the strange surroundings, and the pain they're experiencing, is it any wonder kids need a little relief?

Inside each easy-to-carry Comfort Kit is a prayer card, a journal, a pack of crayons, an "I'm Special" wristband to wear alongside the hospital-issued one, and a plush golden star pillow to cuddle. It's a welcome gift and has a powerful effect in helping to soothe a child's fears.

To learn more about our many nonprofit outreach programs, please visit www.guidepostsfoundation.org.